LIKE YOU'VE NOTHING LEFT TO PROVE

E. L. Massey is a human. Probably. She lives in Austin, Texas, with her partner, the best dog in the world (an unbiased assessment), and a frankly excessive collection of books. She spends her holidays climbing mountains and writing fan fiction, occasionally at the same time.

Also in the Breakaway series

Like Real People Do

LIKE YOU'VE NOTHING LEFT TO PROVE

A NOVEL

E. L. MASSEY

PAN

First published 2023 by NineStar Press
First published in India 2025 by Pan
an imprint of Pan Macmillan Publishing India Private Limited
707 Kailash Building
26 K. G. Marg, New Delhi 110001
www.panmacmillan.co.in

Pan Macmillan, The Smithson, 6 Briset Street, Farringdon, London EC1M 5NR
Associated companies throughout the world
www.panmacmillan.com

ISBN 978-93-6113-924-6

Content Warning: Depictions of homophobia in sports, racial slurs, scenes depicting and discussing a panic attack/social anxiety disorder, injury from sports concussion and epileptic seizures from a brain injury.

1 3 5 7 9 8 6 4 2

Typeset in EB Garamond by R. Ajith Kumar, New Delhi
Printed and bound in India by Replika Press Pvt. Ltd.

FSC www.fsc.org
MIX
Paper | Supporting responsible forestry
FSC™ C016779

To Deacon. My Hawk. The best dog in the world.

1

THE PROBLEM WITH DATING a celebrity is that sometimes they have to do ridiculous things like take a call from their agent on Christmas Eve when they *should* be cuddling with their boyfriend.

Something about a sponsor and a New Year's appearance and an upcoming photoshoot that had to be rescheduled? Eli lost the thread pretty quickly. He watches all of Alex's games and has made an effort to actually understand hockey rules (though what actually counts as goaltender interference is still a mystery to him). He thinks his boyfriending duties are pretty well covered. He doesn't need to know which jockstrap Alex is currently endorsing or whatever.

So Eli is reading *Great Expectations*, proud of himself for getting a head start on next semester's readings, hoping his boyfriend comes to bed soon, and feeling very sleepy. Though that could be the Dickens. Actually, that's not fair. He enjoys Dickens a fair amount. But *Great Expectations* is certainly no *Bleak House*.

He flips the page and glances up as Alex paces into the bedroom from the hallway, where he's been in and out of earshot for the last half hour.

Eli's parents are asleep at the opposite end of the house downstairs, and his sister, Francesca, is still awake next door if the music coming through the shared bathroom door is any indication.

"Hey," Alex says, tossing his phone onto the top of the dresser. "Sorry about that."

Eli waves *Great Expectations* at him in a conciliatory manner. "No problem. But since you're up, I left my Chapstick in the bathroom."

Alex gives him a fond look that Eli is still getting used to: a little squint, a little crooked smile, a raise of one eyebrow. "Is that a request?"

Eli tries to look as cozy and pitiful as possible. "Please?"

Alex rolls his eyes but slips through the bathroom door and switches the light on, painting the wood floor gold.

"I loved him against reason," Eli shouts after Alex, "against promise, against peace, against hope, against happiness, against all discouragement that could be."

"I already said I would get it," Alex shouts back. "You don't need to woo me with Dickens."

"Ah, but I must always woo you, my love," Eli argues, affecting a terrible English accent, "With Dickens or otherwise."

"Can you do your wooing a little more quietly?" Francesca yells from her bedroom.

Eli stifles his laugh in the duvet.

Alex turns off the light, runs into the cedar chest, swears, and then crawls up to flop inelegantly on top of Eli. He tries, very ineffectively, to apply the Chapstick for Eli until, laughing even harder, Eli wrestles it away from him and does it himself while Alex pretends to pout.

"Hey," Alex murmurs, smudging the words into Eli's neck, "do you maybe wanna do that thing where you drag your fingernails up and down my back until I fall asleep completely blissed out on oxytocin?"

Eli slides his book and then the Chapstick onto his nightstand and moves his hands automatically to Alex's shoulders. "How did you know? That's *exactly* what I wanted to do."

"Oh." Alex makes a point of settling in further before going absolutely boneless. "Well, that's perfect, then."

The bruises on Alex's side look particularly stark when painted in moonlight, and Alex is warm and sleepy and vulnerable. His curled fingers in the periphery of Eli's vision make Eli's chest ache in a way he can't explain with anything other than love. This soft, tactile man, who smells like VapoRub and Eli's detergent, is so far removed from the visceral, overconfident Alexander Price, whose skill and notoriety sell out hockey arenas. In the dark and the quiet of Eli's childhood bedroom, it almost feels as if they're two different people. Except Eli is the only one privileged enough to know this gentle night-time version.

"Mm," Eli agrees, dragging his nails lightly, so lightly, up the expanse of Alex's back. "Perfect."

Alex wakes Eli up at 7:00 a.m. on Christmas morning. "Hey," he whispers urgently into Eli's temple. "I want to call James."

"You *what*?" Eli growls somewhere in the vicinity of his sternum.

And, okay. Admittedly, saying he wanted to call his exboyfriend might not have been the best way to go about waking up his current boyfriend.

"Sorry. Sorry. I know it's early but I was laying here thinking. And I realized I'm ready. I'm not afraid to talk to him anymore, and I know he'll be awake but probably not downstairs with his parents yet because his mom likes to sleep in."

He takes a breath. "But I don't have to right now. I can wait until tonight."

"No, no this is good," Eli says, shifting so he can blink up at him, bleary and shadowed in the early-morning light and his hair an absolute disaster.

There are pillow creases on his cheek and his lips are chapped and his morning breath is rank.

Alex loves him.

"I'm good," Eli says, pressing his palms to his eyes. "Do I need to be awake for this, or ... ?"

Alex loves him so much. "No. This is fine. Just ... be here? While I talk to him?"

"Done." Eli yawns, throwing an arm around Alex's waist. "Go for it."

"Okay."

And Alex calls James.

"Alex," James says after the third ring, and Alex has to close his eyes for a moment at the familiarity of it.

"Hey," he says. "Merry Christmas."

"Yeah, Merry Christmas. What are you doing up this early? Isn't it 7:00 a.m. in Houston?"

"I'm not in Houston," Alex says. "But, yeah."

"You're not in Houston."

"I'm not."

James huffs out a laugh. "You're in Alabama, aren't you?"

"I am."

"And you're calling me on Christmas morning instead of cuddling with your—uh. Eli?"

Eli, who can obviously hear James, snickers into Alex's neck.

Alex winces. "Boyfriend. Eli's my boyfriend. We're together."

"I mean, I kind of figured. He said you weren't, though, when he was here."

"It's new. Sort of. We finally got together after Thanksgiving."

"Good," James says after a moment's pause, and Alex thinks he means it. "I'm glad."

"Me too," Alex says.

It earns him a squeeze from Eli.

"Okay," James says. "Well, I'll ask again—why are you on the phone with me instead of cuddling your boyfriend?"

Alex bites his lip.

James sighs at his silence. "Alex."

"I'm ... uh. Those two things aren't exactly mutually exclusive?"

"So. You're calling your ex-boyfriend while cuddling your current boyfriend? On Christmas morning."

Eli turns his face into Alex's collar bone, and Alex can feel him smiling. "Yes."

"I feel like I should be apologizing to Eli right now, but I also feel like he probably knew what he was getting into. Are you all right?"

"Yeah. I'm good. Really good. There are some things we should talk about."

"Okay?" James sounds guarded. Which is fair.

"Um. One thing is personal, and one is professional. Which do you want first?"

"Personal first," James says. "I guess."

Alex takes a breath, and Eli's head shifts on his chest. He smooths one hand down Eli's side, pressing his fingers to the divots between his ribs.

"I'm sorry. For everything. And I miss you," Alex says slowly. "I miss being friends with you. And I understand if you don't want to or if you can't be friends with me again. After everything. But if you do—"

"I do," James says. "I'm sorry too. I'm *so* sorry. I shouldn't have cut you out of my life."

"I understand why you did. I shouldn't have treated you the way I did, there at the end. I was ... uh ... scared. And insecure. And I sort of pushed all of my bad feelings onto you."

"We both fucked up," James says quietly and more than a little resigned.

"Yeah."

"But it also sounds as if we're both trying to handle our problems like adults now, so that's good, right?" James laughs, and Alex's chest feels a little looser.

"So I was thinking we could start talking again?" Alex suggests.

"We could text, maybe. To start with."

Alex makes a face. "Since when do you text?"

"Well. The team has a group chat. And Cody is always texting me. He even taught me how to use emoticons."

Alex glances down at Eli, and they share a knowing look. "Cody, huh?"

"Yeah," James says, completely missing the leading inflection in Alex's tone. "Cody Griggs? He's Eli's friend. The one Eli visited here at

Thanksgiving. He's from Alabama too. He's a smart player. Fast, soft hands, good eye. He's going to be a serious asset to the team next year."

"Yes. I know who Cody is," Alex says dryly, and from the strangled sounds Eli is making, he's either trying not to sob or badly stifling hysterical laughter.

"So," James continues, "you said there was something personal and something professional. Is everything okay with the Hell Hounds? You're playing well. Your whole line is. You really have a shot at the cup this year."

"Yeah, no. Everything is great with the Hell Hounds. That's, um, actually part of—" He takes another breath. Lets it out. Breathes again. "I'm thinking about coming out. I've already talked to management and PR."

"Alex," James says, sounding winded. "Are you sure?"

Alex curls his fingers into the fabric of Eli's shirt. "Yeah, yeah, I'm sure. And it won't be super soon. I'm going to start telling the team at the end of the season, the rest of the organization over the next year. Probably won't go public for another year after that." He takes another breath. "When I do, though, it might implicate you."

James doesn't say anything.

"Hell Hounds PR has been through all our old interview footage and game tapes. Apparently, I wasn't super discreet about my feelings. They think they can play it off as a one-sided crush, but I just wanted to warn you. Especially since two years from now, you'll probably be—"

"In the NHL," James finishes. "Yeah."

And as many years as Alex has spent with him, he has no idea what James is thinking right now.

He wishes he could see James's face.

"I'm sorry," Alex says. "I know that's going to make things harder for you, and I don't want to be the reason for any more stress in your life. I've fucked things up for you enough."

"It wasn't your fault."

"It feels like it," Alex says, rough and quiet and so honest it makes his teeth hurt.

Eli's arm around him tightens.

"It wasn't," James repeats. "And I think it's good. That you're going to come out. After all, if *you* do, then I won't be the first."

It's Alex's turn to find breathing a little difficult. "You're thinking about coming out?"

James doesn't say anything for several seconds.

"Not seriously. Not yet. I want to play at least a couple seasons professionally first. Prove myself, you know?"

Alex does know.

"But I will someday. And I don't want to wait until I retire anymore."

"Does Cody have anything to do with that?" Alex asks.

James's silence is telling.

"Sorry. That's none of my business; forget I asked."

"No. I mean, yes? It's—maybe."

"What's maybe?"

"Cody." James makes an annoyed noise. "He's ... important. And we're not ... uh ... We're not. But ... "

"But he's making you think about it."

"Yeah."

"But you're also still James Petrov."

"Yeah."

"I understand."

"Yeah," James says, laughing a little. "I bet you do. At least you've already proven yourself though. Youngest captain in the NHL for the number one team in your division. Calder your rookie year. Currently first in points and second in goals in the league. You could come out *tomorrow* if you wanted."

And all laid out like that ... James kind of has a point.

Alex swallows, trying to keep his voice steady. "Aw. You still keep track of my stats?"

"Of course I do. But hey, listen. I don't want you to have to lie for me. So just—keep me posted about your plans and whatever PR is telling you, okay? We have time. Who knows how I'll feel a year from now."

"Okay," Alex agrees.

They both go silent, and Eli shifts a little, rubbing his cold nose against the bare skin on Alex's chest. Eli's nose is always cold. Even in ridiculously warm Alabama winter. Alex has no idea why, but it's hopelessly endearing.

"Thank you," Alex says.

James doesn't ask him for what, which he appreciates. Nor does he dismiss the gratitude.

"Yeah," James agrees. And then, "I can hear my parents downstairs. Talk later?"

"Yeah. Merry Christmas, James."

"Merry Christmas, Alex."

He ends the call and lets his phone slide down the pillow, disappearing into the cloud of Eli's duvet. He just breathes for a minute, eyes caught on the dark wood of the peaked ceiling.

He thinks maybe it should hurt that James is considering coming out. That he doesn't want to wait until retirement anymore—something he'd been so painfully adamant about for so many years. He thinks maybe it should hurt that James might be willing to do it for Cody, a kid he's known for less than six months, when he wasn't willing to do it for *Alex*. But it doesn't hurt.

Or maybe it doesn't hurt as much as it could. Because Eli is stretched out in a solid line of warmth next to him, tracing absent patterns on his stomach with gentle fingers, letting him process.

What does hurt is how broken, in retrospect, his relationship with James had been. How disjointed and non-communicative and unintentionally cruel they'd been to each other—both terrified, with no idea how to love someone and no one they could go to for help with figuring out how. He can't say he wishes that first desperate kiss at sixteen had never happened, but he hurts for his past self. For past James. For both of them. It wasn't fair.

He doesn't realize he's crying until Eli makes a distressed noise and sits up, then leans over to thumb away his tears, eyes wide and concerned, and Alex cannot with Eli's stupid beautiful face right now.

He hides in Eli's lap, embarrassed, wraps his arms around Eli's waist, and tries to get a goddamn hold on himself.

"Hey," Eli says, fingers hesitant in his hair. "Is this good crying or bad crying? Because I am really bad at this shit, and I don't know what to do."

"I'm not crying."

"Okay. Well. Are you, um, not crying in a good way or not crying in a bad way?"

He laughs wetly. "Good. I think. Just ... " He breathes for a moment, thinks about being honest and making things simple and saying what he means, and all the other super frustrating shit therapy has introduced to him, which is actually kind of helpful.

"I think I'm sad because James and I had a pretty fucked-up relationship, but we didn't know any better, and we ended up just making things worse for each other. And that sucks. But I'm also relieved? We're both so much happier and healthier now. But then that makes me mad, like, on behalf of my past self. Our past selves. We were just kids. And it's not right that we had so much pressure on us and were so afraid of being caught. It's not fair."

His voice might have broken on the last word.

Eli's fingers move more purposely through his hair. "You're right. It's not. I can't even imagine what you went through, and you are completely allowed to be upset about it. Sad and relieved and angry and happy and whatever else you need to feel."

Sometimes it is abundantly clear Eli is also in therapy.

"But, hey," his voice goes kind of rounded and soft. "Think about the impact you'll have when you come out. You can prove to kids all over the world that living with secrecy and shame isn't the only option. Think about what it would have meant for you, if there had been an out player in the league. And not just an out player, but a captain, with awards and accolades, and ... sponsorship deals with Gatorade."

"I don't have a sponsorship with Gatorade."

"Oh my god, Alex. You know what I'm saying."

He does. And it's ... admittedly not something Alex had thought of previously. But Eli is right. It would have made a difference to have that as a kid. Maybe even a huge difference.

"You're right," he says, face still tucked somewhere in the vicinity of Eli's upper thigh.

"Thank you."

Neither of them moves for several seconds, apart from Eli's restless fingers.

"So," Eli says eventually. "I know we're having an emotionally fraught moment and everything, but I really have to pee, so—"

Alex cracks up, which, judging by the restrained noise Eli makes, probably doesn't help things. "I should shower," he says, resigned, and sits up.

"After I use the bathroom," Eli says.

"I guess I'll allow it."

Hawk, who had slept through the proceedings, wiggles her way up from the foot of the bed to say good morning.

"You want me to let her out?" Alex asks.

"Yes, please."

Alex gets a close-mouthed kiss as he's pulling on a shirt. He catches Eli's hand as he starts to retreat and ducks to press his mouth to Eli's knuckles; he's feeling particularly overcome at the moment, and it seems like the thing to do.

"Thank you," he says, and he's pretty sure if Eli's skin wasn't so dark, he'd be tomato red.

"For what?" Eli asks.

"Being with me."

He feels like maybe that isn't specific enough. Maybe Eli won't understand he doesn't just mean this morning.

But Eli's eyes go wide and serious, and he says, "Of course," in a way that feels distressingly close to *always*.

"But seriously." Eli tugs a little at Alex's grip. "I do need to pee."

2

ELI CAME OUT TO his family on his fourteenth birthday.

It was a Saturday, and he'd spent the morning at the rink with Cody. And then he'd come home, done his chores, because even on his birthday, the goats were needy, adorable bastards. And then he'd collapsed, exhausted, on the couch.

He got to pick what they ate for dinner, and he chose Tres Golpes since breakfast-for-dinner was the best and also Francesca had decided she hated plantains that week and, at eight years old, she was quite possibly the most annoying person ever. Watching her suffer through clearing her plate was its own gift.

He was kind of a dick at fourteen.

But then he'd opened his actual presents and, of course, his mother had bought him clothes and then made him try on the clothes and then nearly got teary when he came out in a button-down that felt too tight around his throat. She hugged him and sighed about her baby growing up and asked if he had plans to ask someone special to the upcoming eighth-grade spring dance. When he said no, she took it upon herself to open his seventh-grade yearbook and go through the various girls she thought might be good candidates, with Abuela occasionally giving her input.

And he knew they didn't mean anything by it. They weren't trying to upset him.

But he was fourteen and full of hormones or whatever, and he'd had a very long, tiring day. Suddenly he was unbuttoning the shirt as if it was the problem, throwing it onto the floor and yelling that he didn't have a crush on any of the girls in his grade, and why couldn't they just leave him alone?

Which, of course, had the exact opposite effect. Five minutes later, he was sitting on the couch half-naked, surrounded by his family and crying that he was maybe, possibly, definitely gay, and please don't send him to a place he'd seen on the news where the kids did bootcamp exercises and prayed a lot until they were "fixed" or whatever. He didn't think there was anything wrong with him.

Surprisingly, it was his father, not his mother, who pulled him into a crushing hug and said, of course, there was nothing wrong with him, and they would never send him to a place like that, please don't cry, and they loved him and would always love him no matter what and maybe go pick up your new shirt before Mamá gets over her shock and remembers that you threw it, tags and all, onto the floor.

So he'd picked up his shirt, laughing a little, and was hugged by first Mamá and then Abuela, who was honestly the one he was most worried about.

"You're not mad I'm gay?" he had to ask.

"There are worse things you could be," she said.

"Like a fútbol player," Francesca said. She was at a stage where anything the other family members liked, she vehemently opposed. Exhibit A: plantains.

"There is nothing wrong with fútbol players," Abuela chided, and then, aside to Eli, she murmured, "Feel free to bring one home."

It was, quite honestly, a little anticlimactic. For years, he'd imagined worst-case scenarios, wondering if he should come out at all or just wait until after college, like Cody planned to do. But he just ... couldn't. College was too far away and, unlike Cody, he didn't think the worst-case scenario applied to him.

He spent the rest of his fourteenth birthday getting—and submitting to—a little more affection than usual. He even got to pick the movie they watched that night, much to Francesca's dismay. By bedtime, Mamá and Abuela were cuddled up on the couch with him, going through the seventh-grade yearbook again, this time, looking at the boys.

It was ... good.

Really good.

And the following Christmas, when he'd come out to the rest of his family, they'd handled things with more or less equal grace. His cousin Toby had been a bit of a dick. But Eli didn't even have to decide whether it was worth punching him over because two of his other cousins piled on Toby a moment later. Then, once Toby's mom found out what he'd said, he didn't get dessert. So that was fine too.

It'd taken Eli ages to fall asleep that Christmas night, watching the shadows shift across the ceiling and imagining maybe, someday, he might have someone else in the bed with him, visiting for the holidays. Maybe, someday, he might actually get the chance to wake up with his boyfriend or his husband in his childhood room, to go downstairs to the madness of his wonderful, ridiculous, family. To perhaps, far off in the future, put to use one of the half-dozen fold-away baby cots his mom has stashed in various closets around the house.

Because that—marriage and kids and family—was suddenly possible. Everyone he cared about knew and still accepted him.

It was probably one of the happiest realizations of his life.

Now, lying curled in Alex's recently abandoned warmth, staring at the same ceiling only five years later, Eli grins up at the rafters. It's happening. And it's even better than he imagined.

Eli decides to go back to sleep once Alex gets in the shower; it's unlikely it will take him less than fifteen minutes. While he can hear his Mamá and Abuela are awake, Francesca definitely won't be up yet, and breakfast won't start until the rest of the family drives in. So he lies there and enjoys the smell of menthol and Alex on his sheets and the soft, indistinct noise of conversation, punctuated by occasional laughter, coming from downstairs. He drifts, not quite asleep, but not fully awake, either, until Alex emerges from the bathroom. Pink-faced and damp-skinned, he jumps onto the bed in a gust of vanilla-scented air. He's only wearing boxer briefs—the black Under Armour ones with neon-green stitching he knows Eli prefers—and he wiggles his way back under the comforter and then drapes himself on top of Eli, grinning.

"Merry Christmas," Alex says, pressing a humid kiss to the little section of skin under Eli's left ear.

"Merry Christmas," he agrees.

And then there's the distinct sound of cars coming down the gravel driveway, followed inevitably by a sudden upheaval of noise downstairs.

Alex sits up, considering.

"Did a child army just besiege the house?"

"Besiege, huh?"

"You used 'besieged' in your paper about the Mesopotamian war," Alex says absently, rubbing his knuckles against the short grain of the shaved portion of Eli's hair. "It's a good word."

"You read my paper about the Mesopotamian war?" Alex looks at him like he's a moron.

"Yes? You left it on the counter. You said I could."

"I know I said you could, but I didn't think you actually would."

"Why wouldn't I? I like history, and I like you. You writing about history is the best. And even if I didn't like history, I would still be supportive. I looked through your calculus bluebook, too, even though I didn't understand any of it."

Eli has to kiss him for that.

Another car arrives, and the noise level downstairs multiplies exponentially.

Alex's eyebrows go up again.

"We should get dressed," Eli says. "Are you ready for this?"

"I don't know, am I?"

"Probably not."

Alex pouts at him.

"I'm the second youngest of six cousins, and all but one of them are married and have at least one kid. None of which are over the age of five. So."

Alex's eyes go a little wide. "Okay," he says seriously, and then—

Well. That's, literally, Alex's game face.

Eli kisses him again since he figures Alex wouldn't appreciate him laughing and then goes to get dressed so they can join the chaos downstairs.

Christmas with his family and Alex is exactly as outrageous as Eli expected. Once everyone is seated at the tables—one main, two overflow—Abuela explains over crying babies and toddler chatter that Eli's boyfriend, Alex, is a closeted professional athlete, and no one is to take or post any pictures of him online under pain of her wrath. This is followed by nearly every adult getting out their phone and googling Alex, much to Alex's dismay.

Eli's oldest cousin, Markus, doesn't have to, however. He lives in New York and gets Rangers tickets from his company pretty regularly. This provides a relieved Alex with a solid twenty minutes of conversation since he's played in juniors with one of the Rangers' new rookies—Jesse Nash. He and Markus fall easily into a friendly argument about the last Hell Hounds/Rangers game. (The Rangers won, but only, Alex maintains, because Kuzy and Matts had both been out with minor injuries.)

When they move into the living room to open gifts, Eli and Alex share a chair that is technically too small for two people, but neither of them complains. They drink eggnog-doctored coffee and laugh over the sheer overwhelming exuberance of the children present.

Later, when the floor is a sea of wrapping paper and empty bags, and the kids are scattered, playing with their new toys, the adults get their turn. It's mostly clothes and home goods, "needs" rather than "wants" as Abuela terms it. Until, of course, they get to Alex's presents.

He's already looking a little sheepish, wearing the handmade crocheted scarf Abuela gave him, and Eli braces himself. He'd given Alex what was, for his budget, a pretty expensive selection of gifts: a very soft, very clingy T-shirt that was admittedly more for Eli than Alex and a new Kindle since he knew Alex's old one was having issues charging. He knows whatever Alex has gotten for Eli—and apparently the rest of his family—probably blows that out of the water.

Alex grins a little self-consciously as Abuela passes out his gifts. He has one arm around Eli, the other awkwardly extended over the arm of the chair so Estaci, Markus's four-year-old daughter, can paint his nails with one of her new nail polishes. She isn't doing a very good job, but Alex doesn't seem to care.

The long, skinny package for Eli's dad is a new pair of DeWalt barbed-wire cutters and a pair of Duluth Kevlar work gloves, which Papá genuinely seems happy about. Mamá is perhaps even more excited, and she moves to hug Alex—gently, so as not to disturb Estaci's work—muttering that maybe now her stubborn fool of a husband won't come home bleeding every time he has to fix the fence. Abuela gets an envelope with a notification that her new yellow stand mixer will arrive at her house in the Dominican Republic the day after her own return in two weeks. She promptly blesses him, his future children, and all his hockey endeavors—in Spanish, of course, but judging by his pleased grin, Alex gets the gist of it. His mom similarly gets an envelope informing her Alex has prepaid for a year's worth of monthly birdseed delivery from Amazon; at which point, she tells Alex he's looking a little hungry and goes to fix him another plate. Eli's mom is just as bad with emotions as Eli is. Francesca gets a pair of Jordans, which she promptly screams about, thanks Alex effusively, and then begs to borrow Mamá's phone so she can FaceTime her best friend to brag.

Eli is the only one who cries, of course, but he's the only one to receive a new pair of custom-made Riedell ice skating boots with John Wilson Gold Seal blades. And he knows they're custom because the black boots have shiny red-lacquered soles—like Louboutins—and he doesn't even want to think about how much trouble Alex must have gone through to make that happen or how much he must have *spent*—

"Oh," Alex says when Eli starts tearing up, one of the new boots cradled reverently to his chest. "No, hey, is—sorry, Estaci. Can I have my hand back?—are you okay? Are the skates okay? I talked to Jeff *and* your coach, but—"

"They're perfect," Eli manages, more than a little strangled.

Alex is perfect.

Oh god.

And maybe Eli has to hide his face in his boyfriend's chest for a minute.

It's fine.

It's not embarrassing at all.

By the time he's managed to get a hold of himself, most of the cousins have migrated to the kitchen and are putting together a fútbol game. Markus is still arguing with Anna about last summer's game, and Francesca is declaring they'll have to replace her; now that she's put the Jordans on, she refuses to take them off. She's certainly not about to get *dirt* on them *oh my god how could you even suggest that*? Eli is glad his parents have held firm on the whole "no phone until freshman year of high school" thing because if she had access to Instagram, the whole feed would probably be the damn shoes for the next month. She is happy, though, and Alex looks endlessly pleased with himself.

"Hey," Markus calls to Eli, "is your boy playing? He can take Francesca's spot."

"Oh, no," Eli starts, but he's interrupted by Alex's even louder, "Sure!"

"You don't have to play," Eli says lowly.

"What? Of course I'm going to play," Alex answers, and the look on his face is—Oh.

Oh no.

"Do you even know how?"

It is immediately clear this is the wrong thing to ask.

"Oh my god. I know how to play soccer, Eli. I was on a team in elementary school. And the Hell Hounds kick a ball around the hallway before every game."

"That's ... really not the same."

Alex makes a dismissive noise.

"So I'll figure it out. I may not know Spanish, but chirping is universal. If I don't play, none of your cousins are going to respect me."

"I mean, to be fair, if you do play, they probably won't either," Eli says, just to make sure his position is clear. His family doesn't mess around with their fútbol. Alex is going to get wrecked, and it will not be Eli's responsibility.

"I'm a *professional athlete*," Alex says, exasperated. "I'll be fine."

"Sure you will, sweetheart."

When they huddle up in their respective teams a few minutes later, Eli interrupts Markus's game-plan speech with a firm warning.

"Do not break my boyfriend," Eli says, looking pointedly at Toby. "I know he's an overly competitive moron, but his ankles are also worth several million dollars. So if any of you so much as thinks about tripping him to prove a point, I will have you excommunicated from this family. Everyone knows I'm Abuela's favorite. I can make it happen."

No one argues. They know it's true.

It turns out Alex isn't, actually, that bad. He can't handle the ball to save his life, but he's fast and arguably the most fit person out there, so he manages to hold his own better than anticipated. Eli's team wins since they have Anna's wife, who played NCAA soccer, which is probably cheating, but Eli doesn't care because it's to his advantage. The other team does care, though, and they all troop back into the house for water, arguing, but too hot to play a second game with new teams. By the time they've all reintegrated in the living room and kitchen with the rest of the family, Alex has been handed a baby.

And honestly.

That's just not fair.

He comes to stand next to Eli, still breathing a little hard, sweaty and smudged with red Alabama dirt, holding a content, ringlet-haired eight-month-old and looking a little concerned about it. He's overly cautious and wide-eyed, one hand—the hand spanning the infant's back—still badly painted with glittery pink nail polish.

Eli loves him so much it's a little scary. "I need to go check on the goats," he lies.

The goats are fine, which isn't exactly a surprise, but as he's walking back to the house, watching Hawk chase grasshoppers and trying to get a handle on his emotions, Eli receives a cryptic message from Cody instructing him to call back when he has a minute alone.

Curiosity piqued, Eli does.

"So," Cody says after the second ring, "Alex is planning a surprise thing for you, but I'm pretty sure it's the type of surprise you'd rather know about in advance."

"Uh. Okay?"

"So do you want to know?"

"Do I? I trust your judgement."

Cody lets out a sigh of relief. "Right. So. Alex asked Mama to borrow her truck tomorrow night and then asked me about typical date places around town as well as typical, uh ... *date* places. I recommended the mill, obviously, but if you'd rather Eddy Spring, I can text Alex directions there instead. I think the mill will be safe since the day after Christmas isn't going to be busy in terms of parking real estate, but it's up to you, obviously."

It takes Eli a moment to compute that.

"Oh my god," he says faintly. "Are you serious?"

"Yup," Cody says, popping the *p*.

"The mill is ... "

Perfect.

Ridiculous.

The location of nearly every embarrassing erotic high school fantasy he's ever had.

"Fine." Eli clears his throat. "Your mom is letting him borrow the truck?"

"Mm-hmm. And it sounds like your grandma is going to supply

him with a bed full of quilts and a picnic to share. Mama and Aba have been texting back and forth all day and are frankly a little disturbingly invested in getting you laid. Not that they've said that. Mama is talking about it as if y'all are going to hold hands and watch the sunset or something. I guess that bodes well for me, regardless though. If I ever decide to come out to them. This is about you though."

"Oh my god," Eli repeats.

"Anyway," Cody continues, "from what I've gathered, Alex is going to take you to an early movie in town and then drive y'all up to park above the spillway and despoil you in the truck bed under the stars which"—Eli makes a noise, but Cody talks right over him—"is a little cliché for my taste but I'm pretty sure is exactly how you'd love to lose your virginity, weirdo that you are."

"Uh. Yeah."

"*Uh, yeah*?" Cody mimics, maybe mocking him a little.

"That would be nice," Eli says delicately. And if that isn't the most massive understatement—"I may have mentioned I didn't get to do stuff like that in high school. So Alex might have remembered."

"Ugh. Y'all are disgustingly cute. So, you're okay with this? I didn't want you to be blindsided."

"No. No, I am. Holy shit, I am. Tomorrow? This is happening tomorrow?"

Oh fuck.

This is happening *tomorrow*.

"Yessir," Cody says blithely, as if Eli isn't having something of a crisis. "So make sure your manscaping is in order. And maybe bring bug spray. I told Alex the mosquitos are no joke out there, and he opted for citronella candles, romantic idiot that he is. Might be good to have a plan B."

Eli isn't really listening because he's going to have sex with Alexander Price tomorrow.

Tomorrow.

"Cody," Eli interrupts, and he stops walking. The back porch is getting a little too close for comfort. Hawk runs into his knees and then sneezes at him to show her displeasure. "Okay. Okay. So. This is happening. Tomorrow. Shit. What do I do?"

"I mean. Suck his dick, probably."

"Cody."

"Well. He's definitely planning to suck yours."

"Cody."

But—

"Wait," Eli says. "He told you that?"

"He didn't need to. Have you seen the way he fellates his mouthguard between plays? That boy has an oral fixation a mile wide."

And.

Yes.

Eli may have noticed that.

Somebody yells his name, and he jumps, squinting up toward the house.

It's Anna, letting him know lunch is ready.

"I have to go," he says. "Thanks for the heads-up."

"You'd do the same for me. Or at least you'd better. Anything you want me to pass on to Alex? Any special requests?"

His voice is dripping with implication.

"Goodbye, Cody."

"All right, all right. I expect deets for my trouble though. Preferably the minute you get home tomorrow night. I'll stay up."

"Goodbye, Cody."

"DEETS, Elijah!"

Eli hangs up on him.

3

"SO," ALEX SAYS THE following afternoon. "Do you want to go take a shower and get dressed to go out?"

Eli blinks up at him from where they're lazily cuddling on the porch swing.

"I don't know, do I?"

"I think you do."

"Hmm," he says, trying not to smile. "What do you mean by 'out'? What would I need to wear?"

Alex clears his throat. "An outfit might have been left for you on the bed."

"Oh, it might have been? That's a masterful use of the passive voice there."

"Eli."

"Alex."

He ducks a little, shoving his face against Eli's temple. "Please go get ready? I'm trying to do a thing."

"Oh, well, a *thing*. Why didn't you say so sooner?"

Alex dumps him off the swing.

There is, indeed, an outfit laid out on the bed, and Eli has a sneaking suspicion Cody was involved in the selection process. The shorts are—short. A pair of pale-blue Chubbies that shrank in the wash and were relegated to the back of Eli's closet sometime last year. They still fit around his waist, but they cling to his thighs in a way that is downright risqué for small-town Alabama sensibilities. Luckily, they're tempered by a plain T-shirt, a thin white button-down, and canvas Vans, brand new and definitely not previously in his closet.

Eli sighs at Hawk because Alex isn't there to sigh at, and then he goes to take a thorough shower and put the damn clothes on. He may need to have another conversation with Alex about his gift-giving proclivities, but he's not going to do it now when a fight would ruin what is hopefully going to be an otherwise excellent night.

When he returns downstairs, dressed and ready, Alex has clearly used a different bathroom and is dressed similarly in jeans and a white button-down—sleeves rolled to his elbows, showing off one of his stupid gaudy watches. He wears a snapback that matches Eli's shoes.

This isn't lost on Francesca, who dissolves into laughter and says they're disgusting before returning her attention to what appears to be a very intense Scrabble game with the cousins. Family tradition dictates players can use any language, and Francesca has been learning French for the past year purely to get a leg up.

"So," Alex says, already pink. "Are you ready?"

"I guess. You going to tell me where we're going?"

"Nope."

"Then, yeah, absolutely, let's go."

Abuela laughs indiscreetly in the kitchen.

"Okay," Alex says. "Can you wait here for a second?"

"Uh. Sure?"

Alex wipes his palms on his thighs, like he's nervous or something, and then just walks out the front door and shuts it firmly behind him. The doorbell rings a few seconds later, but before Eli can open it and ask Alex if he's lost his mind, his father comes out of the kitchen and pushes him gently aside.

Upon opening the door, his father crosses his arms.

"Good afternoon. How can I help you?"

Eli looks back and forth between them, baffled. Apparently, they've *both* lost their minds.

"Afternoon, sir," Alex says, extending one hand. "I'm Alex; I'm here to pick up Eli for our date?"

"Oh my god," Eli says as they shake somberly. "You guys. Stop it."

"Hush," his dad says. "I'm talking to your suitor, here." He then turns back to Alex. "Tell me a little about yourself, Mr. Price. Do you make good grades? Do you have a job? A plan for the future?"

Abuela snickers from somewhere behind Eli, and he glances over his shoulder to find that everyone in the living room has abandoned their various pursuits and is now watching raptly as if Eli's ridiculous boyfriend being ridiculous is some sort of spectator sport.

"Well," Alex says, looking a little bashful. "My grades weren't the best. But I do have a pretty good job."

"Pretty good?" Eli's dad says skeptically.

"Around two and a half million dollars annually if you count my sponsorships. And I have a financial planner guy who's helping me manage things wisely."

"Well. I guess that's acceptable."

Several people in the living room stifle giggles.

"Mr. Price, what are your intentions with my son?"

"Oh, you know," Alex says, grin finally breaking through his serious demeanor, "love him, cherish him, take him to a movie and have him back by 11:00."

Eli's dad glances at the clock—barely 6:00 p.m.—and raises an eyebrow.

"It's a very long movie," Alex says, utterly straightfaced.

"Make it 10:30."

"Yessir," Alex agrees and then turns to grin at Eli, extending one hand.

"Hey, baby," he says, going even pinker. "You ready?"

And yes.

Eli is so, so ready.

Alex holds open the passenger door to Cody's mom's freshly washed baby-blue truck and offers Eli a hand up into the cab even though it's not that high, then makes sure Hawk is settled in the floorboard before tucking her tail out of harm's way and shutting the door. He leans over the gear shift to kiss Eli once he's climbed into the driver's seat.

"How'm I doing so far?" Alex asks, flushed and looking exceptionally pleased with himself.

"Nine out of ten," Eli says.

Alex's face falls. "What did I miss?"

"No flowers?" Eli says, pitching his voice high with a hand to his chest. "Alexander, I expect to be *wooed*."

Alex wrinkles his nose. "You hate flowers. And you're allergic to most of them."

"Mm. True. Then you should have brought something for Hawk instead. We're a package deal, after all. You need to woo her too."

"Next time," he says seriously, and Eli has to kiss him again.

"For real, though, ten out of ten. This is awesome. I can't believe you went through all this trouble. When we get back to Houston, I'm returning the favor."

"Oh yeah?"

"Hell yeah. I'm going to take you on the best date of your life."

"You going to bring something for Bells? Ask her permission to take me out?"

"Obviously."

"I look forward to it."

Once they get to the cinema, they find the theater is empty.

"Why, Mr. Rodriguez," Alex murmurs once they're settled, sliding his arm along the back of Eli's seat. "It would seem we're all alone."

"That we are, Mr. Price. Except for Hawk, of course."

"Mm," Alex agrees, glancing down at her. "Not the most attentive chaperone though. What are your thoughts about PDA?" He ducks to press his mouth to the hinge of Eli's jaw.

"Generally positive, but not when a movie is about to start."

Alex pauses, glancing up to meet Eli's eyes. "Seriously?" There's a little bit of a whine to his tone.

Eli refuses to find it cute. "We paid twenty dollars for tickets to see this movie, Alex. We are going to *watch* it."

"*I* paid twenty dollars," Alex mutters peevishly.

The lights dim, and Eli pushes at Alex's face. "You're dangerously close to losing a point on your date ranking. Shut up and hold my hand."

Alex shuts up and holds his hand.

Except he doesn't just *hold* his hand.

By the time previews are over, Alex's thumb is making a gentle circular pattern against the back of Eli's hand. It seems like an absent movement, at first, something Alex is doing unconsciously, until a few minutes into the movie when he shifts his grip a little so he can drag his fingers in maddening little hitches up and down the divots of Eli's knuckles. And then he shifts again so he's holding Eli's wrist, thumb pressed to the swell of his palm, index finger circling his wrist bone, several seconds between each. Slow. Orbit. Touch so light Eli can barely feel it. And then Alex very intentionally trails his thumb down to trace the tendon in Eli's wrist, turning his hand to lie flat on the armrest between them so Alex can slide his cupped hand—lightly, so lightly—down the length of his arm and back again. His callouses catch in the fine hair on Eli's arm in a way that the gentle pads of his fingers don't, and the dichotomy is strangely, utterly, captivating. And *then*, when Eli finally gets used to that, Alex turns Eli's hand palm up again and trails his fingers from Eli's palm to inner elbow, his nails dragging in light, erratic, goosebump-inciting patterns that start slow and then build in speed and then change direction.

It's utterly distracting.

Possibly even more distracting than making out with him would be.

Somewhere near the end of the movie—there's a lot of explosions and screaming, but Eli has absolutely no idea what's happening because Alex has somehow turned hand-holding into foreplay—Eli gives up and shifts so he's mostly in Alex's lap.

Alex laughs for a solid minute before Eli manages to shove his tongue in Alex's still-grinning mouth, and maybe the twenty dollars wasn't exactly put to good use, but it wasn't wasted either.

When the theater lights come back on, Eli's mouth feels tender.

Alex's hands are halfway up the back of his shirt, and they're both breathing a little harder than is appropriate for a public venue.

Eli pushes his face into the humid pocket between Alex's neck and shoulder and breathes the warm scent of him for several seconds. Eli is wearing really tight shorts, and he's going to need a minute before he can stand up. It's a nice portion of neck, Eli thinks absently, kissing what might be a cluster of freckles or might be a shadow. Good real estate. He could live here happily.

Alex thumbs his spine, sighing, and glances toward the exit where an usher has pulled open the door, talking to someone in the hallway.

"Care to relocate?" Alex asks. That's probably best.

Back in the truck, they hold hands—*normal* handholding—with the windows down, Alex grinning and refusing to tell Eli where they're heading as he takes surreptitious looks at his phone in his lap.

The great thing about bench seats is Eli can slide over and lean into Alex's side, rest his temple on the swell of Alex's shoulder, and revel in the fact that he's in a car with a beautiful boy watching the sun set over a one-lane road that's more pothole than asphalt, with wind in his face and Hawk's chin on his knee and country music on the radio.

It's perfect.

Almost too perfect.

And it makes him anxious, as if surely something will go wrong, *has* to go wrong because he doesn't just get moments like this.

Except maybe he does, now.

He slides his fingers up Alex's forearm, repaying the favor from earlier, tracing one of the veins that stands out, subtle and maddening in the golden-skinned space between wrist and elbow.

Maybe this is just his life, now.

Maybe after everything, maybe he just gets to be happy.

He realizes he's getting a little maudlin, but it doesn't matter. They've hit the river and Alex cautiously takes the right-hand fork from asphalt to red dirt that meanders up the bluff to the unauthorized parking area in the trees that overlooks the mill.

The mill is a monument, one of the few in their tiny town. Every elementary school student visits it on a class trip at some point. It was built in 1901 and restored in the sixties—a shingled building atop a stone dam, dwarfed by the slow-moving, wooden-slatted wheel attached to it. It has all sorts of historical relevance, of course, but it's mostly known for its romantic aesthetic, settled in the gentle bend of the green-blue river, shaded by massive oak trees that turn a host of fiery colors in the fall.

Unsurprisingly, the well-worn grass plain at the top of the bluff is empty, and Alex's eyes are wide and exceptionally blue as he turns off the engine.

"This is ... ridiculously pretty," he says, leaning out the window a little. "I mean, holy shit. This is almost fake pretty."

The sun is mostly set, but the pink-orange on the horizon behind the dam is reflecting below in the water, warped a little by the current. The whippoorwills are out en masse as well, blanketing the trees in a soft susurrus of sleepy birdsong that complements the quiet rush of water over moving paddles below.

Eli allows himself a moment of pride. This is his home. Even if it's only an accident of birth that gives him claim to it.

"Yeah," he agrees, hooking his chin over Alex's shoulder.

Alex turns, his nose wrinkled a little in genuine happiness, and within a few seconds, Eli finds himself knocked over, head awkwardly propped on the passenger door with 185 pounds of professional hockey player stretched out on top of him, mouthing lazily at his neck. He pushes back, redirecting Alex's lips to his own and revels a little in the soft sound of encouragement Alex makes in the back of his throat.

A few minutes later, Eli's gets his hands fisted in the fabric of Alex's shirt, trying to drag it over his head even though his stupid snapback is still in the way.

Alex puts some space between them, laughing. "Hold on, let me—you distracted me. I had a plan."

Eli glances at their surroundings. "Is the plan not sex?"

Alex chokes a little. "It doesn't have to be. I just wanted to give you your high school"—he waves a hand around—"whatever."

"My high school whatever," Eli repeats.

"Yes," Alex says with dignity, pulling his shirt straight again.

"And if my 'high school whatever' involves sex?"

Alex's already pink ears go progressively more red. He hooks his thumb toward the back of the truck. "I, uh, also prepared for that scenario."

"Did you."

"And I definitely promised Mrs. Griggs we wouldn't—that we would keep any, um—"

"Amorous activities?" Eli supplies.

"—amorous activities outside the cabin of the truck."

"Well," Eli says. "I guess we better get out then."

There's a duffel in the truck bed with no less than four quilts—all of them Eli recognizes from various closets around his house—an assortment of throw pillows, and an honest-to-god picnic basket. Alex goes into narrowed-eyed play-making mode, laying out his stash and then consulting his phone before setting up the back of the truck as if he's trying to recreate some sort of romantic Pinterest post.

Which, actually, is likely.

Eli lets Hawk out to explore, knowing she'll stay close. He steals a soda from the picnic basket, sits on the roof, and submits himself to being wooed.

The stars are coming out—bright and startling after so many months spent in a light-polluted city—when Alex jumps off the tailgate to survey his work.

Eli is admittedly impressed.

"So?" Alex says, hands on his hips.

"I'm feeling thoroughly romanced," Eli says. "Ten out of ten for both effort and execution." Eli points to one blanket, still folded over the side. "I think you forgot one though."

"Oh," Alex takes off his hat to scratch at the back of his head before replacing it. "Abuela heavily implied you were conceived under that quilt. Wasn't sure how I felt about that."

Eli grimaces. "Yeah. Maybe we leave that one in the cab."

"Good plan." As Alex leans in the window to deposit the blanket on the floorboard, he makes a revelatory noise and pulls out a plastic Walmart bag. "I can't believe I almost forgot," he says, more to himself than Eli, and then dumps its contents at Eli's feet.

Apparently, Alex has bought out Walmart's citronella candle section. He balances four on either side of the truck bed and beckons Eli down so he can place three more on the roof, then struggles to get them lit in the light wind.

"You know this is ridiculous, right?" Eli says, cross-legged and almost euphorically happy. "Like, you didn't need to do any of this. I'm a sure thing."

Alex looks at him as if he's a moron. He crawls over to sit next to Eli, shoulder to shoulder, eyebrows pinched. "I know. I'm not ... trying to coerce you or something. I just wanted ... "

He takes a breath. Starts again. "You deserve good things. To be treated like—like you're the best thing. Because you are. And I know I'm going to fuck things up. I've never been in a relationship before, and I'm, you know, human. But this is something I can do right. Do better."

"Better than what?" Eli says, maybe a little hoarse. He cups his palm over Alex's knuckles, a sharp jut of bone where he's clenching his hand on his thigh.

"Literally no one but you has ever touched me. Well. Other than me. I've definitely touched ... me." Eli clears his throat, wincing, but at least his awkwardness gets a laugh out of Alex who turns his hand, linking their fingers together.

Alex licks his lips, eyes on their joined hands. "You're giving up a lot to be with me. And I know between my issues and my career and my past, it's going to suck sometimes. Being my boyfriend. Especially when I can't even publicly admit that you are, so ... I just want to do as many things that I have control over right. So maybe the shitty things won't hurt as bad when they happen."

Eli has no idea how to respond to that, except to maybe cry. Because Alex is so—Alex.

And it's more than a little heartbreaking that he thinks he needs to build up some sort of positive-experience buffer so that Eli is willing to stick around.

He lets go of Alex's hand so he can climb into his lap, plants a decisive kiss on his mouth, and then starts unbuttoning Alex's shirt.

"Um," Alex says.

"I love you," Eli says, maybe a little more aggressively than intended. "And I appreciate all this romantic shit. I appreciate that you want me to have good memories or whatever. But I'm pretty sure anything we do tonight is going to be good because it's *us*, and *I love you*. So can we please get naked before these citronella candles all go out and we get eaten alive by mosquitos?"

Alex stifles his laughter in Eli's shoulder, squeezing him so tightly he has to give up on the shirt buttons for a minute. "Yeah," he says, "okay."

And then there's quite a bit more laughter on both of their parts as Alex tries to keep his hat on throughout the process of removing his clothes and actually succeeds despite Eli's valiant attempts to pull the stupid thing off his head. It should be ridiculous, honestly. Alex should look ridiculous, but hockey players' bodies are no joke, and even with one sock on and a half-askew snapback, Alex is—he's—

Everything about him is unfair.

Eventually, Eli wrestles the hat off his head and throws it over the side of the truck, and then things are abruptly a lot less funny and a lot more sexy. There's a whole hell of a lot of naked professional athlete stretched out underneath Eli, and they're kind of sweaty, chest to chest, breathing each other's air which—

Alex sits up a little, one hand spanning Eli's lower back, the other cupped around the nape of his neck. "Hey," he says, "tell me if you don't want—"

Eli does want.

He wants a lot.

Eli touches the pair of freckles just below Alex's right eye, then drags his thumb down to rest on Alex's bottom lip, grinning as Alex exhales, long and slow and a little shuddery.

"Hey," Eli says.

"Hey," Alex agrees.

4

ELI IS HALF ASLEEP WHEN the alarm on Alex's phone goes off.

Alex shifts, rolling away from him, to dig his phone out of his discarded jeans pocket to silence it, and then tucks himself right back into Eli's space, pressing slow, dry kisses to his forehead, closed eyelids, the tip of his nose.

And Alex's mouth is a little rough, his lips chapped and tugging at the sensitive skin on his cheekbone, but whatever. "It's 10:15," Alex says. "We should go. Wouldn't want to make a bad impression on your dad, bringing you home late."

Go? No. Eli thinks that's a terrible idea.

He ducks his face into Alex's neck and groans somewhere in the vicinity of Alex's collarbone.

"Come on." Alex laughs, sitting up. "Just think of the drive home as ... an extended relocation. To your bed. We can pick up where we left off there. Maybe after a shower."

Which—Yeah. A shower might be good.

"Also, we only have one candle still lit, and I'm pretty sure a mosquito just bit me on the ass."

That's also fair.

"So," Alex says, perhaps sensing he's won. "Up. Into the cab. Home."

"Sure," Eli says. "Maybe let me put some clothes on first, though, or we definitely won't be currying favor with my dad."

"All right, smartass."

"You know, when we talked about terms of endearment, that really wasn't what I had in mind."

"Dick," Alex says lovingly, ducking to kiss him.

As long as it took for Alex to set up the truck, it only takes a few minutes for them to pack everything back up, call Hawk out from under the bed where she'd been napping, and maneuver their way to the main road.

They're holding hands again, this time with cooler evening air coming in the windows and a dark sea of fields on either side of the truck's high beams.

"So," Eli says. "I wanted to talk to you about something."

"Oh, me too, actually," Alex says, sounding hopeful. "You go first though."

Eli glances over at him, but it's hard to tell in the dark what Alex's face is doing.

"Okay. Well, there's a New Year's Eve party that Pike House is throwing. One of their juniors is also VP of the Gay Straight Alliance so a couple people I know have invited me. Oh, and the Morgans will be there too."

"Okay?" Alex says.

"I wouldn't be able to bring Hawk, but ... The theme is masquerade, so everyone will be wearing masks, and I thought maybe you could come with me?"

"What if something happened?" Alex asks, and clearly, he's too focused on the whole "Hawk won't be there" that he's missed this is a perfect opportunity for them to do a normal college-aged couple-y thing with minimal risk for outing.

"Then you'll take care of me."

"Well, yeah. Obviously. But you'd have to tell me how. Beforehand, so I'd be ready."

"I can do that."

"Okay." Alex bites his lip, "Are you sure though?"

"Alex. I'm sure. I trust you."

"Okay."

He pauses, hand going tighter around Eli's, and then sits up a little straighter.

"Wait. Masquerade. So no one would know I'm me?"

And there it is.

"Yeah."

"So I could go as your mysterious masked boyfriend, not BFF Alex Price?"

"I can't believe you just said 'BFF' unironically, but yes."

"Oh. Yeah! Holy shit. This is going to be awesome. We only have a couple days to come up with costumes though."

And, of course, that's his first concern.

"We live in Houston. I'm pretty sure we'll work something out."

And the dichotomy—the thought of city lights superimposed over the massive expanse of star-spangled night sky out the windshield is a little funny.

"Point. I think Asher's girlfriend works at a cabaret. I could see if she has any recommendations for us."

"Perfect."

Alex slows at a stop sign, withdrawing his hand from Eli's so he can shift, and comes to a full stop, even though they're very clearly the only ones on the road.

"So," Eli says. "You said there was something you wanted to talk to me about?"

"Oh. Right."

Eli gives him a minute because he's Alex, and Eli has spent enough time with him to know silence isn't bad; it just means he's trying to get his words right.

"I know it's way too soon. And I probably shouldn't even bring it up. But I don't know how far in advance you have to do things, and I don't want you to commit to something else without—uh ... "

He clears his throat. "Obviously you don't have to give me an answer now. But I was wondering if maybe you would think about, possibly, moving in with me next year?"

His voice goes kind of thready and high at the end of the last sentence, and Eli has to punch him in the shoulder. He's already had a very emotionally fraught twenty-four hours, and how *dare* Alex spring something like that on him at a time like this?

"Ow," Alex says. "I'm really, uh, not sure how to take that?"

"Are you *serious*?"

"Of course I'm serious. You hate the dorms, but you have to stay in them since your scholarship doesn't cover off-campus housing. And you already have a bunch of stuff at my place anyway. And you could use the kitchen all the time, and do your homework on the island, and I could help you exercise Hawk, especially during stressful times. And you'd be there after hard games for me, and we could ride to the rink together in the mornings whenever our practice schedules link up and ... We could sleep in the same bed at night. Every night. Except for when I'm on roadies, obviously, but ... It would be nice. I think."

And that is ... a lot.

"Okay. Clearly, you've been thinking about this, but—"

"And I know you need time to yourself sometimes!" Alex says, well, yells. "And I respect that. And—" He swallows, eyebrows going kind of pinched. "And I, uh ... want to facilitate your comfort."

Eli almost laughs since, clearly, Alex is parroting someone else, but that just means he's done research or asked for advice, which is even more hopelessly endearing.

"I wasn't really sure how though," Alex continues, "so I asked my therapist for advice."

There it is.

"And she said maybe we could make the guest bedroom your space, and whenever you need me to leave you alone, you can go in there and I'll just pretend you're not even there until you're ready to deal with people again."

That had, admittedly, been Eli's biggest concern. "That might work," he says, almost without meaning to.

And Alex lights up like the fucking sun. "Really?"

"Yeah. We'd have to try it out and see, I guess. But it's really cool you thought about that."

"Well," Alex says, still grinning. "I had help. Do you want to give it a trial run when we get back? I'm assuming you'll be tired and done with people from the trip, so it'd be a good—"

"Testing environment?" Eli supplies, laughing.

"Yeah. And instead of dropping you off at the dorm, we could pick up some of your things and then just both go back to my place? And then you can do your thing and let me know if there's anything we'd need to change or whatever? We can move furniture around or get new furniture if you want. Or maybe add a TV?"

"That sounds really good. Not the TV or the furniture; that's ridiculous, but ... We can try that, sure."

"Good."

They turn into the driveway, and Eli lets his body go slack, falling into Alex as they lurch their way over the uneven gravel and up to the porch.

Alex is nearly vibrating with excitement, and Eli grins into his shoulder.

"Was this just a ploy to get me to move in *now*?"

"No," Alex says, a little too quickly.

"You realize we've only been dating for a month. Less than a month."

"Technically, we've been dating since August."

"You know what I mean, asshole."

"I do." Alex turns off the engine, sighing. "I know it's probably too fast. But it doesn't seem too fast."

Eli can't really argue with that. "Okay. We'll figure it out."

"Okay."

They just sit there in silence for a minute, leaning into each other, until the porch light turns on.

The screen door opens a second later, and Eli's Papá steps out, looking very intentionally down at his watch.

Eli digs his phone out of his pocket, screen lighting up the cab, to find that it is 10:29. "Oh, shit."

They scramble out of the truck, laughing, and manage to get in the door, dog included, by the time it hits 10:30.

"Cutting it close," Papá says, faux disapproving.

"Do you remember," Abuela says to Papá, from where she's crocheting on the couch, "that one time you say you'll have Alicia home by midnight, and instead, you bring her back three days later and *married*?"

Papá clears his throat. "Well. I hope you boys had a nice night. I should be getting to bed now."

Abuela makes a judgmental noise. Alex subtly high-fives her.

Eli rolls his eyes and heads up the stairs.

He claims first shower and then lies in bed, damp and warm and grinning up at the peaked roof, listening as Alex curses about cold water from the bathroom.

Eli's phone buzzes just past eleven with a text from Cody:

SO? how was the sweet sweet Price loving?

Eli sends a handful of eggplant emojis, the sweat emoji, some fireworks, and a rainbow assortment of hearts because he's a little giddy and basic as hell.

It takes Cody less than five seconds to respond.

Yes? good??Are you even alive rn???

RIP Eli texts back.

The flight back to Houston is uneventful, though Eli and Hawk are both spoiled by first class.

Riding economy will never be the same.

Alex drops Eli off at his dorm with a duffel bag and two boxes (a concession; Alex had been advocating for four boxes initially) for Eli to fill up with whatever he may need for their agreed-upon weeklong cohabitation trial period.

Alex, meanwhile, is picking up groceries since he'd paused his delivery service during the last roadie and forgot to renew it again.

Eli has one box packed when his phone buzzes.

He lunges across his bed, mostly upside down, to collect it from the floor and then nearly brains himself on the nightstand, laughing. It's a five second snapchat of Alex in the produce department holding up an eggplant, leering.

Eli is in love with a fuckboy.

It's less distressing than it probably should be.

It takes them two trips to get their various travel bags, as well as Eli's boxes, up to Alex's apartment, but only a few minutes to unpack everything in the guest room and closet.

Alex hovers awkwardly in the hall afterward, looking uncertain of his welcome.

"So," he says, trying to strike a casual pose and failing as he misjudges where the door frame is. He doesn't entirely fall over, but it's a near thing.

He clears his throat once he's upright again. "Do you want me to leave you alone now, or ... ?"

Eli stifles a laugh, considering. "Not really? We can just sit and not talk for a while, if that's cool. So, I can do that in here or out in the living room with you."

"Can I still touch you? If we sit on the couch together? I could play some NHL16 with the volume low?"

"Are you asking if we can cuddle?"

"I'm asking if we can sit in close proximity with each other. And ... maybe you could play with my hair," Alex says casually. "If you want."

"This is acceptable," Eli answers, face grave.

"Okay. I'll get the good blanket from the bedroom."

Eli does laugh then, just a little. His boyfriend is an epicurean weirdo, and he loves him a lot.

An hour later, Eli is propped in one corner between arm rest and couch back while Alex quietly curses at the TV, head in Eli's lap. Hawk and Bells share the real estate of Alex's prone torso.

The front door opens, and Jeff—holding his key, talking over his shoulder to someone—walks inside. "Oh," he says when he sees them on the couch, "shit."

And then Asher runs into Jeff, where he's stopped in the doorway.

Alex scrambles to sit up, but there's nothing they can do about the fact that they're both shirtless and pressed pretty close together, and Alex's hair looks like they've been doing something a lot less innocent then cuddling.

This is ... not good.

"The hell?" Asher says faintly. "Are you two fucking?"

"Oh, Alex," Eli says, dry as the Sahara. "Why didn't you tell me? I would have put my book down."

And whatever. Sarcasm has always been his first defense, and he's not sure how Alex wants to play this, but he probably isn't ready to come out to more teammates quite yet, so—

"Eli is my boyfriend," Alex says evenly. "If that's what you mean."

Or maybe he is ready.

Jeff whacks Asher on the back of the head so he loses the gape-fish look he's got going on. And Asher hits Jeff back automatically because, apparently, hockey players are all musclebound children.

"That actually makes a lot of sense," Asher says. "Cool."

"I'm so sorry," Jeff says, still slapping at Asher's face. "I left my headphones here last week, and I didn't think you guys' flight got back for another hour. I thought we could just run up and grab them on the way to dinner."

"Wait," Asher says. "You guys spent Christmas together?" He turns to look at Jeff. "You *knew*?" And now he's wearing a kicked puppy expression.

Alex runs a hand through his wild hair and then turns to glare at Eli; yes, he might have started a tiny box braid at the top of Alex's head where his hair is the longest.

Eli is unrepentant.

"Kuzy and Rushy know too," Alex says. "I was planning to tell the whole team soon. It wasn't that I didn't trust you, I just wanted to do it in stages."

Asher nods, but he still looks like a large, sad blond puppy. Then again, Asher tends to look like that most of the time. "I won't tell anyone," he says loyally. "Sorry for barging in. Interrupting whatever you guys were doing."

He grins suggestively, showing his missing front tooth.

"Oh my god," Eli says, gesturing to the paused TV. "We weren't doing anything. Alex was just playing video games, and I was reading."

"Shit, that's even worse." Asher says.

"What? Why?" Alex asks.

"Dude. You were *cuddling*."

"We were not."

"We definitely were," Eli says.

"Alex," Asher asks, squinting at the TV. "Are you playing NHL16 as yourself?"

"Of course, my stats are awesome."

"So, wait," Asher says to Alex. "Back to the cuddling thing. Are you the big spoon or the little spoon?"

"Is that sexual innuendo?" Eli asks.

"No. I'm genuinely curious."

"I'm the knife," Alex mutters.

"He's the little spoon," Eli says.

"Not all the time!" Alex argues. "We take turns!"

"That was almost too easy," Jeff says.

Alex reaches over Eli to pick up a pair of headphones on the side table and throws them at Jeff. "Didn't you say you were on your way to dinner?"

Jeff catches the headphones against his chest, laughing. "All right, all right, we'll go. Let you two get back to cuddling."

"*Goodbye*, Jeff."

The boys head back into the hall, and it's not until several seconds after the door has closed that Alex exhales, slumping back against Eli.

"Well," he says, kind of dazed. "That wasn't so bad."

"Are you okay?"

"I am, yeah. Weirdly okay? I'm not okay with whatever you did to my hair though."

Eli coughs on a laugh. "Sorry. I'll take it out."

He pushes Alex's shoulders down a little so his torso is cradled between Eli's thighs and he can reach the top of Alex's head.

He glances toward the TV.

"Are you really playing as yourself?"

"Yes," Alex mutters. "It'd be weird if I played as anyone else. And only Lachland has better stats, and they're bullshit. I could totally take him in real life."

"I'm sure you could, sweetheart."

"He's old," Alex says, eyes closing as Eli tugs gently on his hair. "And my ass is, like, a hundred times better than his."

"It is. I love your ass."

"Thank you."

5

THE NEXT FORTY-EIGHT HOURS pass in the kind of sweet domestic blur Alex had been daydreaming about. Eli spends most of his time at the rink, practicing for his competition, or reading in the guest room. He still sleeps in Alex's bed at night, quiet and warm and willing to cuddle, if not particularly conversational. So Alex just lets Eli do his thing. He keeps the volume on the TV low and makes sure to put his dishes in the dishwasher when he's done with them instead of dumping them in the sink to do later that night. He doesn't leave his discarded shoes directly in front of the door, and he hangs his towel on the rod instead of over the edge of the tub, and puts clips on the bags of cat and dog food rather than just rolling down the tops. He knows all of those things annoy Eli, and Alex has fully dedicated himself to being the best possible housemate for the following week. He picks up bath bombs from Lush on the way home from practice and leaves them to smell up the bathroom on the lip of the sink. He adds kale chips to his weekly grocery order.

On the third morning, when he brings Eli coffee in bed after taking Hawk out for a morning walk, Eli squints at him.

"I know what you're doing."

"What am I doing?" Alex asks, pressing a kiss into Eli's pillow-creased cheek.

"You're being all—" Eli accepts the coffee mug and then gestures at Alex with it. "—considerate. And perfect. And shirtless."

"I am," Alex agrees, "all of those things. Which makes me a good roommate."

"Oh, really?"

"Really." He kisses Eli again, a little closer to his mouth this time but not on it since he knows Eli is self-conscious about kissing before he's brushed his teeth in the morning.

"I've got to head out," Alex continues. "I'm meeting Matts and Rushy to do our video segment about the All-Star Game before practice."

He stands and retrieves his hoodie from the foot of the bed. Eli stole it the day before, and it smells like him. It also has a significant amount of both dog and cat hair on it.

Alex loves it.

He pulls it on and tucks his nose into the collar. "Hey. You know what would be cool?"

Eli takes a slow sip of his coffee. "Hmm?"

"If you could come with me to next year's All-Star Game."

"You think you're going again next year?"

"Of course. I'm one of the best. And I'm young. I haven't even hit my peak yet."

"I'll block it off in my schedule," Eli says dryly.

And he knows Eli's joking, but it's still kind of a thrill to think about it. To think about introducing more of his world to Eli in a less confrontational, stress-ridden environment. When they can fight over how nice a hotel room Alex is allowed to buy Eli, and they can hold hands under the table at dinner and sneak kisses in empty hallways.

Or.

Or maybe not next year. But a few years from now, when everyone knows that Eli is his boyfriend. When he can dress Eli in his jersey and kiss him on-camera when Alex wins fastest skater. Or maybe accuracy shooting. Or both. If Eli is there, he'll want to show off.

"Alex?" Eli says.

"Hm?"

"You still with me? You okay?"

Alex cups Eli's face between his palms, gently at first, and then squishes his cheeks together.

Eli makes an outraged noise.

"I'm great," Alex says. "I love you. I'm going to practice now."

He kisses Eli's forehead, then Hawk's forehead, tries to kiss Bells's and is rebuffed, and then whistles his way to the car.

It's going to be a good day.

It's a good day.

Making the video about the All-Star Weekend is just as fun as expected.

They start with an interview in which the social media intern asks them to recount the "hockey all-stars" in their lives growing up—coaches, teammates, older siblings, etc. She challenges them to a karaoke battle to see who knows the most of "All Star" by Smashmouth (Matts). And then they all kit up with GoPros and head for the ice where Alex and Matts take trick shots on Rushy before switching to easier shots so Rushy can make intentionally ridiculous saves. The segment ends with Rushy upside down, his right skate stuck in the net, and all of them laughing so hard it takes two trainers to get Rushy untangled.

Practice, afterward, is good too. Matts and Asher are clicking on the ice again, everyone's passes are connecting, Coach is in high spirits, and they're coming off a week-long break that has everyone excited to play that night.

A few of the guys decide to get lunch together after practice, but Alex begs off to Kuzy and Jeff's vocal displeasure. "Alex," Kuzy says sadly, "I'm not see you for so long I forget what face looks like under helmet."

"You're literally looking at my face right now," Alex says.

"I miss you," Kuzy insists, eyes wide.

"Oh my god, I can do lunch with you tomorrow. I already have lunch plans today."

He doesn't have lunch plans, exactly. But he does have pregame nap aspirations that he's hoping to achieve with the aid of Pretty Bird salads and a zucchini brownie.

Eli gets particularly cuddly after zucchini brownies.

He also makes sex noises while eating them, which is nice too.

"Alex," Jeff says, throwing an arm around his shoulders. "It's been too long, buddy. Cancel your other plans and come with us."

"Tomorrow," he repeats, shrugging off Jeff so he can pack his bag. He already called in a takeout order on the way to practice, and he needs to pick it up in fifteen minutes.

Jeff makes a sad noise. "Hey," he whines, "how am I supposed to be a good role model for you if we never spend time together?"

"How am I supposed to be successful if you're my role model?"

"Wow," Jeff says, feigning hurt. "Okay, asshole."

"What about babies?" Kuzy presses, reeling Asher into a hug from behind. "Babies need captain. For grow up strong."

"Asher and Matts are the same age as me, and the rest of the rookies are older," Alex points out.

"Uh, I also can't go to lunch," Asher says. "My parents are in town for the game tonight, so I already said I'd show them around. Sorry?"

Kuzy and Jeff make disgusted noises and finally give up, shepherding the rest of the lunch-goers out of the locker room.

Alex shakes his head, grinning, and heads for the parking garage a few minutes later. He nods at Rads who gets on the elevator with him.

"So, hey," Rads says, eyes on his phone. "We need to talk about your boyfriend."

And Alex's heart just ... stops.

"What?"

"Sarah has started watching Cody and Eli's channel, and she's convinced the store-bought apple butter is fucking up her crumble thing. So either I need to get Eli's actual recipe for her so she can make the damn stuff herself, or I need to get him to send me a few jars. Either way, it's her birthday next month, and that's the best gift I've been able to think of so far. The woman already has everything she wants and gets mad if I spend too much money on her, you know?"

"I—" Alex didn't really follow any of that, though the last part definitely seemed relatable.

"What?" Rads glances over at him and then pauses, frowning. "You okay, kid?"

"You said 'boyfriend.' You know about Eli? About me and Eli?"

"Was I not supposed to?"

"No?" Does *everyone* know? Has he been that obvious?

"I only assumed because it seemed like you were living together when we went to your place for dinner that one time."

"Okay," Alex says, a little breathless.

He doesn't know why this is making his chest feel tight. Rads clearly isn't making a big deal about it. Hell, he's treating Alex like having a boyfriend is totally normal. And several of the guys already know, and Alex is planning on coming out to the entire team soon anyway, so it shouldn't—

Except Anika is always telling him there is no "should" or "shouldn't" with feelings. You just feel them. It's not so much the idea of the team knowing that's freaking him out, even. It's the idea of not being in control of that knowledge. Of things not happening according to plan. Of people knowing and not saying anything. Maybe even talking about him. Him and Eli. Behind his back. And that's stupid because he shouldn't care. Because he *wants* to be out, but—

"Hey," Rads says, and Alex looks up to see that he's holding the elevator door open, dark-eyed and concerned.

Alex walks forward on autopilot.

"Hey," Rads says again, one hand curling around Alex's bicep. "I'm sorry I said anything. I assumed if people knew, they were keeping it quiet. But you have to know I've got your back. *We've* got your back. The whole team would if you do want to tell people."

"I'm—I have a plan to tell people," Alex manages. And it comes out far too soft and cracked, and it's not at all captain-ly. But Rads is one of his A's and nearly two decades older than him and such a dad that maybe it's okay.

Rads pulls Alex to a stop, and he realizes he was about to walk past his car.

"At the end of the season," Alex says. "I've already talked to management. I want—after the last game. Locker clean-out. I'll tell the team then, so they have the summer to, uh, deal."

"End of the season, huh? You should just kiss Eli in the locker room when we're celebrating our Stanley Cup win."

And wouldn't that be something.

Alex laughs, which was probably Rads's intention.

"I was thinking a little more subtle than that. But yeah. After a cup would be nice."

"We'll have to get it for you, then," Rads says, as if this probably isn't *his* last chance for one.

Alex hugs him because he isn't sure what else to do. "Thanks," he says, stepping back and pretending his voice is steady.

"You planning to go public at all?"

"Two years. Maybe less. I'm working out a plan with PR."

"Okay," Rads says steadily. "Whenever it happens, anything you need from me—sound bites, charity stuff, beating the shit out of someone. Anything. You let me know."

And, okay. Rads is a dad, but he's still a bit of a goon. "Thanks, man. Will do."

"But only if you get me that apple butter recipe."

Alex nearly chokes because the laughter is unexpected this time.

"I'll ask. I'm sure he'll be willing to share it for such a worthy cause."

Rads winks at him, sliding down his sunglasses, and turns to backtrack to his car.

Alex unlocks his own vehicle with a long exhalation and goes to pick up lunch with a smile on his face.

When he gets home, he tells Eli about his trying morning, maybe exaggerating his level of anxiety through the Rads conversation. Eli, eating his zucchini brownie, making the kinds of noises Alex would like to recreate in a different context, suggests that maybe some orgasms and a nap would make Alex feel better.

So. Yeah. Good day.

The day might have been good, but the game that night is a shit show.

The Hell Hounds win by one in overtime only because Rushy is a brick wall and has possibly taken up sorcery.

And it's Alex's fault they had to go into overtime at all.

Because he spent what felt like half the game in the box, and it fucked up the lines and put too much pressure on Matts and Kuzy to be playmakers and—

And clearly dealing with his residual anger issues needs to move to the top of the to-do list with Anika.

Because this can't keep happening.

"This" being his stupid, irrational, jealous rages that result in penalty minutes and the inevitable news stories about Alex Price's continued predilection for dirty hockey.

And the worst thing is, he knows it's stupid to care so much. But he doesn't know how to stop.

So now he's at home, icing his neck and staring blankly at the TV and more or less ignoring Eli. He doesn't know how to tell him what's wrong in a way that doesn't seem batshit crazy.

He's three days into their week-long trial run, and he's trying to convince Eli to stay, not chase him in the opposite direction.

Unfortunately, that kind of backfires when, after nearly an hour of silence, Eli moves to sit on the arm of the chair, uncertain.

"Do you want me to go?"

Alex turns to look at him so fast he undoes whatever progress he's made with the ice. "Ow. What? No."

Eli gestures a little helplessly for a moment. "You said—In your list, you had all the reasons you wanted me to move in with you, that it would be nice to have me here after bad games. But I don't know how to be what you need right now. Every time I've tried to talk to you or touch you, all I get is these little one-word answers, or you shift away from me."

"Fuck." Alex has been so wrapped up in not scaring Eli away that he's scaring Eli away. "I'm sorry. Can you—here." He shifts over, and Eli tucks himself into Alex's side, looking relieved.

"You have to tell me what to do," Eli says. "I don't know how your brain works when you're like this."

He doesn't really want Eli to know what his brain is doing right now, but apparently, he doesn't have a choice.

Alex pulls his phone out of his pocket and opens Instagram, finds Kuzy's most recent post.

It's a screen grab of a Snapchat Eli sent to Kuzy that reads "ready for the game." In the snap, Eli's taking a selfie in the bathroom, looking over his shoulder at the mirror, making a face. And the Kuznetsov across his shoulders is big and stark and awful. Kuzy had tagged both Alex and Jeff in his Insta post captioned: *I'm favorite*.

It had taken everything in Alex's admittedly immature body not to throw his phone across the locker room when he saw it. Even though he knew Jessica had told Eli to wear other player's jerseys. Even though he *knew* it didn't mean anything, it did mean Eli was somewhere in the stadium wearing a name across his back that wasn't Alex's.

"I'm a jealous asshole," Alex says, handing Eli the phone. "I saw this right before we started warmups, and I know it's stupid but—I didn't like it."

"What?" Eli says, understandably baffled.

"You. In his jersey."

"Alex."

"I know. I know it's just for avoiding speculation and that you can't wear mine. But still. I didn't like it. And it's not fair. Kuzy can make that post on Instagram and laugh about it and not have to worry because it's not even a big deal for him when that's literally—I want to be able to do that so bad. It's the airport hug all over again, you know? I want to brag about you. That you chose me. That you're mine. I want to post pictures of you in my jersey every damn day. But I can't. And he can. And it's bullshit. We shouldn't have to do this. We wouldn't *have* to do this if I wasn't *Alexander Fucking Price*."

He exhales, surprised at how angry he's getting.

He thought he got it out of his system in the game.

"I hate hockey," Alex says, and Eli raises an eyebrow at the vitriol in his tone.

"No you don't," he says gently and maybe a little resigned. "You love hockey."

I love you more, Alex wants to say, but he's not sure if it's true.

6

GETTING READY FOR THE masquerade party together is the kind of ridiculous domestic shit Alex never knew he wanted in life until he had it; sweating in a steamed-up bathroom, helping Eli tie the back of his corset-looking vest thing and trying to convince him to wear the Louboutins.

"It's an LGBTQ-friendly party," Eli says, sliding his hands down his torso. "But it's still at a frat house. I'm not sure if they're quite up to that level of gay."

"I'll punch anyone who says anything."

"My dear sweet goon," Eli deadpans. "I'll just end up barefoot after half an hour anyway. I'm not going to fuck up my feet dancing in heels all night. And someone will steal them the minute I take them off."

"I'll watch them for you."

"No, you won't," Eli says, going up onto his toes to touch their noses, pushing their hips briefly together. "Because you'll be dancing with me."

"Oh," Alex says. "Cool."

Eli backs up, grinning, to sit on the edge of the tub and pull on a pair of black boots instead. The chunky heels are at odds with the slender line of his black skinny jeans, cinched-in waist, and loose coattails, but it works. The sleeves of his button-down are rolled up to his elbows, the collar is open where it disappears into the top of his vest, and Eli has a lot of smooth, lovely, throat on display. There's already a fading hickey just above his left collarbone, but Alex thinks he should add one to the right side as well before the night is over. Just for symmetry's sake.

"So," Eli says, standing. "Are we ready?"

Alex tugs him over to stand with him in front of the full-length mirror, and they both take a moment to consider their reflection.

Alex has paired a black three-piece Armani suit with a dark-purple shirt, which matches the purple vest thing Eli has on over his black button-down. And Eli got something called hair chalk—also purple—and mixed it with gel to turn Alex's usually blond unkempt hair into something sleek and dark and kind of fantastic. Even without the mask, he looks nothing like himself. He does have a nearly full-face, matte black mask, though, just to be safe. It leaves only his eyes and mouth visible (perfect for kissing, Eli said). Eli's mask, in comparison, is a delicate little lattice of a thing that sits just around his kohl-rimmed eyes. There's glitter highlighting Eli's cheekbones and gloss on his lips, and Alex is more than a little infatuated.

They look good, is the point.

"We look good," he says.

It's an understatement.

They get to the party an hour after its official start time, which seems to be right when everyone else is arriving too. Eli introduces Alex as "my boyfriend Max" to a handful of people, several of whom are from the figure team, and he's briefly met them before as himself.

They play a round of beer pong with the Morgans, lose spectacularly, and then there's a red solo cup in his hand. Eli has his arms around Alex's neck, holding his own cup with lazy fingers, singing along to the music and asking if he wants to dance.

Alex does what any responsible nineteen-year-old would in this situation and gets drunk.

Not too drunk though. He has to remember how to take care of Eli if he has a seizure—which Eli said is likely since things tend to get hot, literally, at parties—and Alex can't take care of him right if Alex is drunk. So he gets just tipsy enough that everything goes warm and bright, and he can dance without being embarrassed that his boyfriend is a sexy, beautiful dancer, while Alex is, by contrast, a flailing potato.

At least Eli doesn't seem to mind.

So Alex sways in what he hopes is an appealing way and touches Eli whenever he's close enough—moves his hands from Eli's back to shoulders to hips and pulls them together to grind during the slower songs, puts his mouth against Eli's ear and tells him how damn pretty he is.

They retreat to the back porch occasionally when Eli thinks he's getting too hot, and Alex makes sure they're drinking equal amounts of water and beer, but Eli clearly does not have the concerns Alex does about staying vaguely sober. By 1:00 a.m., he's adorably lax against Alex; they're pressed together from chest to thighs, not even dancing anymore, just taking occasional breaks from making out to sway a little each time the song changes.

Eli has his head resting on Alex's shoulder, cheek hot where it's tucked up against his neck. He's trying to convince Alex that they should go find an empty room and hook up for the "full college party experience," when Eli brings one hand up to his head, suddenly out of sync with the subtle rhythm they have going on.

"Well, shit," he says. "I'm getting an aura; we need to—" Alex scoops him up in a bridal carry because Alex is not only Extra but currently Tipsy Extra, which apparently, turns him into a wannabe Byronic hero.

"Why are you like this?" Eli says, resigned.

Alex shoves open the first door in the hallway to find a still-mostly-clothed couple attempting to become less clothed and orders them out, not very nice about it, before setting Eli on the bed. He expects Eli to chastise him for his rudeness, but Eli sighs, rolling onto his side, and says something about Alex's "sexy captain voice."

"My what?" Alex asks, but Eli has already gone stiff. He unties and pulls off Eli's mask and then stands back, taking off his own mask. He sets them both aside on a nightstand that is worryingly cluttered with condoms.

Even after the talk Eli gave him, even after the YouTube videos Eli made him watch—it's still scary when Eli starts jerking.

Alex fumbles his phone out of his pocket, drops it, and then counts in his head as he crouches to retrieve it, watching as the quaking in Eli's limbs recedes to tremors, as the tremors finally recede to stillness at eighty-three seconds.

It feels like a lot longer than eighty-three seconds.

Alex kneels beside the bed and checks Eli's pulse and his breathing like they practiced. That all seems fine, so he lies down facing him and waits.

Twenty-three seconds later, Eli opens his eyes.

He blinks slowly at Alex.

"Good news," Eli says. "I didn't piss whoever's bed this is."

"That is good news," Alex agrees. "How do you feel?"

"Weird. I've never done this drunk before."

"You want to sit up?"

"Not yet."

"Okay. Can I touch you?"

"Please."

Alex scootches forward, wraps his arms around Eli's waist, and shoves his face, maybe a little harder than needed, against the bare skin of his upper chest. Eli's heartbeat is a conciliatory thing: loud and regular beneath his ear. "Hey," Eli says, bringing his hands up to slide into Alex's hair. "I'm fine."

"I know."

"Are you okay?" Eli laughs, and it sounds self-conscious. "Not having any second thoughts?"

Second thoughts?

"What? No."

"I'm just saying. I would understand if you were freaked out. It's okay."

"I want to marry you," Alex says, and that is ... not what he meant to say.

Shit.

"And I know I'm not supposed to tell you. Because it's way too soon, and I'm still pretty fucked up, and you're eighteen and barely know who you are yet much less what you want from someone else but—I want to be what you want. So this is—There are no second thoughts with us. Okay?"

Eli's eyes are wide when Alex looks up at him. "Oh," he says, sounding a little gut-punched. "Really?"

"Yeah." And Alex is committed now, so he might as well, just—"I want the whole everything with you. Joint Christmas cards and buying a house together and stupid inside jokes. And kids. Maybe. Someday. Mite hockey. Or figure skating. Or nothing on the ice at all. Maybe, like, chess. Just ... Whatever they want. To be happy. I think we'd be really happy. You make me happy."

"You're a little drunk right now," Eli says, and his voice is still funny.

"I am," Alex agrees. "But it's true. I'm just saying what's in my head all the time when I look at you."

And wow. Maybe he's a little more than tipsy. He should probably drink some water.

Eli doesn't say anything for several seconds, twisting the hair at the back of Alex's neck into tiny curls around his fingers. "That's a lot, Alex. *I'm* a lot. To deal with. And I don't think you realize how much yet but I'm—I think I want all of that, too, someday. If you do."

"Yeah?"

"Yeah."

"Good."

"We should probably talk about this again when we're sober," Eli says dryly.

"Probably."

"And after we've been together for, uh ... longer."

"Yeah," Alex agrees, thinking about his game schedule.

"Maybe in April?"

"April," Eli repeats. "Okay?"

"Because we'll need to figure out our summer plans around then anyway. So if we're going to be having a serious conversation, we can just have this one, too, and get it all out of the way at once."

"Summer plans," Eli repeats.

"Well, yeah. I was planning to stay in Houston, but if I can get some rink time in Huntsville, I could come visit you at home for a couple weeks in June, maybe. And I'd like to bring you with me on whatever post-season vacation I take. But I know you'll want to argue about me spending that kind of money before you'll even give any input on where we go, so."

"Okay," Eli says, "first of all—"

"Shhh," Alex interrupts. "We'll talk about it in April."

Eli whacks him gently on the head, trying not to laugh.

Alex kisses the dip between Eli's collarbones.

"Fine," Eli concedes. "April."

He laughs again, dragging his fingers down the side of Alex's neck. "We're getting purple from your hair all over this poor kid's bedspread."

"I imagine hair chalk is the least problematic substance on these sheets," Alex says.

Eli makes a face. "I think I'm feeling up to leaving now."

"Yeah? You wanna go home?"

"Mmm. Home. Shower. Clean sheets." He pauses. "Well. Moderately clean sheets."

"Home, then," Alex agrees, sitting up.

And he likes the way that sounds.

They've been living together for two weeks and three days when Eli points out over breakfast that they've been living together for two weeks and three days.

"Has it been that long?" Alex asks, like he hasn't been gleefully keeping track. "I guess time flies when you're cohabiting with someone perfectly suited to you."

"Oh, really?"

"Really. More coffee?"

Eli doesn't say anything else, and Alex is frankly baffled that worked.

He leaves the next day for Dallas feeling particularly optimistic. The Hell Hounds play the Stars on Friday, and he's staying overnight to see Eli compete in Plano on Saturday. Eli is driving into Dallas with his team on Friday, but they got permission from his coach for Alex to fly back home with Eli's team on Sunday night.

He wasn't able to convince Eli to let him upgrade their seats this time, but it's a short flight, and they'll be in bulkhead with Hawk anyway.

Alex can't wait.

The Hell Hounds win handily against the Stars. Since it's an early afternoon game, the team is going straight from the locker room to the plane to fly home, so they'll have two nights back in Houston before they leave again for Anaheim.

"Well," Alex says to the room at large, zipping his duffel shut, hair still wet from the shower. "I'm headed back to the hotel. Nice work out there tonight, guys. I'll see you on Monday."

"Actually," Jeff says casually beside him. "You'll see some of us tomorrow."

Alex pauses, lifting the strap of his bag over his head.

"What?"

"We got Coach to make practice optional," Asher says from his stall, grinning. "So we can stay and watch Eli compete."

"Surprise!" Kuzy says, and then, more seriously, "We're making signs, yes? Like at airport. But better. More big. More glitter."

"I—sure? Who all is staying?"

"Me," Jeff, Kuzy, Asher, and Rushy all say.

"And Rads and Matts," Asher says, pointing toward the shower.

Which—Matts? Interesting.

"You guys," Alex says. "This is—Thank you."

"Not doing it for you, bro," Jeff says. "We just wanna see Eli kick some ass."

"Fair," he agrees.

They all end up eating dinner together at the hotel that night, then go on a craft-supplies shopping spree first thing the following morning. They shove several of the tables in the dining area together at their complimentary continental breakfast and make signs while trying and mostly failing to keep glitter out of their food.

They get a lot of dirty looks from waitstaff.

Alex makes sure to leave a big tip.

At 12:30, they share two Ubers to get to the Dallas Stars Plano facility, which is hosting the regional competition, and they find a place midway up in the stands to sprawl out with their various smuggled-in snacks. They're a lot bigger and a lot louder than most of the other people in the stands. Within thirty minutes, they attract a fan—the younger brother of a competitor—who is delighted to find professional hockey players (even if they beat his team last night, he tells them somberly) at a figure-skating competition.

"For sure! Figure skating is the shit," Asher says earnestly.

Jeff sighs, and the kid giggles behind his hand.

"Dude. He's like, eight," Matts advises, sotto voce.

"Oh," Asher says. "Right. I just mean—Figure skating is really cool? Our friend Eli is competing today, so we came to cheer him on."

"Cool," the kid says and then asks if Rushy will share his Doritos.

He's handing them over, a little grudgingly, when the kid's dad comes over, apologetic, to drag him away. They offer to take a picture with him before he goes, counteracting a looming tantrum. Then Eli's name is being announced over the PA system, and they all have to stand in their seats and wave their signs and scream really loud.

They attract a few more dirty looks.

Eli glances briefly at them, smiling, but then settles into his beginning stance, serious, and Alex hushes the other guys, pulling them back down to sit as the music starts.

And god, Eli is beautiful on the ice.

That's his *boyfriend*.

How *lucky* is he?

Alex has watched Eli do this routine dozens of times. Heard the music so often it sneaks into his dreams sometimes.

So he notices when things start to go wrong.

He notices before anyone else around him does, is standing and shoving his way to the aisle before the first shocked gasps of onlookers start.

It starts with the barking.

About two-thirds of the way through Eli's routine, from somewhere off the ice, just down the tunnel, Hawk starts barking. And Hawk doesn't bark when her vest is on. Ever.

It's barely audible underneath the music coming through the PA system, where the climax of the song is building—when Eli is spinning, tight and perfect and so fast he's little more than a blur in the middle of the ice. If Alex weren't intimately familiar with both the music and Hawk, he might dismiss it.

He doesn't.

And then Eli wobbles in his transition from sit spin to layback spin. Alex may not know much about figure skating, but he knows quite a bit about Eli's skating, and he's never once had an issue with that transition. The choreography doesn't call for his hands to move up to his head, either, and he totally skips the fancy footwork he's supposed to do before readying for his final jump. That's when Alex stands, not waiting for the others to move their legs, not even able to articulate why he needs to get out, not knowing where to go but only that he needs to.

Jeff is yelling his name, trying to follow him, when the lady in front of him with the massive purse blocking his way lets out a soft, shocked noise.

Eli has stumbled to a stop and is hunched over, one hand on his head, the other braced on his upper thigh.

He straightens, clearly off-balance, and tries to skate for the exit, where his coach is moving forward to help him, but before he can get there Eli just—stops.

And Alex knows exactly what's about to happen, but there's nothing he can do. So he just watches as Eli falls, completely slack, like a puppet whose strings have suddenly been cut.

His head hits the ice. It bounces.

His *head*.

Alex steps on the woman's purse.

When he finally shoves his way into the aisle, trying to watch where he's going and what's happening on the ice at the same time, Eli's coach has scooped him up and is carrying him down the tunnel yelling something at the guy in a medical smock beside him. Alex gets a final glimpse of Eli's red-bottomed skates jerking over the coach's arm, and then they're gone.

The music for Eli's routine is still playing.

Alex grabs the jacket sleeve of the first security guard he can find, maybe a little too roughly, and points wildly toward the ice.

"How do I get down there? That's my—my best friend. He's having a seizure, and I need to get to him. Can you—"

"I'm sorry," he says. "If you don't have a badge, you're not allowed access."

"Hey," Jeff says, and oh, thank god, Jeff is here.

"Can you tell us where they're going to take him?" Jeff asks. "Which hospital?"

"Uh." The security guard's eyes have gone a little wide.

Alex glances behind him to find the rest of the guys have followed Jeff and are now blocking the aisle.

Faced with a good portion of the Hell Hounds starting roster, even if the majority of them are covered in glitter, the security guard takes a step back. He says, "Texas Presbyterian."

Jeff's hand is on his shoulder before Alex can even turn to look at him. "I'm getting us an Uber now; let's go."

They go.

The six minutes they have to wait on the curb are possibly the longest six minutes of Alex's life.

And then there's *traffic*.

Alex sits in the back seat of the Uber sandwiched between Jeff and Rads, with Kuzy in the front seat, anxiously glancing back at him every few seconds. He can't stop pressing the home button on his phone, not computing how abruptly the morning has gone from euphoric to disastrous. He should be able to call someone. But he doesn't know anyone's numbers. Not Eli's coach or the Morgans or anyone. And he doesn't want to call Eli's mom without knowing if Eli is okay. If she hasn't been contacted yet, he doesn't want to scare her, but—

They get to the hospital only a few seconds before Asher, Matts, and Rushy in their own Uber, and they all enter the emergency room doors together—causing something of a hubbub when one of the intake nurses recognizes them. "Oh my god," he says. "You're Alexander Price. And Justin Matthews. And Dmitri Kuznetsov. And—"

"Yes, hi. We know who we are," Jeff interrupts, and it's probably the rudest thing Alex has ever heard Jeff say to someone off the ice. "Our friend Eli just had a seizure at the Star Center down the street, and he was brought here. Elijah Rodriguez. Can you tell us—"

"Alex!"

Alex spins to see one of the Morgans jogging toward him, a too-big windbreaker over her velvet skating uniform. Her eye makeup is smeared.

"I'm so sorry," she says. "I don't have your number, or I would have called—"

"It's fine. Is he okay? Have you seen him? Where's Hawk?"

"I don't know. They won't tell us anything because we're not family. Coach rode with him in the ambulance and he had Hawk but he's not answering his phone and I don't know—"

"Okay. Okay, did Eli wake up? After his seizure? Did you see him before they brought him here?"

"I don't know. I mean, yes, I saw him, but it was really fast and they had him on one of those board things with a neck brace and stuff while they were putting him in the ambulance. He wasn't moving though. I didn't see his eyes open." Her voice goes quiet. "His head was bleeding."

"Fuck. Okay." Alex turns back to the nurse at the front desk. "Elijah Rodriguez," he says again. "Can you tell us what's happening with him?"

The nurse pauses, glancing at his coworker and then at the waiting room full of hockey players and interested onlookers.

Apparently, they're causing a bit of a scene.

"Are any of you family?" the nurse asks.

"No, but his family is in *Alabama*. Please, can you just—"

"I'm sorry, sir."

And Alex knows he's starting to get a little hysterical, probably more upset than he should be if he was just a concerned friend, but he's *not* just a concerned friend.

"Can't you just tell us—"

"I'm sorry. If you're not family—"

Alex wants to hit him with something

Like his fist, maybe.

"Look," the guy says, maybe realizing this. "Our system hasn't updated yet since he was just admitted. I couldn't give you much information even if you *were* family."

"So what are we supposed to do, just *sit* here?" Jeff asks, which is a nicer version of what Alex was going to say.

"Yes. Sorry."

"I'll try Coach again," Morgan says and puts her phone to her ear.

Kuzy tugs on his arm.

They go sit.

For an hour.

If the six minutes waiting for the car had been interminable, an hour in a plastic hospital chair is a new form of purgatory. Alex has never felt so useless in his whole goddamn life.

And then he hears the distinct noise of Hawk's toenails on linoleum.

"Coach," Morgan says as a man in a HU sweater comes through the internal double doors. He's pale and harried-looking and probably the best thing Alex has seen all day.

"Is he okay?" Alex asks, standing, and the next thing he knows, Hawk has pulled her leash out of the man's hands and is crashing into Alex's shins. He goes to his knees automatically, folding around her, attention still on Eli's coach.

If he's surprised to see a half dozen Hell Hounds players in attendance, he doesn't show it.

"Eli is in intensive care," he says. "But he's stable. I've called his mother, and she's on the next flight out."

"Intensive care," Alex repeats. "Why? What does that mean?"

"He has a concussion. Grade three. From hitting his head on the ice. And his brain is swelling. It's not bad enough yet that they think they need to intervene surgically, but since he already has a traumatic brain injury, complications are more likely. They're keeping him asleep, and they'll monitor his progress for the next twenty-four hours. And I know that sounds scary, but it's really more of a precautionary measure. They're hoping they can wake him up in another day or so once—"

And the man is still talking, saying more things about decompression, but Alex doesn't hear them.

He's stuck on the word *asleep*. Because he's pretty sure that's a nice way of saying "induced coma." Which, yes, is pretty damn scary.

He doesn't realize he's crying until Hawk starts licking his face.

"Where is he? Will they let us see him?" he interrupts, scrubbing one arm across his eyes.

"He's up on the fourth floor. Room 423. But no. Once they moved him to the ICU, they made me leave since I wasn't family. His mom should be here by 2:00 a.m., but until then—"

And no.

No.

Eli is not going to be in a fucking hospital bed with his *brain swelling*, alone. Not for ten more hours. Not for ten more minutes.

Alex gathers Hawk's leash in his hand with studied calm, loops it around his chest the way he's seen Eli do it a thousand times before, and walks back to the nurses' station.

He lays both palms flat on the counter.

"Elijah Rodriguez. Room 423. I need to see him. You can call his mother—she's his primary emergency medical contact. She can't be here until tomorrow, but she'll tell you to let me stay with him until then."

"I'm sorry," the guy says, and Alex is getting really tired of hearing that phrase. "If you're not family—"

"Please," Alex says, and it sounds a little bit like a sob, probably because it is one. "*Please*."

Alex realizes if he doesn't get it together, he's going to out himself. In front of a waiting room full of people, at least one of who has their phone in front of their face and is probably recording Alexander Fucking Price's glorious emergency-room breakdown for posterity.

Good, he thinks, a little deliriously. Then it would be done. All of it. All of the hiding and the anxiety. And he and Eli could just be together—Eli. Who he loves. Who is somewhere in the hospital right now, alone.

And the realization is both terrible and a little cathartic:

Eli is worth it.

Eli is worth risking hockey.

Not at some indistinct time in the future, but now.

Right now.

"He's my boyfriend," Alex says. "Please, he's my boyfriend. You have to let me see him."

7

ALEX'S PHONE STARTS RINGING in his pocket forty-five minutes later, when he's resting his forehead on the back of Eli's slack hand, praying for the first time in years and probably doing a really terrible job of it.

It's Jessica. "What," he says.

And the way she says his name tells him everything he needs to know.

"How's Eli?" she asks.

"I don't know," he says. "He's—"

Asleep is too gentle, but he can't make himself say the word coma either.

"Sedated."

Hawk, stretched out over Eli's feet at the foot of the bed, picks her head up to look at him.

"Is there anything we can do?" Jessica asks. "I can get the head of our medical team on the phone for you if you need recommendations for a specialist."

"No," Alex says. "Or. I don't think so. His mom should know, but she won't get here until early tomorrow."

"Okay. Alex, I need to talk to you about—"

"Someone posted a video, right?" he says, watching Eli's chest move. "Someone in the waiting room."

"Yes. We're trying to get it taken down."

Alex isn't naive enough to think that will matter.

He considers apologizing but can't bring himself to do it because he's not sorry.

It worked.

He's holding Eli's hand right now, and he can't be sorry for that.

"You have to tell us how you want to proceed here," Jessica says quietly. "We had a couple different contingency plans that we discussed with you last month, but we didn't actually expect to need any of them so soon."

"I don't care," Alex says, and he doesn't.

The fact that he was ever so worried about coming out, as if that was some big terrible life-altering thing, seems trite and ridiculous when Eli is so, so, still, surrounded by blinking monitors and the quiet, anxious, hum of hospital noise outside the door.

"We can give you some time to think," she says. "I understand you're more focused on Eli right now than dealing with media, but if we can get ahead of the story—"

"I don't care," he repeats.

One of the numbers on the IV stand monitor ticks up, but Alex doesn't know what it means.

He needs to google it.

"I have to go."

"All right," Jessica sighs. "How about I call you again tomorrow morning once you've had some time?"

"Okay," Alex agrees, knowing he has no intention of answering when she does. "Tell Coach I'm not leaving until Eli wakes up."

She pauses. "Do you have an estimate on when that will be?"

"No. Hopefully within twenty-four hours."

"You'll miss the Anaheim game if you don't fly out by tomorrow afternoon," she says, like maybe he's forgotten. Like the very concept of him being a healthy scratch is anathema.

Maybe that's fair. He's never missed a game for any reason other than injury. Hell, he hasn't missed plenty of games he *should* have because of an injury.

"Yeah," he agrees. "I will."

She doesn't say anything for several seconds.

"Okay. I'll let him know."

By midnight, Alex knows what all of the numbers on all of the monitors mean. He's called Cody to tell him what little he knew and talked briefly to Jeff to update the guys and have them locate and retrieve Eli's backpack so Alex could feed Hawk. After several false starts—because what if something happened while he was gone?—Alex took Hawk for a quick bathroom break outside. Then he used Eli's laptop to start researching traumatic brain injuries, which probably hasn't helped his anxiety level.

James calls just before 1:00 a.m.

Alex doesn't want to answer.

He doesn't know if he can handle answering right now. Especially if James is angry. But considering Alex has potentially just outed James as well, he figures he owes it to him.

"Hey," he says, uncertain.

"Hey, Alex."

And no. James isn't angry. That's the voice from the good memories Alex has with James. Well, not the *good* good memories. The good memories were winning games, crashing into each other for a celly, going for runs together in the early mornings and doing homework on the bus, and secret week-long summer vacations to the cabin at the lake. But there were other memories too. There were good/bad memories. When his birthday would pass without a call from his mom; or he couldn't get the puck to sit on the goddamn ice, and he went five games without a point; or when his billet-family's dog, who'd taken to sleeping in Alex's bed, was hit by a car, and he didn't find out until hours later, over the phone in a hotel room after a game that they'd lost.

That's the voice James would use when he didn't know how to help but wanted to. When he didn't have words, so he'd just say Alex's name, as if asking for permission. And then he'd awkwardly crowd into Alex's space and tuck their gangly teenaged bodies together, like maybe if James smothered Alex with empathy, things would be better. Like maybe he could share his demons for a while. And it did, help. Sometimes. When Alex would let him.

But James isn't here right now, and Alex feels as if he's drowning.

"James," he says, closing his gritty eyes.

"Are you okay?"

And that's the first time anyone has asked him that. "I'm fine."

"Alex."

"No," Alex says, after a stubborn pause. And he's cried more today than he has the rest of his adult life combined, so why not start again? "I'm not fucking okay."

"Yeah," James says quietly. "I guess that was a stupid question. What can I do?"

"Nothing. There's nothing—We just have to wait."

"You were never any good at that."

Alex laughs wetly. "Asshole."

"Cody wanted to fly there tonight, but I convinced him to wait since they wouldn't let him see Eli right now anyway. Would it help you, though, if we came?"

Alex rubs his palm into one eye.

"We?"

"Oh. Well, I wouldn't want Cody to go alone. He's pretty upset. And ... " James clears his throat. "I'm worried about you too."

"Don't you have games?" Alex asks because he's not anywhere near ready to deal with the latter part of that.

"Some things are more important than hockey," James says.

"Yeah," Alex agrees, looking at Eli.

"So?"

"I mean. Come if you want? But coming now wouldn't help Eli or me. I'm not leaving his room until he wakes up, except to walk Hawk, so ... Y'all would be in the waiting room alone."

"Y'all, huh?"

"Shut up."

"Okay. I figured. And, from what Cody has told me, once he does wake up, they'll send him home pretty soon afterward."

"If there aren't complications," Alex says darkly.

"Right."

Neither of them says anything for several seconds.

"Okay," James says finally. "Well. I wanted to call. I'll let you go though. You should probably try to sleep some, right?"

"Yeah. Wait. Have you been online?"

"Of course. Cody and Muzz have a whole system set up with, like, a spreadsheet, tracking news sources and stuff. The rest of the boys are taking turns being, uh, 'trolls'? In the comment sections of articles?"

"Right."

"Pretty dramatic," James says. "That video. You never could do anything by halves."

"I'm sorry; what was that, Mr. Pot?"

James huffs. "Fair."

"So," Alex says, still uncertain despite everything. "You're not—I thought you called because of the whole ... 'if I'm out people might start asking questions about you' thing."

"No," James interrupts, surprisingly sharp. "I called for you. And Eli. I figured you didn't care about the rest of it right now."

"No," Alex agrees. "I really don't."

He doesn't know who is more aggressive with their hug when Alicia gets there just after 2:00 a.m., but her presence is such a relief he finally feels as if he can breathe again.

She demands to speak with whatever doctor is on call and is

impressively calm, collected, and assertive through a list of questions and demands, using words Alex only occasionally recognizes from his couple of hours of reading. Once the doctor leaves, though, she wraps Alex up in another hug and proceeds to cry on him.

It's fine.

Neither of them sleeps much that night.

They take turns sitting with Eli, lying on the rollaway bed the nurses set up in the corner, and walking Hawk.

Alex mostly ignores his phone.

They don't turn on the TV, and Alex doesn't check any of his social media accounts.

They wait.

And then, finally, the doctor says it's safe to wake Eli up and move him out of the ICU, and they let out a collective sigh of relief.

Alicia warns him that Eli probably won't be coherent at first, but it's still kind of a shock when he opens his eyes the first time, says a string of completely unrelated words, and then goes right back to sleep again.

She seems confident after talking to the doctors and seeing Eli's scans that he's going to be just fine, but Alex is thinking about all the potential complications the doctor mentioned.

Like issues with speech and motor function. Like memory problems. He saw a movie about that one time. Where the girl lost her memories and her husband had to get her to fall in love with him again. Except, he isn't sure how he managed to get Eli to fall in love with him the first time. He might not be able to do it again.

He does more, ultimately unhelpful, research through four more rounds of Eli waking briefly—sometimes unresponsive, sometimes making no sense—before blinking his way slowly back to sleep.

The sixth time he wakes up, Alicia isn't there, and Alex is exhausted and expecting more of the same.

"Hey," he says tiredly.

"Hey," Eli says, sounding perfectly rational. "You're really cute."

Alex sits up from where he's slouched over. "Oh my god," he says. "Do you know who I am? Do you remember me?

Eli squints at him. A little judgmentally, honestly. "Yes?"

Alex can't decide if he wants to laugh or cry. "Okay. That's good. I was worried maybe you had amnesia or something."

"Well, that's dumb," Eli says, slurring the 's' a little. "You'd be cute whether I remembered your stupid face or not. I do though. So don't worry about that. Why are you worried about that?"

Eli runs his tongue around his mouth, squinting a little harder. "Did I hit my head?"

Alex makes a pathetic noise and buries his face in Eli's wrist because Eli is talking and remembers him and is moving all of his fingers and his toes, and he's okay.

"Hey," Eli says, sounding a little alarmed. "Hey, no. Don't cry. I love you."

And that really doesn't help on the emotions front.

"Yeah," Alex says. "Yeah, you hit your head. Is—Can I hug you? How do you feel? I don't want to hurt you."

"I think I'm on a lot of drugs," Eli says. "I can't really feel anything. But yes, you should hug me. Actually. You should just—come up here."

Alex does, gladly.

"What happened?" Eli asks once they've got him tucked comfortably under Alex's arm, leaning into his chest. Alex cups his hand around Eli's elbow, sneaking his fingers up the sleeve of Eli's gown to pet the soft skin of his inner bicep.

Alex opens his mouth and then closes it, remembering what the doctor had said. "What do you remember?"

Eli considers this for a minute. "Um. Skating. Competition. I was—Hawk was barking during my routine. Wait. Where's Hawk?"

"With your mom."

He startles, glancing around. "Mamá is here?"

"Yeah. I got her a room at the hotel so she could have a shower and change. She took Hawk with her to get some more food because we ran out. They'll be back soon. Can you tell me what you remember?"

He brings one hand up, searching, until he finds the line of stitches on his temple. "Shit. I had a seizure on the ice, didn't I?"

"Little bit, yeah."

"I hit my head."

"Yeah."

"Fuck."

"Yeah."

He exhales slowly. "How long did they have to keep me sedated? Were there complications?" He reaches back up to his head. "Did they have to—?"

"Hey, easy," Alex says. "They kept you asleep for thirty hours, and you've been in and out for another six or so since then. They moved you out of ICU last night. It's Tuesday. There weren't any complications, and they didn't have to do anything surgical. But you do have a serious concussion, um, grade three? So, there might be—"

"Lasting unknown effects," Eli finishes, expression pinched. "Because I already had *one* traumatic brain injury, so this is just icing on the shit cake."

"Not exactly how I would have characterized it. But yeah," Alex agrees. "Do you want me to get the doctor? Or call your mom? You've been awake a couple times since they first woke you up, but this is the first time you've been coherent and didn't immediately fall back asleep."

"No. I actually do kinda just want to sleep some more. Can I sleep some more?"

"Yeah, of course."

"Gunna sleep on you," Eli asserts, making himself comfortable.

"Okay."

"Don't leave."

"I won't."

Eli wakes up again two hours later and submits to being cried on by his mother. This time, they do call the doctor, who walks Eli through his tests and treatment plan and recovery time. Alex leaves after he's got the gist of things to take Hawk for a walk around the grounds and give Eli and his mom some privacy.

Except within a minute of exiting the south lobby doors, before Hawk can even find a nice tree to pee on, someone is taking his picture.

Several someones, actually, jogging from around the corner, where they must have been initially waiting at the north entrance, holding telescoping lens cameras and yelling his name.

And *shit*.

He'd forgotten about the real world.

Or maybe Eli is the real world, and all of this is just bullshit.

He turns and walks right back inside, where a security guard is already moving in front of him to block the photogs from following.

"Excuse me," Alex says to the woman at the front desk. "There's a garden with benches and a grassy section I can see from the window of my—" He almost censors himself but realizes he doesn't have to. "—my boyfriend's room. Can you tell me how to get there?"

"Are you Alexander Price?" she asks, glancing at the people outside.

"I am," he agrees, strangely calm.

"Why don't I have someone from security escort you there, just to be safe?"

"Thank you. I'd appreciate that."

He returns to Eli's room forty-five minutes later to find him alone, sitting up in bed but staring at the wall blank-eyed and hollow. Alex has a sudden, visceral, memory of the way James looked shortly before he cut Alex out of his life completely.

Alex nearly has a panic attack right there in the doorway. "Hey, no," he says, "what's wrong? What's happened?"

He kicks off his shoes and climbs back into the bed, wraps himself around Eli, and just clings, a little desperate, a little afraid of his answer.

"I'm done," Eli says, and his voice is all wrong. "With skating. I can't—He said it'll be at least three months before I can get on the ice again, and I can't do anything that will put me at risk for another fall for at least six months but—"

And oh. Oh no.

Alex feels like someone has punched him in the stomach.

"He says even after that, competitive skating is—it's too big of a risk. That I was lucky this time."

And, yeah.

Alex can see that.

"But." Eli stops. Starts again. "I was supposed to be this inspirational story." His voice is brittle. "The Olympic hopeful who came back against all odds. That's what got me through my recovery the first time. The idea that this was all just some additional thing I would add to my underdog story once I was successful. The gay, Latino, Black kid from Alabama, who nearly died in a car accident, who persevered through adversity and won medals and started a skate school and helped underprivileged youth achieve *their* dreams. I was still supposed to—to—" He exhales, shuddery and a little wild.

"But that's not going to happen."

Alex can hear Eli trying to hold back tears, and that's probably even worse than if he was actually crying. "Hey," he says, "it's okay."

Except it's not.

What a stupid thing to say.

"You can't think in circles like that. You'll drive yourself crazy if you do."

"Alex, I can't skate anymore," Eli says. Well, sobs more than says, really. "I *am* going crazy."

And Alex had never really understood when people said they wished they could take someone's pain for them. To feel it instead. He'd never actually believed anyone could be that level of altruistic.

But he gets it now. And he'd do it too.

He'd do anything to make the expression on Eli's face go away.

"I'm sorry," he says. It's true, and he doesn't know what else to say. "I'm so sorry."

Eli folds himself into Alex's chest, face damp, breath humid against his throat. "I yelled at my mom," he says. "I was angry, and I took it out on her."

"Do you want me to go find her?"

Eli's fingers hook into the fabric of his shirt, pulling it taut against his back. "No. Please stay."

The last forty-eight hours really have been an exercise in showing Alex the limits of his own humanity. Because, once again, he's powerless here. He's gotten used to being able to fix things with hard work or money or his name. But he can't. Not here. And he doesn't know what to do.

"What can I do?" he asks, mouth against the top of Eli's head, more than a little desperate. "How can I help you?"

Eli shakes, and the whole world shakes with him. "I don't know," he says. "I don't know."

And that might make it even worse.

8

ELI WAKES UP FEELING strangely okay.

Well. Not okay. They're clearly weaning him off the pain meds, and his head feels like someone took a pickaxe to it. His vision is kind of blurry, and he cried so hard it made him nauseous earlier, which probably isn't helping things.

But his puffy, aching face is pushed into Alex's neck. Alex is warm and solid and still has one sleep-slack arm wrapped around Eli's back. He kind of smells a little, probably because he hasn't showered in a while, but Alex is making the little whistle-y breathing noises he always makes when he sleeps on his back, and the familiarity is nice.

Eli still feels hollow. But not—not the way he had earlier, the way it'd felt when the doctor said he shouldn't skate competitively anymore. Because the key word there is *competitively*.

And he doesn't even *like* competing.

He knows some people live for it, for the drama and the adrenaline and the prestige, but he's never been one of them. Sure, it feels good to win, especially when people automatically make assumptions about him because of the way he looks or the state of his skates or second-hand uniforms. But it feels just as good to land a new trick in practice, to hit up free skate at his hometown rink, show off a little, and coerce wobbly kids away from the boards. Helping out at the Breaking the Ice event with the Hell Hounds was probably the most fun he's had while skating in months. So, no. He won't miss competition.

Competition is the worst part of skating. It's stressful and harrowing and, yeah, puts him in a pretty damagingly aggressive headspace. The problem is that competition has always been tied to his ability to skate at all; he had to *earn* ice time to prove to himself, if no one else, that the lessons and the gear and all that money was worth it. But that's not really the case now.

Especially—

Well.

Especially because of Alex.

Because if he asked, Alex would find a way to make sure he has ice time every week.

Probably every *day*. And *that* is something Eli may very well let Alex do.

And he's always wanted to teach kids someday when he retires. Maybe he just has to ... skip ahead in his planned timeline a little. It's not the death sentence it had felt like initially.

He's not losing the ice. Or his memories on it.

He shifts a little to look at the time—11:40 p.m.—and then rolls the other way to see if his mom is still there. She is, curled up on the rollaway bed with Hawk, despite both Alex and Eli trying to convince her to go back to the hotel for the night.

And ...

... wait.

He admittedly has an excuse for being so slow, but it occurs to Eli that Alex hasn't left his side for more than an hour in probably around three straight days. He's *missed a game*.

And he shouldn't even be in the room with Eli right now according to hospital procedure, much less in the bed with him.

"Hey," Eli whispers, poking Alex's cheek. Alex startles awake. "What? Are you okay?"

"Shh. Mamá's still asleep. How are you here?"

"What?"

"You've been here, with me. The whole time. Even in the ICU."

Alex blinks at him, still mostly asleep. "You remember being in the ICU?"

"Not really? I sort of remember you were there though."

"Oh."

"But they shouldn't have let you," Eli presses. "You're not family. You shouldn't even be here *now* because it's not visiting hours. So how are you here? And what about the team? What did you tell them? You had a *game* yesterday."

It's dark, and Eli has a little bit of double vision going on, and his head really is hurting after all the thinking he's been doing. But despite that, he can tell Alex's face is doing a thing.

A scared thing.

Like he really, really doesn't want to answer those questions.

"Please tell me you didn't bribe the medical staff," Eli says. "Getting the hotel room for my mom is one thing, but—"

"No. No, I didn't bribe anyone." Alex swallows.

"What?"

"I just—I don't know if you're going to be mad or not, and I don't think I can handle it right now if you are."

"Alex, hey, it's okay."

"I told them I was your boyfriend. So they had to let me see you."

He—what?

"You *what*?" Eli says.

"And then, when they tried to make me leave the first night, I said—" Alex gnaws on his bottom lip for a minute, and it's clear he's been doing that a lot because it's red and ragged and angry-looking.

Eli presses his thumb to Alex's mouth. "Stop. And put on some Chapstick in a minute. What did you say when they tried to make you leave?"

"That I'd tell my 900K Instagram followers the hospital wouldn't let me stay with my partner, who was in the ICU, and that I was pretty sure there was a discrimination lawsuit to be made there." Alex sighs. "I wasn't very nice."

"Oh my god," Eli says faintly. "Did you make them sign non-disclosure agreements? Have you been checking online to make sure no one has said anything? I mean, doctor patient confidentiality is one thing, but if anyone was listening—"

Alex laughs, and Eli doesn't understand why right up until Alex says:

"Someone recorded it—me telling the nurse that you were my boyfriend. It's been online pretty much since the minute it happened. I can't leave the building from any of the main entrances now without vultures taking pictures of Hawk and me."

And Eli just ... doesn't know what to say.

This is everything they've been trying to avoid, and they aren't ready yet.

They were supposed to have more time.

And now they have to deal with this on top of everything else, and—

This wasn't the plan.

This wasn't the plan at all, and it's *his fault*.

"I'm sorry," he says. "Alex. I'm so sorry."

"What? No. *You* didn't do anything wrong. Jesus."

"What are people saying? Is the team—" Eli brings the hand not attached to an IV up to Alex's face. "Are you okay?"

"I'm fine." Alex says. "Mostly. I talked to Anika for two hours yesterday morning before you'd really woken up, and that helped. A lot of the guys have texted their support. But I haven't really—I've been ignoring my phone after the first call from Jessica on Saturday afternoon. She said we needed to figure out what statement I wanted to use and all this stuff, and I was just—It was so stupid that I was even expected to think about anything that wasn't you. So I told her I didn't care what they did and just ... hung up. Haven't responded to anyone's calls or texts since, except for Cody and a few of the guys. I haven't even been online."

"Okay," Eli says and takes a couple of mindful breaths. "Okay. This is fine. We just need to—"

Well. They don't. Not if Alex has been avoiding social media for a reason.

"Would it be a problem, for you?" Eli asks. "To check and see what people are saying?"

"I have no idea."

"Can we try? Because I want to know. And I can't look at screens. So ... "

Alex laughs.

"Sure." Alex shifts, reaches for Eli's backpack on the floor, and pulls it up onto the bed. "So"—he slides out the MacBook—"you seem better. Than you were before, I mean."

"Yeah," Eli agrees. "Sorry for ... you know ... all of that. Earlier."

"No, it's fine. I don't even want to know how I would feel if someone told me I couldn't play hockey anymore. Deal with it however you need to. I just want to help, and I don't know how, and you were kind of scaring me."

"Sorry," Eli says again. "I'm going to be sad for a while. Maybe angry. I don't know. I should probably apologize in advance for future shitty behavior. My mom can tell you, I'm not the best patient in recovery."

"If you'll remember, neither am I," Alex says and does one of his little self-conscious smiles that makes the corners of his eyes go crinkly.

"True. Anyway. I think the most helpful thing you can do right now is distract me. So I'm just going to close my eyes, and you can tell me what the internet is saying about us, cool?"

"Cool," Alex agrees.

Eli makes a show of settling back against the pillows as Alex pulls up a web browser. "We should probably set some ground rules before we start though."

"Uh, okay?"

"Are we going to read comments sections?"

Alex pauses. "I don't—yes? Just to see what people are saying?"

"Then we need to agree beforehand that we don't respond to them. Even if people are saying terrible things. Even if they're wrong," Eli says pointedly.

Alex grimaces a little. Eli definitely has his number.

"That's reasonable."

"And—" Eli reaches out, not looking at the screen but rather the place where his fingers come to rest on Alex's cheek. "If it's too much for either of us, we stop. No questions asked. Okay?"

"Okay."

Eli rubs his thumb against Alex's poor mangled lips. "Good. Now put some Chapstick on, and then kiss me."

"Okay." And he does.

Eli settles back in the cup of his shoulder, leaning his head into Alex's neck, eyes closed. "All right. Let's start with Instagram first. Yours and then mine?"

"Yeah," Alex agrees, game face engaged.

And they get to work.

Alex falls asleep a little past 2:00 a.m., his running dialogue getting more blurry and incoherent the later (earlier?) it gets. Eli waits until Alex's breathing has evened out—gone soft and deep for several minutes—before he shifts the MacBook off Alex's thighs and onto his own lap.

Slow.

Careful.

Usually, once Alex is asleep, he stays that way regardless of Eli's trips to the bathroom, Hawk's pointy elbows, or Bells's subtle attempts at smothering them both in their sleep. But Eli is still cautious, turning the volume even lower than it'd been before.

And then he finds the video.

It's really good quality. There's no mistaking Alex, kneeling, curled around Hawk like she's the only thing holding him upright. And Eli's coach is saying something indistinct, too quiet for Eli to discern with the volume so low. Then Alex is looping Hawk's leash around his chest and walking purposely up to the nurses' station, his captain voice wavering into something like desperation. Eli realizes he's leaning forward without meaning to, reaching to pull the screen closer instinctively.

"Hey," Alex mutters sleepily. "What are you doing?"

He's my boyfriend, the Alex on the screen says, utterly wrecked. *Please, he's my boyfriend. You have to let me see him.*

And Eli really needs to stop with all the crying because it's not helping his head at all. "You are a romantic fucking idiot," he mutters, closing the laptop and shoving his face into Alex's neck.

"Uh. Yeah?" Alex says, because there's really no arguing with that. "Do you—" He swallows, loud in Eli's ear. "Do you wish I hadn't?"

"No. No, I'm so glad you did. And maybe that's selfish, but ... "

It occurs to Eli that he hasn't actually thanked Alex for that.

"Thank you," he says, and it feels woefully inadequate. "I am. So. So angry that you didn't get to come out on your own terms. And—" Well, if he's being honest, he might as well be brutally honest. "I'm pretty scared about what's going to happen once we leave the hospital. But having you here for the past few days will probably be worth the fallout. For me, at least."

Alex pulls away from him a little, enough to look at his face, eyes all squinty in the darkness. "You think it won't be worth it for me?"

Eli's head really hurts.

He probably should have waited for this conversation.

"I think ... it's never good when someone comes out because they feel like they have to. Especially when it's for another person, rather than themselves."

"Hey, no." Alex's hands come up gently to frame his face. "I didn't do it for you, I did it for me. Because if I had to spend one more minute in that goddamn waiting room, I was going to kill someone. You didn't need me then. You were asleep. I'm the one that needed you. To be with you. I don't know how else to—"

Alex's voice goes a little waver-y, and he stops, clearing his throat. "I don't think you understand how much I fucking love you."

He might.

Eli tips up his chin a little, and it's a familiar enough gesture that Alex ducks to kiss him automatically.

"I do," Eli says. "I had a minor breakdown about it, remember?"

"Yeah." Alex sounds pleased.

Eli leans back in to kiss Alex again, Alex's bottom lip in particular, the ragged mess that it is.

"Put some more Chapstick on your poor mouth, and then come cuddle me. My head hurts."

"Okay," Alex agrees.

9

ALEX LEAVES THE NEXT day.

He waits until the last possible minute because, of course, he does. But by 8:00 p.m., Alex has been smuggled out an employee exit, taken to the airport, and flown back to Houston on a chartered plane just for him.

Because that's the kind of thing a multi-millionaire can do when they're hiding from the media.

It's all very cloak-and-dagger according to the occasional phone updates Alex gives him, and Eli is disappointed he misses it. However, he's not ready to leave the hospital yet. Getting his catheter taken out, submitting himself to an endless battery of tests, and relearning how to walk with his new (old?) balance issues takes precedence.

The good news is that his mother prepared for the possibility his balance would be a problem again and brought Hawk's original mobility harness with her from Alabama. So Eli is strolling a slow, wobbly, circuit of the ward—leaning heavily on Hawk but doing better than the doctor anticipated—by the time Alex calls to tell him he's home and half the Hell Hounds were waiting in the lobby of Alex's building when he got there. Alex had told Kuzy and Jeff about his flight plans, and one of them is, apparently, incapable of keeping a secret.

Eli's money is on Kuzy.

Eli tells Alex to see to his team and returns his attention to completing a second lap of the ward. If he can do three circuits and pass a memory test the following morning, the doctor said he could leave. And Alex has already booked him a ticket to Houston for that afternoon because Alex views everything as a competition, and obviously, he thinks Eli is going to *win*. He's also booked Eli's mother a ticket back to Alabama, and Eli hasn't checked, but he's going to go ahead and assume they're both first class. He's a little too overwhelmed with everything to care, though. God knows his parents are going to have even more medical bills to pay now, so at this point, Eli will let Alex buy his Mamá as many flights as he wants.

Eli takes a break at the nurses' station to surreptitiously listen to the TV. Of course they have it turned to some sports channel, where they keep interrupting actual sports news to let large men stuffed into suits gleefully rehash what little they know about Alex and Eli's relationship every half hour. They've only added two pieces of information since his last pass by the desk.

The first is that someone (unsurprisingly) noticed that a good portion of the Hell Hounds roster was camped in the lobby of Alex's building, and shortly after they congregated there, they were escorted upstairs by concierge. So the hypothesis is that Alex is home.

The second new bit is that Hell Hounds management confirmed Alex would play in the home game against Arizona the following day.

The newscasters present the fact that Alex has likely returned to Houston as if it is world-altering news. They then return to familiar waters—Eli's YouTube channel and Alex's troubled past.

Eli rolls his eyes and heads back to his room.

Finding it empty, Eli takes the opportunity to call Cody back for the fourth time that day.

They've been playing phone tag since 10:00 a.m., when the doctor said he could have his phone back as long as he only used it for calls. Cody's voicemails each time they miss each other have gotten progressively more bitchy.

"About time," Cody mutters in lieu of 'hello'. "How many tests have they dragged you to today?"

"A lot," Eli confirms. "Hi."

"Hi. I'm going to try really hard not to cry on you, but it might happen anyway, fair warning."

"Noted."

"Okay, so," Cody says, more exhalation than words, "how are you? Physically. Mentally. Spiritually."

"Geographically? Ecumenically?"

"Shut up, I'm serious."

"I'm okay. My balance is fucked again. They said it should probably resolve a lot quicker this time around, but it's still pretty shitty to feel like I've regressed so far. At least Hawk hasn't forgotten how to brace me."

"How's your head?"

"Pissed. Constant headache. All the standard vision issues. No migraines or aphasia, though, and no seizures since."

"Good." Cody pauses. "Have you seen the video?"

"Oh. You mean the one where my romantic fool of a boyfriend outed himself in full Hallmark Fashion so he could sit tearfully at my hospital bedside?"

"Yes," Cody says dryly. "That video."

"I have."

"Were you able to see what the internet is saying, or do I need to give you the rundown?"

"Alex did some investigational research for me last night, but I'd be interested in your one-minute takeaway."

"One minute? That's cruel, Elijah. Well. Let's see. General population, I'd say, is about 80 percent supportive, 20 percent neolithic simpletons. Hockey world, probably more like a 60–40 split, unfortunately. Maybe as good as 70–30? And lots of support from players and franchises on Twitter and Instagram—whoever runs the You Can Play social media accounts is fully in love with you, by the way. But even players who I thought were Alex's mortal enemies are tweeting nice things."

Cody makes a noise that's the verbal equivalent of a shrug. "Now, granted, this is all early stages. The real test is how things go after Alex starts playing again. Lip service is all well and good, but if he's targeted on the ice, and if the refs don't call it—But once you two go on a press tour and delight the free world, maybe things will shift more in your favor."

"Oh my god, Cody. We're not going to start giving interviews."

"Of course you will. I'll bet you—I'll bet you my stand mixer one or both of you have invitations with talking heads within the next week. This is a big deal, Elijah. And frankly, y'all have a sickeningly good meet-cute story."

"I don't need your stand mixer; I have my own, now. Besides, it's not like James wouldn't just buy you another one, so that's not really high stakes."

Cody is strangely silent.

Eli glances down to see if the call is still connected.

"Hey. Did I lose you?"

"No, I'm here. You think James got me the mixer?"

Eli resists the urge to roll his eyes only because he knows it would hurt. "Yes," he says patiently. "Of course James got you the mixer."

"But he didn't even like me then. If anything, he hated me!"

"James Petrov has never hated you. The man called Alex within hours of me being hurt to talk logistics about flying out with you—*missing a game* so he could fly out with you—to make sure you were taken care of while you were so worried about me."

"We're teammates," Cody says. "James would do that for any of us." But he sounds uncertain.

Eli is very tempted to just tell him James is probably in love with him but manfully resists. "Is that honestly all you two are?" he asks. "Honestly."

Cody sighs, all in a rush, and it sounds as if maybe he's pacing. "I don't know. Sometimes I think—The night we found out you were hurt, I went to the house to make biscuits and gravy because I needed some comfort food—"

"Of course you did."

"And then it got late, and I used up all the butter and decided around 1:00 a.m. I needed to just go get on a plane. But James talked me into waiting until morning and said I shouldn't walk across campus so late with it snowing, so he said I could stay. And we could sleep in his bed together. Like he and Muzz do sometimes, but—"

After the surge of words, the sudden silence is jarring.

"But what?"

"There was definitely cuddling. He was holding me. And the bed is small, so maybe that was necessary. But he did this thing, where he was sort of rubbing his thumb up and down the back of my neck, and it *really* didn't feel platonic. But then the next morning, he was back to his normal 'Griggs, we're going for a run; personal tragedies are no excuse for losing muscle tone.' And I'm pretty sure he's been avoiding me since Alex called and told us you woke up, so ... " Cody sighs. "I don't know. Maybe your whole—"

Eli can tell that Cody is gesturing.

"—thing is just throwing me off."

"My whole what?"

"I mean, statistically speaking, it's really unlikely two gay kids from Alabama will fall in love with professional hockey players and both have it ... actually work out. And you're kind of cornering the market there."

"James isn't a professional hockey player," Eli points out.

"Yet," Cody says darkly.

Which—point.

"I keep reminding myself," Cody continues, "that just because you've managed a happy ending with your originally unrequited hockey crush doesn't mean I'm going to get one too."

"Cody."

"It's fine. I'm sorry. I know I'm being dramatic."

"Cody, seriously."

"But let's get back to you!" he says faux cheerfully. "Tell me about how ridiculous Alex has been, please. I need some humor in my life."

"Fine," Eli says. "I'll drop it. But just do me a favor. The next time y'all have a kegger and you get table-dancing-drunk? Pay attention to where James is. And the way he looks at you. And the way he doesn't *stop* looking at you. Okay?"

Cody doesn't say anything for several seconds, then, "Really?"

"Really."

"Huh."

Eli's mom gets back from the hotel, dragging her carry-on and talking on the phone with a lilt to her Spanish that can only mean Abuela. She tosses Eli her little travel bottle of oil and nudges Hawk to one side so she can sit in front of Eli on the bed, then slaps absently at his legs so he'll sit up.

He dutifully does so. Using the dropper to make a little pool in the cup of his hand, he then rubs his palms together. She tips her head back, still a little damp from her shower, and he starts to work the oil into her scalp with the pads of his fingers. It's familiar, something they've been doing since he was ten and so full of excess energy she decided to—in her own words—put his fidgeting to use before he put her in an early grave. They tried to twist his hair one year, but his curls have never been tight like hers. She nearly put *him* in an early grave because he couldn't sit still for more than a few minutes, so that idea was discarded rather quickly. But he still likes helping her with her hair; it's something they can do together without talking or arguing, as is often the case, so that's nice too.

Apparently, tonight they will be talking, though. When she hangs up the phone, she pats his knee in thanks and says, "So. Be honest with me. Do you want to take a semester off and come home? How are you feeling?"

He's feeling as if she purposely engineered this so she wouldn't have to look at him while they're talking about Serious Things.

"No," he says. And it's the truth. "I'm not really worried. Since the semester just started, I'm still in the drop window if I need to lighten my course load. And Alex would be willing to help if I need it."

"Yes, but will you *ask* for help?"

He rubs, maybe a little harder than necessary, at the crown of her head.

"*Yes.*"

"Well," she says, sighing. "I don't doubt that Alex will try. That boy is ... certainly something."

She twists one of her locks absently at the root, pressing the fluffy little baby hairs into place. "He loves you. I don't know if he's told you yet, but he does."

"He has."

Mamá tips her head back, one eyebrow raised at him, waiting.

He pushes her upright again. "I love him too."

"Do you."

It's not really a question.

"He's a good boy," she says, which is the closest he's going to get to a ringing endorsement. "Maybe a little rough around the edges—"

And, yeah, she's definitely been listening to some of the news stories talking about Alex's past exploits.

"—but a good boy. Although," she pauses, clearly choosing her words. "He does not have the best, hm, impulse control, I've noticed."

Eli isn't sure where she's going with this.

"So," she continues. "I expect it to be a long, *long*, engagement if he comes anywhere near you with a ring within the next year."

Eli manfully does not choke on his own spit.

He focuses on adding a little more oil to his fingertips.

"We're talking about that in April."

"You're talking about *rings* in April?" She turns to look at him. "Elijah. I was joking. You are *eighteen*—" He can tell she's about to dissolve into Spanish because her face is doing the "I can't deal with you in English anymore" thing, so he really needs to stop that line of thought.

"No!" Eli says. "I mean, we talked about how we were moving a little fast, maybe, and that we should wait to really start talking about the future until we've been together longer. So we're going to talk about things in April."

"Things," she repeats flatly.

She mutters something about rich hockey gringos with stupid heart eyes. "I thought you said you were moving slow at Christmas. It's been a *month*."

"I guess we, uh, sped up?"

She sighs. She turns away from him, nudging his knee so he'll get back to work. "This isn't the kind of thing I ever thought I would need to prepare for as a parent."

"What do you mean?"

"Well," she says wryly. "The gay thing, I could research, and I did. But I somehow doubt there are books about how to be supportive when your son is dating the first-ever out NHL player. Especially when that NHL player is—"

"Alexander Price," Eli supplies.

He only barely manages saying it without the 'fucking' in the middle.

"Yes," she agrees.

"Well," he says, and it's stilted because they don't do this. "You're, um, doing a pretty good job so far?"

She pats his knee again.

"And," he says. "About before. Yesterday. I didn't—I was angry, and I didn't mean what I said. I'm sorry."

"I know you are, baby."

They lapse into silence, and he focuses on the little spaces behind her ears, breathing in jojoba and argan. If he closes his eyes, he can almost pretend he's thirteen again and sitting on the couch at home.

He clears his throat. "I, uh, I really appreciate all the sacrifices you and Papá made the first time I was hurt. And I know I wasn't very nice when I was recovering then, so ... I'm sorry for that too. And you were great, have been great, about everything with Alex. And you did research when I came out—a lot of kids don't have that. So ... thank you."

She glances over her shoulder at him, eyes wide. "Are you talking about *feelings* with me, Elijah?" And the disbelief is fair.

"Yeah, I guess."

"Since when do you do that?"

"Alex makes me, sometimes. It's healthy."

"Well," she says, and good lord, they are just as bad as each other. "That's—good. I—you know your father and I would do anything for you. We—love you very much." She clears her throat. "Even when you don't call."

Eli laughs a little, which was probably her intention.

"So," she says. "Do you ... want to talk about feelings some more?"

"Nope."

"Do you want to see if there's anything on TV?"

"Please."

10

ALEX HAS A MEETING with management before practice the morning of the Coyotes game that is just as awful as he anticipates.

Well.

Not awful.

No one is cruel, or even judgmental, but they have a franchise to run, and Alex just became an important, and somewhat volatile, pawn in their game.

After nearly an hour of passive-aggressive, politically correct, gentle bickering with the GM, Alex agrees to read a statement after the game that night. He then makes his excuses to leave because practice is starting; he is here, after all, to play hockey.

They can't really argue with that, and Alex practically runs for the locker room after being dismissed, hands fisted in the front pocket of his hoodie.

Except then he gets to the door of the locker room and can hear the guys inside getting ready and that's—That's a whole new brand of anxiety.

If he wasn't the goddamn captain, he would just duck in with his head down and skate hard and try his best not to talk to anyone. But that's not an option because he *is* the goddamn captain, and at this point, everyone in the room has seen the video, where Alex begged to see his boyfriend—desperate in a way that would be utterly humiliating if it wasn't desperation about Eli.

It's going to be weird, he thinks. It's going to be so, so, weird.

He pushes open the door and walks purposely to his locker and ...

It's weird.

He'd told the guys who came over the night before to just act normal, and they do, mostly. Except the noise level ratchets way down upon his entrance and just ... stays that way.

Like they're waiting.

Alex takes a deep breath through teeth still-clenched from the meeting and considers, briefly, how Eli would handle this situation.

He grabs his helmet from the top cubby of his locker and bangs it a few times against the side of his stall until everyone goes completely, expectantly silent.

"So," Alex says. "I'm gay."

Jeff coughs on what might be a laugh next to him.

"It's not a big deal," Alex continues quickly because it's clear Kuzy is readying a sarcastic response. "People are going to try to make it a big deal. PR and other teams and whatever the fuck else. But don't let them. I'm still here to play hockey and I'm still here to win and that should be everyone else's focus too. Okay?"

He gets a handful of affirmations.

"I'm only going to make one statement tonight, after the game, and I'll ignore all media after that. I'd appreciate it if you don't comment on my relationship with Eli if you're asked, or that if you do comment, it's without giving them any actual information. Hopefully after a few weeks, people will get bored and move on. But I don't know how this is going to go down at first. How other teams will react. Other fans."

"I can guess," Rads says darkly.

Alex nods, resigned, already feeling exhausted.

"I won't apologize for coming out or for, uh"—and after everything that's happened, the word still sticks in his throat—"being gay. I'm not sorry. But I do apologize for how this will affect you. It shouldn't. But it will. And I know that."

"Got your back," Kuzy says and is quickly echoed by Rushy, Asher, and a couple other indistinct voices.

"All Russians got your back," Kuzy continues. "I'm talk to them.

They all promise. No dirty hits. No, uh ... " He glances at Oshie and says something in Russian.

"Homophobic," he supplies.

"No homophobic talk," Kuzy finishes.

"Oh," Alex says. "Thanks."

"You talked to *all* of the Russians in the NHL?" Asher asks, sounding kind of awed. "How? Do y'all have, like, weekly secret phone meetings? Do your families all know each other? Is there really a Russian Hockey Mafia?"

"No," Kuzy says patiently, as if Asher is particularly stupid. "We have group chat. WhatsApp."

"Oh." Asher looks disappointed.

"But if *is* a Russian Hockey Mafia, I'm boss."

"Of course," Jeff says.

"How's Eli?" Rushy asks. "Are they letting him go today?"

Alex brightens. "Probably. He passed his mobility and physical tests first thing and was about to do the mental tests when I talked to him last." Alex pulls his phone out, but he doesn't have any missed calls. He shrugs.

"If he passes them, will he come to the game tonight?" Asher asks.

Alex gives Asher a disbelieving look. "He can barely walk, and he's dealing with fucking concussion symptoms. You think I'm going to ask him to navigate the maze that is our stadium and then spend three hours around flashing lights and screaming fans?"

"Not to mention he'd be mobbed the minute someone recognized him."

"We could get him a wheelchair!" Asher argues. "And some hearing protection! And we could sneak him in. Put a hat on him or something."

"You gonna put a hat on Hawk too?" Jeff says.

Asher deflates. "Oh. Right. I guess the dog is a little conspicuous."

"A little," Jeff agrees.

"Maybe the next home game," Alex says and tries not to get his hopes up about seeing Eli finally wearing one of his jerseys in the stands. "But tonight, I'll just be happy to go home to him."

Kuzy makes a gagging noise, and Alex flushes because that was, admittedly, pretty gross.

Feelings are the worst.

"*Anyway*," Alex says, "if anyone has any problems or, uh—questions? Talk to me privately. But otherwise, let's just keep playing the way we've been playing."

Jeff clears his throat, and Alex glances at him.

"Also, Jeff would like to say something," he says dryly.

That gets a few laughs.

"As most of you know," Jeff says, "I do a lot of work with You Can Play and hockey camps for LGBTQ youth."

Kuzy makes a faux surprised noise. Rushy punches him in the spleen.

"I tell the kids that, sure, some guys are still assholes, but on the whole, NHL teams are about brotherhood, are like family, and that gay or bisexual players—" He nods to Rushy. "—aren't treated any differently than the straight ones."

"You know a lot of gay NHL players?" one of the call-ups asks, not mean, just curious. Maybe a little disbelieving.

"I know a few," Jeff says. "Shockingly, when you're an outspoken advocate for the queer community, queer people tend to trust you."

"Oh. Right."

"Now," Jeff continues. "Complete acceptance isn't, unfortunately, the truth. Most guys? Sure. But some dealt with, or are still dealing with, a lot of shit when teammates or staff found out about them. Some got traded and got more careful. But none of that has ended up on the news. So this is the first time the hockey world at large has really had to confront a situation like this. And because it's *Alex*—"

Several of the guys whoop.

"—I don't need to tell you this is a big deal. That even with Alex making a statement, the media is going to be watching his every move."

"Thanks, bro," Alex mutters.

Jeff rolls his eyes. "Alex isn't the only one who's going to be watched though. We will be too. And if there's even a hint of division or discomfort from anyone on the team, the media is going to latch onto it and exploit it. They don't want a happy story, here. They want blood."

And Alex ... hadn't thought of that.

"I know Jessica is already planning to talk to everyone before the game tonight, but until then—think long and hard about anything you post on Instagram. Anything you snap, anything you text your friends or other guys in the league. The last thing we need is a screenshot of someone's shitty locker room joke ending up on Deadspin."

Alex glances around the room and all of them are paying attention. Even the ones not looking at him—taping their socks or lacing their skates—are nodding along.

"There are kids all over the world right now who are going to watch how this whole thing plays out and use it as a determining factor in their own lives—whether they'll keep playing hockey or quit. Whether they'll come out or stay in the closet. We can't control how other organizations react, but we can make damn sure they see a united, supportive team behind Alex. Okay?"

Alex has to sit down through the yells of agreement.

And maybe he pulls his shirt off a little slower than normal so he can hide his face for a minute.

It's fine.

He leaves his phone with one of the trainers, just in case, as they head onto the ice. Ten minutes into practice she waves at him. He has a voicemail. It's from Eli, saying he just barely made his flight but has boarded, and Alex makes the mistake of excitedly telling Kuzy that Eli will probably be back at Alex's place before practice is even over.

Because of this, he finds himself escorting a half-dozen freshly showered hockey players home with him two hours later.

Alex texts Eli a heads-up, but doesn't get a response. He's trying to shush the guys in the hallway, hoping they don't wake Eli up if he's sleeping, when he realizes there's music coming from his apartment.

Alex pauses at the door, imagining Eli in the shoes, dancing in the kitchen. But he remembers pretty quickly that Eli still needed help standing, much less walking, the last time he saw him. Dancing, especially dancing in heels, is probably off the table for a while.

He takes a steadying breath and opens the door.

Eli is leaning against the center island, back to the door, cutting something while swaying slightly to the music. Hawk, still wearing her mobility harness, is pressed up against his left leg.

Eli is wearing one of Alex's long-sleeved raglan shirts, the green apron, and a pair of knee-high wool socks. He might be wearing shorts, but also might not be. If he is, they're very short and hidden under the hem of the shirt.

It's a good look, but he clearly isn't expecting anyone other than Alex.

"Oh my god," Eli says, fumbling for the handle on Hawk's harness. "Uh. Hi?"

"Eli!" Kuzy yells. He doesn't seem to care about the Schrödinger's Pants situation. "Hug okay? Don't want to hurt."

"Oh, yeah, go for it."

Kuzy folds himself down, very carefully, to envelop Eli and ... yeah. Alex kind of gets why the internet thinks they're so cute together. Not cuter than Alex and Eli. Definitely not. Just. They are kind of cute.

Eli excuses himself to go put on a pair of Alex's sweats a moment later—no shorts, then—before the rest of the guys say their hellos.

When Eli finally gets passed to Alex, Alex wraps him up in his arms, not so gently, and then just clings. For a minute.

"Jesus," Jeff says.

Judging from the other guys' laughter, Eli flips Jeff off behind Alex's back.

They separate a moment later, though, and Eli turns to face everyone again, stabilizing himself with Alex on one side and Hawk on the other.

"Bro," Asher says. "You're really wobbly. Are you okay?"

Kuzy slaps the back of Asher's head.

"Ow," Asher says, slapping Kuzy back. "I wasn't trying to be mean. He *is* wobbly."

"I am," Eli agrees. "It's fine."

"See," Asher says, hopping backward to avoid a kick Kuzy aims at his shins.

"You think this is what having kids is like?" Alex whispers.

"Yes," Rads says.

Eli pointedly clears his throat, and they settle down. "I don't know how much Alex has told you—"

"Next to nothing," Rads supplies.

"But I have a TBI—again—and a concussion. I'm recovering really well, but it'll probably be a few months until I'm back to normal."

"When can you start skating again?" Rushy asks. They're all athletes, and that's the first question any of them ask when teammates are hurt.

"Well. Eight weeks, best case."

Alex pulls Eli a little closer.

"But I can't skate competitively anymore."

"At all?" Asher asks, looking horrified.

"Not competitively, no." Eli says. "But it's okay. It doesn't mean I'm losing skating. I mean, next semester, as long as my balance is better, I'll probably try to find a coaching job. And Alex's already promised to get us ice time the day I'm allowed, so."

"Coaching?" Matts asks, and it's the first thing he's said all morning. Alex is still a little baffled Matts decided to come at all.

"Yeah," Eli says. "Like, teaching kids? There aren't a ton of programs in Houston for figure skating, but I can probably find some part-time work somewhere with the résumé I have. I'm maybe a little overqualified, honestly, but they'd have to be willing to work with the whole"—he gestures to Hawk—"seizure disorder thing."

"Do you *like* teaching kids?" Matts asks, strangely intense, and ... that's admittedly a pretty important question.

"I do," Eli says, grinning. "I always used to volunteer to help out the younger skaters on my teams growing up. My mom says I just enjoy bossing people around, but—" He shrugs. "You remember how much fun we had at the Breaking the Ice Event? With the kids there?"

"Yeah," Matts agrees. "You're, um, you're really good with them. Kids. You even taught *me* something."

"Put that on your résumé," Rushy advises Eli.

That devolves into another fight, and then Alex corrals everyone into the living room, where he starts up Mario Kart to distract them before returning to check on Eli.

"Hey," he says, looping his arms around Eli's waist. "Should you be spending this much time standing up?"

Eli elbows him gently and slides a pile of finely diced red pepper into a bowl. He reaches for a stalk of celery next. "I'm fine. The doctor was actually really impressed with how much I've improved. She said I can move around as much as I want, provided it doesn't exacerbate any of my head issues—which it hasn't. Oh, and I start physical therapy on Monday."

"Okay." Alex smudges the word under Eli's ear, then kisses the skin there just to be thorough. "What are you making?"

"Comfort food. Habichuelas guisadas. Abuela's recipe, of course."

"Of course," Alex agrees. "Do you want any help?"

"What I want," Eli says darkly, "is Amazon Now to deliver plátanos, but apparently, that's too much to ask from the largest internet retailer in the world."

"Uh," Alex says. "I'm sorry?"

Eli sighs, leaning back into him. "Not your fault. I just wanted to make tostones."

Alex has no idea what that means. "Do you want me to write an angry letter to Amazon?"

"Would you?" Eli says faux seriously.

"For you? Of course."

That gets him another kiss.

"Okay," Eli says, "stop distracting me. And go make sure the boys don't destroy the living room."

"Okay." Alex squeezes him a little. He then vaults over the couch onto Jeff's back, ensuring he drives right off the rainbow road.

Jeff does not take kindly to that.

It's amazing his couch has survived as long as it has.

Half an hour and several outraged losses later, Alex notices Matts edging his way out of the living room. When he finally commits, rounding the island to approach Eli, now working at the stove, Alex gets up too.

Matts looks nervous more than anything else, so Alex pauses, leaning against the wall, and watches Eli's back as Matts draws to an awkward stop next to him, in front of the sink.

Eli glances over at Matts briefly, then a second time when it's clear that he isn't there to wash his hands or something. "Hey," Eli says.

"Hey," Matts agrees. "So. Do you want to coach professionally? Like when you're done with college? Or would it just be a side thing?"

This is also something Alex has been wondering.

Why *Matts* is asking it, he has no idea.

"Oh," Eli says. "Well, I don't know. I wouldn't ever want to coach Olympic hopefuls or anything, just kids who are starting out. Less expectations. Less stress."

"More fun?" Matts supplies.

"Right," he agrees. "But that doesn't usually pay well, so." He shrugs. "Then again, thanks to Alex, my YouTube channel is making a little profit off ad revenue, and some big brands have been DMing me on Instagram about doing collaborations. So maybe if I can grow that a little over the next few years? I guess that may be an option. I've got time to figure things out."

"But you don't even—"

"What?"

"I think I was about to say something that Jeff would give me a lecture for."

"Oh? Well, say it anyway. I've had a disclaimer, and now I'm curious."

Matts glances toward the living room, where Rushy has Kuzy in a headlock, yelling about Russian espionage, and Alex pulls back into the hall a little so he won't be seen.

He's eavesdropping and he shouldn't be, but—

"Well," Matts says, voice low. "Do you really even *need* to work? Alex has a shit ton of money. And he's totally gone on you. After the hospital, I kinda figured you two were end game."

"End game," Eli repeats.

"Um. Going to get married?" he says, even quieter.

"I know what *end game* means," Eli mutters.

"So," Matts continues. "You could do whatever you want? Regardless of if it pays well."

"Potentially," Eli allows.

And that's ... It honestly hadn't even occurred to Alex. That if he and Eli do end up together—even thinking the word "married" is kind of terrifying—then Eli will be a millionaire by, like, proxy.

It's a good thought. That maybe Eli wouldn't object to Alex spending money on him anymore if the money was officially *theirs*.

"Are you okay?" Matts asks, and Alex returns his attention to the kitchen where Eli has stopped moving.

"I'm good," he says, sounding a little breathless. "Just—trying to adjust my worldview a little."

"Okay," Matts says, uncertain. "So, if money wasn't a problem? What would you do then?"

"Probably the same thing, I guess. I'd still want to coach, but maybe as a volunteer? For kids who can't usually afford lessons? And keep up with my channel."

"Cool," Matts says decisively. "All right, well. I've got to go nap, but it was nice seeing you. I hope you feel better."

And then he walks away.

Alex watches, stymied, as Matts collects his coat, yells a goodbye that no one acknowledges—because Mario Kart—and then heads out the door.

Eli watches him, similarly baffled, and then shakes his head, returning his attention to the stove.

Alex retreats to the living room with the mental equivalent of a shrug.

Hockey players are weird.

Especially about their pregame naps.

A few minutes later, Eli sets the oven timer, takes Hawk's harness off, then more or less collapses in Alex's lap.

Alex turns the volume on the TV down, just in case Eli's head is hurting, while Jeff happily updates Eli on the current standings: where Alex is dead last.

"Hey, Jeff," Alex says. "Did you know that somewhere in the world, there's a really rude goat named after you?"

"Oh, no," Eli says.

"There's a *what*?" Jeff says.

11

NAPPING WITH ELI IS one of Alex's favorite things in the entire world.

Eli isn't clingy, but he doesn't seem to mind Alex's predilection for wrapping around him like a body pillow. Which means Alex wakes up in the exact position he fell asleep: warm and happy and with his mouth against the vertebra of Eli's neck, just beneath the fuzz of his hairline. Alex leaves a sloppy kiss there, because he can, and then eases his way out of bed and into the bathroom.

Where he promptly remembers he's about to go play his first NHL game as an out gay man under the watchful eyes of a sold-out stadium and hundreds of thousands of TV viewers.

He leans against the counter and takes a minute to breathe.

Then another minute.

Possibly a third.

The duvet crinkles in the bedroom, and he hears Eli talking briefly to Bells before telling Hawk to go get her harness. Alex listens as Eli buckles her into it and makes his way out of the bedroom. Then Alex glances toward the not-quite-closed bathroom door as Bells shoulders it open and joins him, a little judgmental at his hunched-over position.

She jumps up onto the counter, knocks her head against his wrist briefly, and settles herself primly in the bowl of the sink.

"Okay," he says firmly. "I should get ready."

Bells blinks approvingly at him.

Alex straightens, rubs his knuckles once over Bells's bony eyebrows, and goes to change into his nicest game-day suit.

He can't control what the media will say about him tonight, but he can make damn sure he looks fantastic in any of the photos they publish.

When he makes his way back out to the living room, shoes shined and hair at least sort of gelled into submission, Eli has a Hozier record on and is doing something that seems needlessly aggressive to a chicken breast.

Alex just watches him for a while; he has a few minutes before he needs to leave, and there's something innately calming about the way Eli moves around a kitchen, even when he has to pause every now and then to find his balance—to brace his hand against the counter or lean into Hawk.

When he's finished brutalizing the chicken, he adds it to a pan that's already making low, spatter-y cooking noises; "simmering" is the word? Maybe? Alex is trying to build his cooking vocabulary, but it's a work in progress. Eli then moves to preheat the oven.

Alex's phone buzzes with a text, letting him know his driver is in the parking garage, and he takes a bolstering breath.

It's not really effective.

He comes up behind Eli as he's opening the fridge, wraps his hand around Eli's on the handle, presses his opposite palm flat to the face of the freezer door and then just ... holds him there: The front of Alex's body tucked flush to his back. Head ducked. Nose crushed almost uncomfortably into the side of his neck.

"Oh," Eli says. "Well, hello."

Alex breathes him in.

And then exhales.

Slowly.

"Hey," he says, maybe a little sheepishly.

"Hey," Eli agrees. "You okay?"

"I am now."

"Okay."

Eli closes the refrigerator, turns so they're face-to-face, and leans back against it. "Do you want me to ride with you to the arena?"

"No. Jessica said there will probably be protestors. You don't need to see that."

"Neither do you," Eli says quietly.

And then he pets the side of Alex's face. Gently. Like Alex is someone who deserves gentleness.

Alex clears his throat. "No," he says again. "Really. It's fine. You stay and don't overexert yourself. Call Cody. Take a long bath." He pauses. "Maybe not at the same time."

Eli rolls his eyes and mutters something about him being a possessive moron.

"I'm a possessive moron that ordered a box full of new Lush products for you to try. They're in the cabinet."

Eli braces his hands on Alex's shoulders and very carefully goes up onto his toes to kiss Alex's nose. "FYI, you can't just buy your way back into my good graces when you're being problematic. But thank you."

It's a joke. Alex knows it's a joke because Eli is still smiling at him. But there's an undertone that makes Alex think maybe they're going to need a conversation about his gift-giving proclivities soon.

He's not looking forward to it.

Maybe he should ask Rads for advice.

"Okay," he agrees. "I should go."

"Hey." Eli laces his fingers behind Alex's neck. "Whatever happens tonight, I love you."

Alex kisses him.

Takes his time.

Commits it to memory so he can think about it later, when things inevitably go to shit.

"Love you too," Eli says.

Jessica was right.

There are protestors.

He thought he was prepared for it, but he really isn't. At all. Not because it's horrifying or anything, but because it's absolute madness. The entire street in front of the arena is filled with people, easily double, maybe even triple the normal amount of pregame pedestrian traffic. There are police barricades and people with signs and flags and bullhorns. Except he realizes very quickly as the car creeps through traffic along the boulevard that a good portion of the crowd, maybe even a majority of them, is decked out, not in Hell Hounds reds, blacks, and whites, or even Coyote reds and tans, but all sorts of colors. Pinks and neon-greens and turquoises.

Rainbow colors.

People are wearing tie-dyed jerseys. Homemade shirts. Dresses. Kilts.

There are kids on shoulders with glittery rainbow faces and women wearing pride flags like capes.

There are several men in full-body paint posing for pictures together at one of the police barricades while a giant, bearded guy in Alex's winter classic jersey and a pink tutu juggles his beer and a phone to take the photos.

There's a pair of (probably) teenagers in rainbow morph suits, dirty dancing in front of a man with a sign about Alex going to hell.

And yeah, sure, there's definitely that: the requisite God Hates Gays posters and a guy screaming through a bullhorn about the wages of sin being death. There are a cluster of people who proudly hold aloft tatters of what used to be Price jerseys. There are signs with slurs and badly photoshopped pictures of Alex and angry, red-faced, middle-aged men shaking them in people's faces. But.

They're the minority.

Alex was never good at math, but. They're the *minority*.

He laughs a little hysterically as a woman dips her girlfriend? wife? convenient bystander? and kisses her right in front of one protestor, both of them flipping the man off.

Alex has to sit back in the seat and close his eyes and breathe a little.

"Mr. Price?" the driver says a few minutes later.

Shawn? Alex thinks his name is Shawn. Shawn deserves a substantial tip when this is over.

"Yeah?" Alex says. "We're here."

Alex steps out of the car in the parking garage to find Jessica waiting for him.

She's in her usual black suit, but there's a tiny rainbow maple leaf pin on her lapel.

Normally Alex would make a Canadian joke, but he doesn't.

He just. Hugs her. Quickly.

And doesn't say anything; he doesn't know if he can without his voice doing something embarrassing.

And he thinks: *maybe this won't be a disaster after all.*

It's a disaster.

The game is an absolute disaster.

And it's not even really the Coyote's fault.

Well, it is. A couple of them are opportunistic douchebags. And the refs certainly aren't helping as it seems they've been rendered temporarily deaf and blind. But the primary reason the Hell Hounds are down by two at the end of the first is entirely because his team has *lost their fucking minds*.

Jeff gets four minutes for slashing less than a minute into the game after Booker hisses something at Alex that contains multiple slurs.

Kuzy joins him in the box for high-sticking thirty seconds later.

Rads gets in an all-out brawl with a defenseman after they have an exchange in front of the goal, and Rushy probably would have joined in if a ref hadn't dragged him by the tail of his jersey back into the crease.

Asher gets five for fighting.

Rads gets four for slashing.

Kuzy gets ten for misconduct after Alex gets cross-checked in the head and the refs don't call it and Kuzy decides to take justice into his own hands. "Justice" apparently being immediate death. Right there on the ice.

Jeff gets five for fighting.

They're playing three on five for over half the first period, Coach is well on his way to an aneurysm, and the only reason the Coyotes haven't racked up more points is because of Rushy, who looks equally ready to drop his gloves at any moment.

When time runs out and they file into the locker room, cursing, Alex throws his helmet and, with a nod from Coach, yells:

"*What. The actual. Fuck.*"

The guys all mutter about the asshole Coyotes and the fucking refs, and no one will meet his eyes.

"I said," Alex starts lowly, "to treat this like any other game. Coach said to treat this like any other game. Jessica said to be on your best behavior because this game will be under extreme scrutiny, and you—"

"But Booker—" Asher starts.

"I know. I *know* what Booker's been saying, and Nooks, and Pevs, and I'm ignoring it."

"But we can't let them get away with it!" Asher says, a flush riding high on his cheekbones. "It's bullshit!

"Yeah!" a rookie agrees. "The refs aren't doing anything, and the things they're saying—"

"*None of this is new*," Alex yells, and several of those who had started to object go quiet.

"None of it," he repeats. "I've been hearing the same fucking shit since I was in peewee. Hell, I've *said* worse on the ice than the things I've heard tonight, and I'm pretty damn sure everyone in this room has as well at some point in their careers."

"*I* haven't," Jeff says mulishly, tonguing the cut on his lip.

Everyone ignores him.

"Well, yeah," Matts says. "But never to someone who was *actually* gay."

Alex just stares at him until Matts realizes how stupid that just sounded.

"Look," Alex says, running a hand through his hair. "Someone tries to check me in the head and the refs don't call it? Fine. Punch their fucking teeth out."

Kuzy preens.

"But in the second period, I don't want to see a single person draw a penalty for anything less than that. If teams realize that talking shit about me results in our entire second line in the box for—for defending my honor or some shit, we are going to lose every single game we play from here on out. If I can ignore the shit being said about me, you can too."

"Or not ignore," Kuzy says. "Talk back. Make, uh—" He consults quietly with Oshie for a moment, then, "Make them uncomfortable. So they stop."

"What do you mean?" Alex asks guardedly.

"Example. Little angry forward—long hair?"

"Peverly," Alex supplies, sighing.

He'd actually played with Pevs in juniors. Nooks too. He'd thought they were good guys.

"Okay. Peverly says bad things, beginning of period against the boards when I'm fight him for puck. He says Alex bad captain—blah blah. And I'm say yes, Alex *very bad* captain. I ask, every day, for threesome with Alex and Eli, and Alex say no. Because he's jealous. If we threesome, Eli knows I'm best at sex, and then Eli like me most, and then Alex is sad and alone and only cat loves him—"

"Oh my god," Alex says. "Seriously?"

Kuzy looks pleased with himself, shrugging. "It worked! He's shut up, now."

"I like that," Asher muses. "Can we do that?"

"Sure," Alex says, resigned. "Whatever. Just no more penalties."

"Unless they hurt you," Kuzy reminds him, picking torn skin from his knuckles.

"Right," Alex sighs. "Unless they hurt me."

"Then we punch their fucking teeth out," Rads agrees.

Coach sighs, louder than Alex, and shakes his head. "Okay, boys, focus. Let's talk about the second period."

Alex is thinking about what Kuzy said when he lines up for the first face-off of the second period with Booker. He's been ignoring him so far, but ...

"Fucking cocksucker," Booker hisses.

And.

Well.

Alex glances at the ref who is still pointedly pretending he can't hear them.

"Uh, yeah?" Alex says, tightening his grip on his stick. "I'd be a pretty shitty boyfriend if I wasn't."

Booker's face goes blank. "What?"

"It's not like it's a hardship, though, let me tell you. Eli's dick? Very nice, as far as dicks go. A little bigger than you'd expect for someone his size but not *too big*, you know?"

"The fuck?"

"And he's definitely a grower, not a shower, which threw me off at first because I'm not a size queen or anything, but I have to admit—"

"Jesus," Booker says viciously. "Shut the fuck up."

"Hey man, you brought it up. Anyway. Back to Eli's dick."

Booker loses the face-off.

Booker also retreats to stony silence, and Alex finds himself grinning for most of the rest of the game. Because, firstly, they quickly tally two points in the second to tie, but secondly, he keeps hearing little snatches of conversations: Like Rushy shouting advice to anyone near the net on where to get good sex toys in town since clearly the Coyotes are a little too keyed up and need to get laid—even if it's only by themselves.

Or Asher talking about the pros and cons of oil versus water-based lubricant—possibly unprovoked—to a rookie as they battle over the puck.

Or Jeff inquiring if a red-faced defender might himself have latent homosexual desires judging by his apparent obsession with the male phallus.

They win the game.

And when the buzzer sounds, seconds after Alex's empty-net goal, Alex just stands at center ice for a second, leaning on his stick, smiling so hard it hurts.

No one is leaving the stands.

It's a wall of colorful noise—so many people standing up and screaming and—

He doesn't think he's ever heard the Houston arena this loud before.

Jeff crashes into him a few seconds before Kuzy and then Asher and then Rads and then there's a pile of Hell Hounds on top of him all yelling indistinctly like they've won game seven in a tied-up playoff run.

He loves his team so much.

"Hey," Jeff says, catching Alex in a headlock so he can yell in his ear. "Looks like your boy is here."

"My what?"

Jeff points, and some of the other guys start howling and—

Yes.

Eli is on the Jumbotron sitting next to Jo in one of the private boxes, wearing sunglasses and hearing protection and smiling so wide it looks like it hurts.

Alex knows the feeling.

Alex points to him with his stick, and Eli stands, a little slow, a little shaky. Alex doesn't understand what he's doing at first until Eli has turned to show his back to the camera.

He's wearing Alex's jersey.

Price 23.

Eli grins over his shoulder, and the stadium maybe gets even louder.

And *oh*.

Alex didn't know it was possible to love someone this much.

12

ALEX LETS RUSHY HANDLE the media on the ice because he was the star of the game, and Alex has a press conference scheduled in ten minutes. At the very least, he wants a shower, a solid liter of Gatorade, and maybe a hug from his boyfriend beforehand. As he strips off his pads, Alex hopes absently that Eli isn't getting mobbed as he tries to leave the box. Jo probably has that handled, but—

"Hey," Alex yells to Devonte, one of the trainers. "Can you make sure Eli is okay?" Alex pauses, glancing around the locker room. The guys have all been more or less supportive so far, but there's a big difference between inviting his friend, who happens to be gay, into the locker room and inviting his boyfriend. So he isn't sure—

"Bring Eli here," Kuzy yells from his stall, mostly naked. "We protect best."

"Yeah, we do," Asher agrees, high-fiving and then chest-bumping him.

Okay, then.

"Can we get him down here?" Alex asks Devonte.

"Security has him already, I think. Jessica arranged it with them beforehand."

Jessica. Of course. Alex should have known.

He gets in the shower, and by the time he's out, less than five minutes later, Eli is sitting in his stall grinning as Hawk, vest off, attempts to lick all of the sweat off Rads's calves.

"Hey," Alex says, a little breathless.

He just finished a hockey game. Breathlessness is allowed.

"Hey," Eli agrees.

He's not wearing the hearing protection anymore but still has the sunglasses on.

Alex's sunglasses actually. The custom ones Oakley made in Hell Hounds colors just for him. They have little 23s on the frames and everything.

They look good on Eli.

"You're here," Alex says inanely.

"I am."

"Are you okay? I mean, is it okay that you're here?"

Eli laughs a little. "I'm fine. I even checked with my doctor to make sure. And Jo and Jessica helped. It's been very low-stress, all things considered."

"You're welcome," Jo says from Jeff's stall. She's curled up like a cat with a highlighter tucked behind one ear and a large beat-up paperback textbook of some kind ruthlessly folded in half in her hands.

"Thank you," Alex says solemnly.

"Shh," Jo says. "I'm reading."

Alex rolls his eyes and drops his towel.

He gives the room another glance, but most of the guys are doing their own thing or are occupied with trying to entice Hawk away from Rads. Regardless, Alex waits until he's dressed again to pull Eli up and into a hug.

"I can't believe you came."

Eli pushes Alex's damp hair back off his forehead. "You really thought I was going to let you do this alone?"

Uh. Yeah?

"You were in the *hospital* this morning," Alex reminds him.

"I'm not right now though."

"But you acted like you didn't want to come. We didn't even talk about it."

"If I'd told you I wanted to go, you would have argued with me and it would have been exhausting. Now I'm here and everything is fine and we skipped fighting about it."

"Uh-huh."

"Alex," Jessica yells, poking her head in from the hallway. "Media is ready when you are. Dmitri and Derek, you have ten minutes."

"Oh, shit," Rads says and stands to finish stripping and hit the shower.

Asher takes the opportunity to cuddle Hawk.

"Wait," Alex says as Eli calls Hawk away from a disgruntled Asher. ("But, Eli, I *just now* got my turn with her!") "You're coming? To the press conference?" Alex rakes his hair back and settles his favorite Hell Hounds snapback on his head.

Eli gives him a patient look. "We're in this together. Like a team, right? What kind of teammate would I be if I let you deal with those vultures alone?"

Alex refuses to get choked up before he has to go talk to the press. "Oh," he says.

There's been enough time since the final buzzer that he doesn't really have an excuse for his breathlessness anymore.

"Boys," Jessica says from the doorway.

"Right. Sorry. Okay."

Alex offers his arm to Eli on the side opposite of Hawk.

"Ready?"

Security takes them in a golf cart to the largest conference room, where Alex then goes to sit at the table front and center, backgrounded by the wall with the Hell Hounds logo all over it. Alex squints against a flurry of flash photography from a hoard of journalists. He should have requested more time so he could put his suit back on. He's still sweating, and his damp hair drips down the back of his neck.

He pulls the notecards Jessica made for him from his pocket and clears his throat, glancing over toward the door where Eli stands, smiling at him.

Alex taps the cards against the table and leans forward so he can talk into the microphone.

He hates that press conferences are always configured this way, where he always feels like he has to hunch over in order to be heard.

He notices absently that his hands are shaking.

He clears his throat.

"Uh, hi," he says. "I've prepared a statement. And I'll take a few questions afterward, but I'd appreciate it if you keep the focus on me, hockey, and the Hell Hounds organization. Specifically, going forward, I would also like to ask that you respect Elijah's privacy. As a public figure, I understand I can't expect complete anonymity, but Eli is just a college student."

Alex glances up.

"He doesn't have a PR team or media training or any of that. I signed up for this, but he didn't, and his recovery is going to be difficult enough without people following him around with cameras. So. If people can—" He consults the card again. "—uh, respect that, I'd appreciate it. Thank you."

He looks toward Jessica, who's squinting at him.

Ok, so he went a little off script there.

He shuffles his first prompt card to the back of the stack and continues.

"Last week, my privacy was invaded in a completely unacceptable fashion when someone posted a video online of my interactions with hospital personnel at Texas Presbyterian. My boyfriend"—he manages not to stumble over the word, a small victory in and of itself—"Eli, had been placed in an induced coma after an accident, and I was—"

He glances over at Eli, who's biting his bottom lip.

Eli nods encouragingly.

"I was pretty upset." Alex swaps cards again, glancing up a little ruefully at the reporters. "Which you know is an understatement if you've seen the video."

That gets a few laughs.

Out of the corner of his eye, he sees Jessica shaking her head at him, and he sighs.

Right.

Stick to the cards.

"Anyway, uh. What should have been a deeply personal conversation is now public knowledge, and frankly, I hadn't anticipated having this conversation so early in my career."

That gets a few murmurs.

"I've never wanted to be the first out—" He swallows because this is the word that always gets stuck in his throat. "—uh, the first out gay NHL player. I don't think of myself as a role model or want to be the face of a movement. But I realize, circumstances being what they are, people are going to treat me like a representative for the queer community, and I want to apologize in advance if I'm disappointing in that role. I'll, um, I'll do my best though."

He swaps cards.

He knows he's supposed to be glancing up and making eye contact and doing other things Jessica has tried to coach him through during media training days, things that make him more personable and engaging and shit, but he just keeps reading. That's the best he can do right now.

"My team is and has been supportive. Several of them knew about my relationship with Eli before that video was taken, and I appreciate the environment of acceptance and encouragement the Hell Hounds coaching staff and management team have cultivated."

He manages a nod in Jessica's direction.

"I'm proud to call Houston my home. And I'm especially thankful for the fans who've been supportive online and in person tonight, outside the stadium as well as in the seats. I'm glad we could get a win for you tonight."

Card swap.

"But that being said, I am an athlete. And I don't want conversations about my sexuality or the relationship I'm in to interfere with my job."

He takes a breath.

"I'm gay"—he says it with more confidence this time—"and I have a boyfriend, but I just want to play hockey. So I'd appreciate it if, from here on out, media outlets could just let me live my life without speculation or judgment"—not likely, but it's worth a try—"and treat Elijah and me like any other couple in the organization. Thank you."

The words are barely out of his mouth before questions are being shouted at him, and Jessica steps forward.

Everyone quiets down.

She has that effect.

"Alex?" she says.

"Uh. Right."

He points to a guy close to the front of the room wearing a *Washington Post* hat.

"Mr. Price," the man says, "you mentioned you didn't anticipate having this conversation so early in your career—does that mean you *were* anticipating having it?"

"Not initially, no. I'd decided pretty early on I wouldn't come out until after I was retired."

"Why's that?" another man calls.

Alex laughs. Or he tries to. It maybe comes out more like a verbal grimace. "Were you watching the game tonight?"

Jessica clears her throat, and he rocks back in his chair for a moment. He takes off his hat, runs a hand through his hair, and replaces it.

Alex leans forward again, fingers damp, exhaling. "I knew there'd be people who would respond badly if I came out. That, best case, it would be a distraction, and worst case, it would mean the end of my career. I didn't know how much opposition I'd face, and up until I met Eli, I wasn't willing to find out."

"Are you saying your boyfriend pressured you to come out?" a woman near the back of the room shouts.

"No. Definitely not. I just hadn't ever considered that an option before. If I wasn't with someone, I didn't have a reason to take that risk."

"But you *were* more recently planning to come out prior to retirement? Since you're currently in a relationship?"

"I was, yes. I'd already spoken to management and was tentatively thinking about going public in two years."

"Why two years?"

"Well, I wanted at least one cup first."

That gets a couple laughs.

He points to a woman with bright red lipstick in the third row.

"Can you comment on your expectations for the All-Star Game this weekend? Have you spoken to other players in the league since coming out?"

"Oh." He glances at Jessica, who nods.

"I'm no longer attending the All-Star Game for personal reasons." Alex is thankful Eli had slept through most of that discussion at the hospital, where Alex and Eli's mom had a perfectly civil whispered argument over whether Alex really had the capability to care for Eli during the weeks it would take for Eli to regain complete independence again. "But I'm sure Rushy and Matts are going to represent our team really well. As for speaking with other players, I've received, well—honestly a pretty unbelievable amount of supportive text messages and phone calls and snapchats and whatever from guys all over the world who I've played with or against. So that's—I appreciate that."

He points to another woman, this one tiny, who's standing on her chair in order to see him. She reminds him of one of Eli's Morgans.

"I know you said no questions about Eli," she says, and Alex sighs. "But there's a lot of speculation online; could you comment on how you two met?"

He glances at Eli, who grins. That he can do.

Alex laughs, rubbing his palms together, and ducks his head.

"Uh. I guess I can. Eli sure likes to talk about it anyway. Mostly because it's embarrassing. For me."

And he realizes, somehow, that several journalists are only just now noticing Eli is in the room. Which is dumb because A. Eli is probably the most beautiful person ever; how do you just *miss* him? And B. There's a whole German Shepherd standing right next to him, which isn't exactly inconspicuous.

"Hey," Alex says sharply as people shift to take pictures of Eli. "Did you not hear what I, literally, just said, like, five seconds ago?"

The camera clicks die down.

"Okay, so. We met at the practice facility actually. I, well, I was running a little late, and I parked in a handicapped spot."

"Two!" Eli yells.

Alex makes a face. "Okay. I parked across two handicapped spots."

"The only two at the north entrance," Eli adds.

"Do you want to come tell the story?"

Eli demurs, laughing.

And Alex realizes he's smiling even though his hands are still shaking.

"Anyway. It's really—It's not funny. It was a shitty thing to do. It was selfish and entitled and"—he glances up, trying to make eye contact with a few of the video cameras—"it's really important that disabled people have access to parking like that. So even if you don't mean anything malicious by it and you're just in a hurry or whatever, you should never take a handicapped space unless you need it."

"Two," Eli repeats barely audibly.

"And you *definitely* shouldn't take two spaces," Alex adds, rolling his eyes.

"So. Eli came to the end of Hell Hounds practice, and I tried to pet his service dog like an idiot." He looks up at the cameras again. "That's also not good, by the way. You should always ask first because most service dogs can't be distracted if they're working. But anyway, I was basically striking out in terms of making a good impression. Once he confronted me about the handicapped space, I apologized. And Jeff convinced him I wasn't actually an asshole, and Eli let me take him to lunch, and we just—became friends. After that."

"When did your romantic relationship start?" a guy from the back calls.

"I don't think I want to comment on that. But I knew pretty much immediately that I, uh—That he was—" Alex gestures for a minute, trying to think of a less horribly cliché way of saying "special" without success. "—special," he finishes, wincing a little.

He glances down at the final prompt card. "Can we refocus on questions about hockey and the organization?"

"Mr. Price," a man in the second row calls. "Are you worried that your coming out will affect team dynamics?"

And thank god, a question Jessica had prepared him for.

"Of course I'm worried about that. It's the primary reason I hadn't publicly come out until this point. But hockey is my focus and will stay my focus. I think the game tonight illustrated there will be some obstacles, but I'm lucky to be part of a team that's willing to face those obstacles with me."

Jessica nods approvingly, and Alex starts to relax.

Maybe this won't be so bad after all.

He should know better.

"Speaking of the game," a guy says, well, leers really. "Can you talk about what happened in the first period?"

Alex opens the water bottle beside the microphone and takes a sip, mostly as a stalling method.

"It took us a while to settle into the first period, to focus on connecting passes and finding our chemistry. There were—I don't think some of us were fully prepared for some of the things said on the ice, and we took some penalties we shouldn't have."

Understatement.

"But we got our heads right before the second and came back strong, and I'm really proud of the effort we put into the third. Rushy had thirty-two saves, and Matts really showcased his abilities as a playmaker tonight."

"You mentioned there were things said on the ice," the *Washington Post* guy says. "Things like what?"

"I'm not comfortable repeating them."

"The refs didn't make any unsportsmanlike conduct calls," a woman points out.

"No," Alex agrees. "They didn't."

"Is that a criticism of—"

"Next question," Jessica interrupts.

Things only go downhill from there.

After the fourth person has essentially repackaged the same question (will Alex's sexuality be a distraction/problem/spectacle affecting his performance/the Hell Hounds/the league), trying to get an answer other than "I'm here to focus on hockey and my team is as well, and I appreciate the Hell Hounds organization's support despite any obstacles my coming out may produce," Alex is 98 percent done.

And then the leering guy from before pushes him to 99 percent.

"You keep saying you can't control how other teams or fans react to your sexuality and you recognize the team is going to face obstacles. But if you knew it was going to be controversial, why come out in the middle of the season knowing this could affect your playoff run?"

"I'm sorry," Alex says tightly. "Can you restate the question?"

Jessica starts to move forward again, but Alex holds up his hand and—yeah, she's probably going to kill him for that, but she goes still.

"I mean," the guy says patiently as if he's talking to a child. "As a young captain with a history of questionable, some would say 'selfish' behavior—in fact, I think you yourself said it earlier—do you think your actions were impulsive when—"

And there's that last 1 percent.

"Okay, no," Alex interrupts, and the guy smiles, sharp and mean. Clearly, his objective is to get Alex to go off-script. And—Congratulations. Objective achieved.

"First of all, I didn't come out. I was *outed*. And yeah, it absolutely was impulsive and selfish of me to tell the people at the hospital that Eli was my boyfriend. Because he was in a *fucking coma*. I wasn't thinking about obstacles or playoffs or hockey or anything except—the person I care about most in the entire world was—that he might not—*Oh my god*, yeah, it was selfish. But I won't apologize for something that none of my teammates would do *any* differently if they were in my situation and it was their wife or girlfriend. Jesus."

Jessica's hand had closed over his shoulder at some point, firm but not painful.

She waits until he's finished talking and then says, "No further questions for Alex. Derek and Dmitri will be available momentarily to discuss tonight's game, and then Coach will wrap things up for us."

She emphasizes "tonight's game".

Alex stands on autopilot and lets her push him toward the door, as if he needs any incentive to go grab the hand Eli is holding out to him and escape into the hallway.

"Well," Eli says after they've walked a few feet. "That was shitty."

Alex stops to lean against the wall and, groaning, lets his head fall back against the cinderblocks. "I shouldn't have let him get to me."

"He was a dick." Eli rubs one hand up and down Alex's arm. "You hung in there longer than I would have. You want to go home? You need to eat something. I made a new kind of chicken chili for you to try."

"Yeah," Alex says, not moving. "We should go."

He takes another moment, thankful Eli doesn't push, and then straightens. "Are you okay?" it occurs to him to ask. "You're probably really tired, huh? Let's get out of here."

"Not that tired." Eli leans into him. "But yes, we should definitely get out of here."

Alex doesn't get it at first.

Not until Eli glances around surreptitiously—the only person in the hall is the security guard with the golf cart, waiting for them to get their shit together—and sneaks a hand up the back of his shirt, palm cool against his sweaty skin. He uses his hand as a brace to go up on his toes and bite softly, just a tease, at Alex's ear lobe.

"Oh," Alex says. "*Oh*. Is that allowed?

"Yep. I asked the doctor and everything. Sex is definitely allowed. As long as we're careful." Eli throws a hand up to his forehead, pretending to swoon. "Can you be gentle with me, Mr. Price?"

Yes.

Alex can be gentle.

Eli laughs at whatever Alex's face is doing. "So," he says, slipping his hand from Alex's back to his side, walking his fingers absently up and down the ladder of Alex's ribs. "Home? Chili?"

"Yeah," Alex agrees. "And then I want to find out what publication that guy works for and make sure he's banned from any future Hell Hounds press conferences."

"Sure. But maybe we can save that until after we've had a couple orgasms."

"A couple? That seems a little ambitious."

"We're literally teenagers. It's not ambitious. It's realistic."

Alex grins. "Oh, the places you'll go with warming lube and a can-do attitude?"

"That's the spirit."

13

THE NEXT WEEK IS ...

Well.

Idyllic, might be the word.

Alex takes Hawk to run with him in the mornings and stick-handles tennis balls around the house for her to chase in the afternoons. He drives Eli to his therapy appointments and drops him off and picks him up from class. They cook together, on camera and off, and cuddle on the couch while watching the All-Star Game coverage, even though Eli technically isn't supposed to have screen time yet. ("Alex, no. Don't turn it off. I'm not looking at the TV; I'm looking at the wall next to the TV!")

After the second grocery delivery where Eli says probably unkind things in Spanish and bemoans a lack of plátanos, Alex Google translates "plátanos" and then sacrifices fifteen minutes of selfies in the line at CVS to purchase a dozen bananas on his way home from the gym. When he proudly presents them to Eli, however, Eli is confused for several seconds and then just ... laughs.

Uproariously.

For a while.

"Oh my god," Eli says. "You silly gringo. You brought me bananas."

"Uh, yeah? Because you keep complaining that Amazon won't deliver them with our other groceries? Which seems dumb, by the way, because I don't even *like* bananas, but I know they're super common."

Eli just laughs harder.

"Is that not—Google said plátanos is Spanish for bananas." Alex pulls up the search screen on his phone from earlier that day. "Look. See? Plátanos. Bananas." Alex shoves his phone back in his pocket and crosses his arms. "*Why* are you laughing at me?!"

"Oh, no," Eli says, still giggling but grabbing one of Alex's wrists. "No, no. I'm sorry; I'm not laughing at you."

"Well, you're definitely not laughing *with* me," Alex mutters, pulling away from him.

Okay. He doesn't really pull away. Just pretends to. Eli's balance has improved, but it's not back to normal yet and the last thing he wants to do is contribute to a fall.

That, and the fact that if Eli is touching him, even if Alex is kind of pissed at him, he doesn't ever want Eli to *stop* touching him.

"No, I know," Eli says, clinging a little harder anyway. "Hey. I'm sorry. I love that you brought me bananas." He kisses Alex's chin. Goes up on his toes to reach his mouth. "I really do. Thank you."

Alex is mollified. "Then why are you laughing at me? I was trying to do a thing. A nice thing."

"I know, baby. I know you were. It's just—" He badly suppresses another laugh. "I meant plantains. In the Dominican Republic, plátanos are plantains. That's what Mamá and Abuela call them, so I do too. Bananas are guineos."

"Then why did Google say—"

"In most other Spanish-speaking places, plátanos *are* bananas. You didn't do anything wrong; it was really sweet, just ... funny. And I need to call Mamá and tell her right now. This is literally the cutest thing."

Alex gets another kiss for his trouble and then is left glaring at a dozen bananas while Eli alternates between cooing and cackling loudly in Spanish from the guest bedroom.

Great.

Alex may or may not spend fifteen minutes locked in the bathroom later that evening, feverishly googling where to find plantains in Houston, which seems to be ... most grocery stores.

But that doesn't seem good enough. He wants *specifically* Dominican plantains. So he has a whispered phone conversation in the closet with the owner of a Dominican restaurant who imports their plátanos directly and agrees to pay what is probably an exorbitant price for a box of them—available for pick up the following day—and then tries to exit the bathroom casually.

Eli asks him if they need to start upping the fiber content in Alex's food.

Alex throws a banana at him.

The following day, Alex picks up his order on his way home from the gym, to the extreme amusement of the restaurant owner, who feels the need to be present when Alexander Price of the Houston Hell Hounds comes to collect a box full of plantains for his boyfriend.

She calls him a good boy, and she's definitely laughing when he leaves.

He manfully ignores it.

He's expecting more laughter when he arrives home and presents Eli, napping on the couch, with his spoils. Instead, Eli just stares at the box in his lap for a minute, and then his face kind of squinches up, and he bites his lip and—

Well shit.

"Hey, no. Don't—hey," Alex says, shifting the plantains off Eli's lap so he can pull Eli into his. "I don't understand. They're plantains! You said plantains. Are they the wrong kind? Are there *kinds* of plantains? Is this why the lady at the restaurant was laughing at me?"

And Eli just collapses into his chest, and he might be laughing now rather than crying, but Alex can't tell.

"Okay." Alex rubs Eli's back with one hand and cups the nape of his neck with the other. "You need to talk to me because you're kind of freaking me out."

"I'm sorry," Eli says somewhere in the vicinity of Alex's neck. "I'm fine. I am."

"Are you sure?"

"Yeah. I'm just extra emotional or whatever right now. I can't help it. Concussion. And you—"

And then they're making out, apparently.

So. The plantains are probably okay, then.

Eli makes them tostones with dinner—which is not nutritionist approved but really, really good. Then he makes mangú with breakfast the following morning and lets Alex help with the mashing, and there's just a lot of love and plantains and kisses in his life for the next several days.

It's a good week.

But then the break is over, and it's February. Alex leaves for a roadie with the team and comes back to an Eli who is struggling through assignments that are taking three times as long to complete as they did the semester before. An Eli who sometimes mixes up his words and doesn't want to use Hawk for balance even though he still needs to; an Eli who gets stress migraines, which means he's turning in assignments late or incomplete. He won't tell Alex how many seizures he's had, but Alex has been present for two in the three weeks since Eli was released from the hospital, so he knows it's probably not a good number. And he doesn't want to push, because Eli isn't a kid. Alex wants to allow him his autonomy or whatever; he definitely doesn't want to scare him away back to his dorm by stifling him, but—

He cares.

So much.

And most of the time, Eli doesn't let him show how much he cares, which—Maybe Eli is completely normal, and Alex is just clingy and overbearing. But after two more weeks of Eli getting more and more frustrated—stressed often to the point of tears—and not letting Alex do anything to help, Alex feels like he's losing his mind.

He should probably talk to his therapist about it, except he's already back to seeing her every week again, sometimes more, and they usually spend all their time dealing with hockey stuff.

Because the hockey stuff is ...

Bad.

Not his team. Not the Hell Hounds. Even the call-ups are mostly behaving themselves.

And honestly other teams, as a whole, are too. But there's usually a handful of guys every game they play who, even if they aren't being directly malicious, are using the gay thing to try to get penalties. Then there are the occasional ones who are malicious—who spit venom and make illegal hits and leave him bruised like he's in the playoffs. Dealing with that every other night is exhausting. Dealing with refs who ignore it all is exhausting. Dealing with media who desperately want to break his Jessica-approved demeanor to talk about the language or the hits or the refs is exhausting. Trying to encourage his team through it—because he's the captain and they didn't sign up for any of this shit anyway—that's exhausting too.

So Alex is dealing with shitty players and shitty refs and shitty media, and then having to put on a good face for his team, and he comes home so, so, tired, and then he has to worry that his boyfriend is slowly killing himself.

It's not good.

So maybe Alex overreacts one day when he gets home. Eli isn't there yet, even though he should have gotten out of class over an hour ago. His phone is going straight to voicemail, the Morgans haven't seen him, and Cody hasn't talked to him since the night before.

Alex is seriously considering driving to campus—and he doesn't know, wandering around the quad yelling Eli's name?—when the door finally opens.

"Where the *fuck* have you been?" Alex says, which is ... probably not the best way to start a conversation.

"What?" Eli says, kicking off his shoes. "Shouldn't you be on your way to the arena?"

"Yeah," Alex agrees. "I was supposed to leave twenty minutes ago except you weren't here, and you weren't answering your phone, and no one I called had any idea why you weren't here or answering your phone."

"The bus was late," Eli says, still taking off Hawk's vest as if everything is fine and normal, "and my phone died. It's not a big deal."

"The fuck do you—*Yeah*, it's a big deal. You're over an hour late. And I thought you weren't taking the bus anymore. We talked about that."

Eli's face is starting to go pinched. "It's hard to be late when we didn't have plans. And you may have talked *at* me about not taking the bus anymore, but we didn't make an agreement."

"I gave you the number for the car service and put you on my account for a reason. *This* reason. So I wouldn't have to be sitting here fucking up my schedule on a game night wondering where the hell you are."

"Oh," Eli says sharply. "Okay. So this isn't about you being worried about me, it's about inconvenience. Because you've made me part of your *pregame rituals*."

And that's. Not true at all.

"No," Alex says. "I put you on my account because everything is hard enough for us without dealing with shitty public transportation and the shitty people who use it."

Eli sighs, letting his backpack fall off his shoulders and into the crooks of his elbows. He dumps it gently on the floor. "So, poor people."

"What?"

"The shitty people who use public transportation? You mean poor people. Newsflash, Alex, I *am* poor people. And I'm not some charity case you can just throw money at."

"No, you're not a charity case; you're my *boyfriend*."

"So that makes it okay? Well, shit. I guess I don't get any say in the matter. I can't take the bus with the peasants anymore because god forbid Alexander Price's boyfriend be photographed sitting next to a homeless person."

"That's not fair. That's not what I'm saying at all."

He means the assholes Eli complains about, the ones who take the handicapped seats and touch Hawk without asking, the ones who touch *him* or stare at him or ask what's wrong with him as though it's somehow an acceptable thing to say to a stranger.

Alex is trying to formulate this into words, but he doesn't get a chance.

Eli says, "My head hurts," and walks toward the guest bedroom.

And that's just perfect. It seems like any time they disagree about something, Eli's head hurts and that's the end of things because only an asshole would keep talking after that point.

Apparently, Alex is an asshole today.

"Your head always hurts," Alex says. "And your balance is shit, and your aphasia is fucking up your grades, and you're having more seizures than normal, and you're stressed out all the fucking time. And that sucks. And I wish I could do something about it, but I can't. What I *can* do is get you a car service so you don't have to deal with the bus, or a new phone that can hold a charge for longer than an hour, or one of those stupid wedge pillows that's supposed to help with your neck or—With all the other shit we're dealing with, coming home to you should be the best part of my day, but it's almost worse because you're so upset all the time and you complain about shit but then you won't let me do anything to try to *fix* any of it."

"I'm sorry this is so *hard* for you," Eli snarls, and that's—okay. This is not working.

"Oh my god," Alex exclaims. "Why are you *like* this? You're not *listening* to me, you stubborn asshole."

And Eli might not be listening, but he is crying now.

Fuck.

He made Eli cry.

He did that.

Jesus.

"You should go," Eli says lowly, smearing the back of one hand over his eyes. "You're going to be late for warmups."

He's right.

Alex walks out the door; if he stays any longer, he's going to say something he regrets. Well. Something else.

Eli doesn't come to the game.

Alex doesn't play like shit, but he's definitely off. Luckily, Matts is on fire—getting his first hat trick as a Hell Hound—and they win handily. Also luckily, the Avs don't seem interested in taking advantage of the gay thing either, or Alex probably would have just said fuck it and punched someone in the face.

The problem is, the person who probably most deserves a punch to the face right now is him. Because, yeah, Eli is emotional and dramatic. But he's also an eighteen-year-old college student with a concussion and a seizure disorder, currently recovering from a *second* traumatic brain injury while trying to deal with his boyfriend being a newly out professional hockey player. Like—he has an excuse for occasional irrational or frustrating behavior. Alex throwing their circumstances at him, as if it's somehow Eli's fault that Eli's recovery is slow and he's overwhelmed and stressed out, isn't fair.

He tells Jeff as much as they're showering, dragging out putting his clothes on; he's honestly a little afraid to go home.

Because what if Eli isn't *there*.

"You just need to talk to him," Jeff says. "And apologize. Probably apologize first before the talking."

"Yeah, but aren't you supposed to give people gifts when you apologize? To prove you mean it? I feel as if that would make things worse in this scenario."

"Maybe?" Jeff says. "I usually do, but not really expensive stuff. Just stuff Jo likes. Anthologies on bat migratory patterns. A bottle of wine. Debts of servitude. Sexual favors."

Alex coughs on a laugh.

"But for real," Jeff continues, "maybe you could get him some more plantains? That seemed to work out well for you."

It definitely had.

Martin Cook, or Cookie, one of the call-ups who will probably stick around considering his numbers, makes a confused noise next to them. "Can't you get him flowers or chocolates or something you'd get a girl? Or shoes, right? I saw that Instagram post."

Alex pauses.

Jeff makes a resigned noise.

"So," Rads says casually, pulling on his shirt. "Because Eli is gay, Alex can treat him like a girl?"

"Uh," Cookie says, suddenly noticing a good portion of the locker room's attention is on him. "Yeah?"

Logan Roy, or Moose, the other call-up (large, Canadian, the nickname had followed him since juniors, apparently), shakes his large Canadian head. He may be new, too, but he at least knows that's not the right answer.

"Alex is gay," Kuzy points out.

"Huh?" Cookie says.

"Alex is gay," Kuzy repeats. "We treat him like a girl too?"

"What? No. That's different."

"How?" Jeff asks.

"You know," Cookie says, gesturing with his nearly empty Gatorade bottle. "Alex is Alex. He's—"

"What?" Rushy says innocently. "Like, the guy in the relationship?"

"Yeah," Cookie says, relieved.

"Oh," Alex says because it's about time he says something. "So you think since I fuck Eli, that makes him the girl?"

"Uh—"

"If that's the case," Alex says with a gentleness he doesn't at all feel, "I have some shocking news for you."

"Wait," Moose says. "Does that mean—"

"If I recall," Asher muses, toweling off his hair, "Alex said he and Eli take turns being the little spoon."

"Oh, my god," Alex mutters. "That wasn't what I was talking about."

"Actually, I'm pretty sure Alex said he was the knife," Jeff says.

"What would that even mean in this context?" Rads asks.

"The point," Alex says, exasperated, "is that Eli isn't any less of a man because of the clothes he wears or what he likes in bed. He's a person, not a stereotype. So when I'm apologizing for being shitty, I want to treat him like a person."

"While we're being progressive and shit," Jeff says dryly, "I'll also point out that *women* are people too."

"This is good point," Kuzy agrees wisely. "Some women not like flowers. Or shoes. Or Cookie's face. It's—" He glances at Oshie and says something in Russian.

"Personal preference," Oshie supplies.

"Yes," Kuzy says solemnly, "it's personal preference."

The laughter starts.

Cookie shoves his pink face through the collar of his shirt and flees the locker room.

Asher nods after him, one eyebrow raised, and Alex waves him away, smiling slightly as Asher jogs after Cookie. The kid is clearly just a little ignorant, not malicious, and while some embarrassment will probably do him some good in this case, Alex doesn't want him to feel as if the team is judging him. Asher will make sure he's taken the lesson in good humor, and if he hasn't, Alex will talk to him.

After procrastinating for several more minutes, he packs up. He stops at CVS for some dog treats. It's one of the few things Eli has never gotten mad about him buying. Then, driving slower than the speed limit and wondering if maybe he should stop and top off his two-thirds full tank of gas, Alex heads home.

He's expecting the apartment to be dark. For Eli to be in the guest bedroom or maybe not even there. And Alex is trying to make the best of it—at least he'll have the rest of the night and early morning to organize his thoughts and his words and maybe not fuck up too badly when he tries to apologize.

But the lights are on when he gets home.

Just the under-the-cabinet kitchen lights and the dim recessed lighting in the living room.

But it's more of a welcome than he thought he'd get. The guest bedroom door is closed, but Eli's keys are in the entryway bowl, his backpack is on one of the bar stools, and Hawk's harnesses, both of them, are hanging on the low hooks by the door. So. At least he stayed.

Alex drops his bag in the hall, downs a glass of iced Gatorade, and then pushes open his own bedroom door. He toes off his shoes and tosses his hat toward the chair and—

Hawk sits up, stretching, and Alex freezes, hopping on one foot, midway through pulling off a sock.

Because Eli is in his bed. Their bed.

And with Hawk's movement, Eli props himself up a little and squints against the light coming in from the living room.

"Uh," Alex says, "hey."

Eli blinks at him and then rolls back over, pulling the duvet with him.

Okay.

Alex finishes getting undressed, turns off the lights, and texts Jeff, a little frantically, asking for advice. He takes another shower as a stalling method, brushes his teeth for well over the dentist-recommended two minutes, and then sits on the toilet playing angry birds for several more minutes. Jeff doesn't answer; he's probably asleep like a sane person.

Resigned, Alex creeps back into the bedroom and sits on the edge of the mattress.

Eli ignores Alex as he slides under the covers on his side of the bed.

Alex is exhausted, but the tension is palpable, and even the animals can't seem to settle.

After several minutes of Eli shifting, Bells making annoyed noises, and Hawk getting up to recircle occasionally at their feet, Alex sighs, sitting up.

It feels like there's an ocean of cool sheets between them.

"I can go. If you want. To the guest bedroom. Or even to Coops's place, if that's—"

Eli sits up, too, with a disbelieving noise. "What the fuck? Go to Jeff's?" He pauses. "If you want to be alone, then fine, but *I'll* leave. This is your home."

"No! I don't—Please. Stay. I'm just—not ready yet."

"What?"

"I really am sorry," Alex says, wishing there was some light so he can see Eli's expression. "But I haven't had a chance—I need time to figure out how to apologize. And try to explain what I meant better. "

"Okay."

"Okay?"

"I mean. I'm still mad at you."

"That's fine. You should be."

"But I know I overreacted, and I haven't been—the easiest person to be around. Lately. And I know you need time to process things and get your words right. So."

"Yeah. I do."

It's quiet save for Bells, who's started up a low creaky purr up by the headboard.

"So. Is it—Do you want me to sleep with you in here?" Alex asks.

"Alex." Eli says patiently. "I'm in your bed. If I didn't want to sleep next to you, I wouldn't *be* here."

"Oh."

Alex is so relieved he doesn't know what to do with himself for a minute. So he just continues to sit there. Like an idiot.

"Oh my god," Eli says, lying back down. "Come here, you moron."

Alex obeys.

14

ELI WAKES UP BEFORE Alex, which isn't a surprise considering how long Alex took before coming to bed the previous night.

Alex isn't wrapped around him quite as thoroughly as usual, but he is tucked up against his back, knees butting up behind Eli's, the fingers of one hand curled loosely in the fabric of Eli's shirt.

He extricates himself easily enough and takes Hawk out to do her business.

When he gets back upstairs, he opens the door to a rumpled, slightly frantic Alex coming out of the guest bedroom

"Oh," Alex says, trying and failing to look casual. "Hi."

"Hi," Eli agrees. "What are you doing?"

"Nothing." He says it too quickly, then seems to realize this. "I just needed to check," he murmurs, running his fingers through his hair.

"Check what?"

"I woke up, and you were gone. So I needed to make sure." He sighs. "I needed to see if your stuff was still here. Hawk's things."

Hawk recognizes her name and wags her tail helpfully. It whacks Eli on the thigh.

He takes off her leash so she can give Alex a proper morning greeting and tries not to find the bright flush riding high on Alex's cheekbones incredibly, horribly endearing.

He is not successful.

"I wouldn't just leave," Eli says.

"I didn't think you would," Alex says. "Not really. I just—I don't know how this works."

"How what works?"

"Fighting. In a relationship. And I've heard stories from the guys—but I know we're not like them. I just don't, uh, have a playbook, here."

Playbook.

Jesus.

"I mean. Neither do I," Eli points out. He moves into the kitchen to pour a Gatorade over ice because Alex is a terrible influence, and despite the fact that it's only February, Houston has apparently decided to skip spring and go straight to summer. "You're my first everything, remember?"

Alex doesn't even attempt to suppress a smug look. "Yeah."

"So I think we can just—decide how we fight? Together?"

"Oh. Yeah. Okay."

"So," Eli says, "I don't have class until 11:00. You want to talk this through now, or do you need more time to think?"

Alex straightens from where he's petting Hawk. "It's Thursday," he points out, like he's trying not to cause problems.

"Yep," Eli agrees.

"Isn't your English class at 10:00 on Tuesdays and Thursdays?"

"It was. I withdrew last night. The papers for that class were causing me the most problems. I think I can handle the rest of my workload a lot better if I don't have to worry about that one anymore."

Alex looks as if he isn't sure if he's allowed to be happy about that.

"You're allowed to be happy about that," Eli says.

Alex moves around the island to wrap Eli in a hug. "Good," he says into his hair, and then they stand there for a minute, breathing and being solidly together.

Eli touches his cold glass to Alex's neck, and Alex bites his ear gently in retaliation.

"I'm ready to talk now, I think," Alex says. "If you want to. We should probably eat something first, though, so you can take your pills."

"True. Do you have practice today?"

"Not until 11:30." Alex brightens. "That means I can drop you off on the way. Or—" He pauses and tries again. "—if you want, I can drop you off on the way?"

"Nice save. That works for me. Pancakes first?"

"Pancakes and then talking?" Alex clarifies, like he's preparing himself for battle.

"Pancakes and then talking," Eli agrees. "I need to use up the last of those frozen bananas."

Alex groans. "Bananas? Again?"

"You're the one who bought them."

"Because I thought *you* wanted them. The whole dozen cost two dollars. Just throw whatever is left out."

"We do not waste food in this household, Alexander Price."

Alex makes an aggrieved noise. "Can they at least be peanut butter banana pancakes?"

"Deal."

Eli makes peanut butter banana pancakes, and they watch ESPN while they eat, then Alex cleans the kitchen afterward so Eli can shower.

When Eli returns to the living room, Alex is sitting on the couch, television off, glaring at his phone like it has personally offended him.

"Everything okay?" Eli asks.

"Yeah. Just—trying to organize my thoughts."

"Oh. Okay."

Eli doesn't know if he should sit next to him or not. "Are you ready to talk?"

"I think so. You want to sit?"

"Yeah. Okay." Eli sits.

"Cool," Alex says, nodding.

"Cool," Eli agrees. He bites his lip. "We're really shitty at this."

Alex exhales, half laugh, half something else. What, Eli isn't sure. "We really are."

"Should we talk about that first?" Eli asks. "Make, like, rules about how we fight?"

"Oh. Sure. Here, let me—"

Alex gets up to retrieve the little whiteboard he keeps in the hall closet for thinking out plays. He uses the cuff of his hoodie to erase what's already on it and snags a marker from one of the kitchen drawers. He sets the whiteboard on the coffee table and kneels on the floor, writes across the top in all caps: RULES FOR FIGHTING. Then he sits back on his heels, looking pleased with himself.

"Okay," he says, and Eli tries not to laugh because he's got his Captain Voice on and he probably doesn't even realize it.

"Rule number one," Eli says, "No yelling."

Alex blinks at him. "You were yelling last night. We were both yelling last night."

"I know. And it was awful. And I don't want to do it again. Didn't you hate that?"

"Yeah," Alex agrees. "Yeah, I did. Okay."

He writes it down. *No yelling.*

"Rule number two," Alex says. "Nobody leaves. I mean, going for a walk or going to a different room is fine. Or going to Jeff's or the gym or something, to blow off some steam. But not—"

"Home by bedtime?" Eli suggests.

"Yeah. Is that okay?"

"Yeah."

Alex writes it down. *No leaving—home by bedtime.*

"You realize the assumption there is that this is my home," Eli points out, a little belatedly. "We never did have that talk after our supposed trial period of me living here."

Alex winces. "We can ... do that now?"

"Nah," Eli says. "I'm too spoiled now. I'm not going back to the dorm."

Alex looks incredibly relieved. "So," he prompts. "Rule three?"

"Um. Not letting things ... fester?"

"Fester is a gross word," Alex says. "Rule number three is that we don't ever use the word 'fester.'"

Eli rolls his eyes. "Fine. We don't let things ... build up. We should have talked way before last night."

Alex nods and writes it down: *No build up*.

"I might need time to pause and think about things though," Alex says. "So can we have a caveat for that?"

"Maybe just, Rule number four. Time and space when needed."

"That works."

It goes on the board: *Time & space when needed.*

"Okay, what else?" Eli asks.

"Um, I'm not really sure how to say this nicely."

Eli leans forward, elbows braced on his knees. "Well. Hit me, I guess."

"I don't think you should be able to use your health as a way to get out of arguments."

Eli bites back the automatic retort. "That's ... fair. I *have* done that, but I won't anymore. You need to trust me to do that though. And believe me if I say I need time because I'm too tired or my head hurts for real. I guess that falls under both number three and four."

Alex hesitates, marker poised over the whiteboard.

"Should we just know that, or do we need to make it a separate rule?"

"Well, we're running out of space, so."

"True. All right. Anything else?"

They both think for a minute.

"I feel like maybe we shouldn't talk about our private business with other people?" Alex says. "I hear guys bitching about their girlfriends in the locker room, and I don't want to be that person. And I really don't want to think about you talking about me like that either."

"Uh. I don't know if—What about Cody?"

"Oh. That's true. I might want to talk to Jeff. I did yesterday. About this."

Alex goes to run his hand through his hair, forgetting he has a marker in his hand, and ends up with a smear of red on his forehead.

Eli licks his thumb and rubs it off because he's helpful.

"So," he says, while Alex swats him away, "Rule number five. No telling people our business unless it's someone close, and it's done privately?"

No public diss tracks, Alex writes.

Eli resists the urge to kick him.

"Anything else?" Alex asks.

"No? We should probably revisit our rules sometimes though."

"We should probably also schedule time to talk every now and then. So we can make sure nothing is ... "

Eli can tell Alex is thinking the word "festering" just from his facial expression.

" ... building up," Alex finishes.

"What, like a monthly airing of grievances?"

"That sounds bad. More good things *and* bad things maybe? Like when you're in high school and you have to say one positive thing for every critical thing when you're editing someone else's paper?"

"That could work."

"So." Alex stands and walks over to the calendar by the door. "Same day next month?"

"You want to plan our next talk before we've even had this one?"

"Yes?" Alex says, looking unsure.

"Well. Sure."

Alex draws a big red heart with the Expo marker on the calendar.

"You realize the guys are going to see that and think it's some special anniversary," Eli points out. "Or a sex thing."

"It could be a sex thing," Alex says hopefully.

"Focus."

"Right." Alex returns to the living room, sits on the couch next to

Eli instead of the floor this time, and they consider the whiteboard. "This is all very idealistic."

"Yup," Eli agrees. "Should we try them out?"

"Guess so. Can I go first?"

Eli gestures for him to continue.

"All right." Alex consults his phone. "So. I think there were two misunderstandings last night. The first one is that you thought I have an issue with poor people or think I'm better than them or something, and I don't. The second thing was that you thought I was mad you hadn't made it home because it fucked with my schedule. Which wasn't true at all. But I realize the way I was phrasing things probably made it seem as if it was all about me and less about ... actual concern for your well-being. So I apologize for that."

"Apology accepted," Eli says. "If we're giving, uh, overviews here, I don't honestly think you have an issue with poor people. Or that you only cared about where I was because of your pregame rituals. I was—I *am*—pissed off and don't have an outlet. Because skating has always been my outlet." Eli shrugs a little helplessly. "Anyway. You might have phrased things kinda shitty, but I was intentionally taking them the wrong way, too, and I apologize for that."

"Apology accepted," Alex says promptly.

"You know, maybe we won't be so bad at this after all," Eli says.

Alex laughs a little shakily. "I'd still like to argue about you taking the bus."

"Why?"

Alex looks stymied. "What?"

"Why don't you like me taking the bus?"

"Oh." He consults his phone again. "First, you hate taking the bus. You complain about people touching Hawk and taking up the only handicapped seats. And how waiting outside makes your headaches worse. And second, if the bus is late, you could be late for appointments or class. Which would just add to your stress level. You're stressed out enough with school, and I'm stressed with hockey and this is something I can *fix*. I can't change the refs or the homophobic assholes or the questions I get asked in the post-game interviews. And I can't change how the computer screens hurt your head and words are hard sometimes and your balance gets fucked up when you're tired. But. I can fix this. And it's so small and stupid in comparison to all the big things I can't fix, so I don't understand why you won't let me. I just—I love you *so* much, and I feel like you're not *letting* me."

"Okay," Eli says.

"Okay what?" Alex says, a little breathless.

"Okay. Those are good points. I'll start using the car service."

"Really?"

"Really. But there are two things I need you to do for me."

"Shoot."

"Well, first, we probably need to make a distinction between when I want help and when I just want to talk. If I've had a shitty day, I want to be able to complain to my boyfriend about things without him trying to fix them all for me. I just want to vent, sometimes. And I don't want to, like, have to censor myself in my own home—" Alex looks pleased at that terminology "—whenever my back is hurting or something because I'm afraid you'll immediately go on Amazon and buy sixteen different products that supposedly help with back pain."

"That's fair," Alex says, sheepishly.

"Secondly, or maybe just part B of that, we need to put a limit on your gift-giving. You're letting me live with you for free and paying for all of my food, and *now* my transportation. And I know I'm cooking all your meals, but that's still not an equitable trade off."

Alex opens his mouth, but Eli holds up a hand.

"And that's okay. I'm a college student and you're an ... NHL superstar or whatever."

"Or whatever," Alex agrees gravely.

Eli rolls his eyes. "And I can live with that. But the other gifts ... Look, if you want to get me stupidly expensive shit for Christmas or my birthday, fine. But I don't want you spending more than, like, twenty dollars on me outside of that. No more random Louboutin purchases."

"Twenty dollars?" Alex says. "You can't get *anything* for twenty dollars."

"How much were the plantains?" Eli asks.

"Twenty-five."

"Well, you were swindled, but fine. No more than twenty-five."

"A hundred," Alex counters.

"This isn't a debate."

"That's exactly what this is."

Damn him.

"Forty, and I'll let you go up to one hundred for Valentine's Day."

"Seventy-five, and two hundred on Valentine's Day."

Eli considers this. "Fifty, no more than once a month, and one fifty on Valentine's Day.

"Fifty," Alex says slowly, "no more than once a month, up to one fifty on Valentine's Day, and I can give you Hell Hounds merchandise or stuff from my sponsors whenever I want."

"Deal."

They shake on it.

"Well," Alex says. "That wasn't so bad."

"Right? Look at us. Being all mature and shit."

Alex reaches a little, tugs a little, and Eli climbs into his lap because he's accommodating like that.

"Hey, so." Eli nods to the heart on the calendar. "Scientifically speaking, it is beneficial to positively reinforce good behavior. And we've got forty-five minutes before we need to leave. If you still wanted this to be a sex thing."

Alex grins. "I guess we'd better make it a sex thing, then," he says solemnly. "For science."

"For science," Eli agrees, equally grave.

15

THINGS GET BETTER.

Well. Some things.

Over the next week, Eli turns in all his assignments on time. He makes a video for his channel, manages Tuesday and Thursday—his lightest work days—without having to use Hawk's mobility harness, only gets one migraine, and doesn't have any seizures. He and Alex also don't fight about anything. It's a good week.

Mostly.

"Mostly" because *other* people are still terrible. Eli has been ignoring comments and private messages on Instagram, but he makes the mistake of scrolling through some of them while waiting for Alex to pick him up from class on Wednesday. And ... well, there are a lot of nice things, but there are also some scary things.

Like death threats.

Actual real-life people. Strangers. Who want him dead. For corrupting Alex or for just generally being gay or—he doesn't even know.

The following day, Jessica calls him (likely because Alex called her) and convinces Eli to give his Instagram, Twitter, and YouTube passwords to one of the Hell Hounds PR interns, who is now in charge of managing his accounts. Not posting anything, she assures him, just deleting all the bad comments and reporting people who cross the line of ugly to potentially dangerous.

So that's—He wouldn't necessarily term it "good," but at least he's not afraid to look at the comments on his posts now. He's also talked to Jessica about some potential PR opportunities with Alex—ways to humanize him, she said, to help move his narrative from bad boy to role model. The Hell Hounds really want to work the "confused gay kid made some bad choices, but now he's Out and everything is awesome" angle. Which feels a little gross, but Eli sees why it's necessary, and it is at least partly true. So he agrees they can talk more about including Eli in smaller, controlled pieces of media: a behind-the-scenes tour for Hell Hounds social media of Alex's apartment—when Eli happens to be cooking—and curating a few intentional Instagram moments in a couple more weeks when he's back, literally and figuratively, on his feet.

Things are good. Mostly. And Eli is trying not to get his hopes up as February progresses. The whole "never had a boyfriend before" situation also meant he'd never celebrated Valentine's Day before. And he knows Alex has ideas and $150 to spend on him. Well, probably $200 if he's being realistic. By the morning of Valentine's Day, Alex hasn't spent any of his allocated monthly $50. It probably means he's planning to add it to the Valentine's provision since they hadn't made any stipulations about that. Eli finds himself unable to be mad about it.

The Hell Hounds have a game that day, but it's at home, and it's a matinee on a Saturday. So Eli, Jo, and Sarah—Rads's wife—sit in the box together and wave their special commemorative Hell Hounds Valentine's Day game towels and bemoan that their menfolk will likely be too tired to really celebrate that night.

Jo and Sarah both have plans the following day. When they ask what Eli and Alex are planning, Eli has to admit he doesn't know. When he and Alex talked about it, Alex said he "had this one," and that it "was a surprise".

So, while Alex is gone for practice, Eli calls James and gets a rundown of all of Alex's favorite foods from his childhood and films a special episode for his channel dedicated to making those foods. Eli spends most of the episode attempting to talk about why he loves Alex so much. Which is harder than any of the actual cooking as talking about emotions will never be his forte. But they now have a refrigerator full of food and a truly sappy video Alex can go back and watch whenever he wants. It's not much, but Eli thinks Alex will be suitably pleased.

He's looking forward to getting back to the house and showing off his work, maybe having a little living room picnic that maybe leads to ... other things. But they have to get through the hockey game first, and the Leafs are apparently not amenable to letting this be an easy win.

Four minutes into overtime, with the score tied 2–2 at the end of regulation, Alex's left skate gets hooked in front of the Leaf's goal, and he does an unintentional split that has Eli wincing in sympathy.

He manages to hobble off the ice with help from Matts but immediately goes down the tunnel, and Sarah sighs something about how groin injuries are the worst.

And, yeah.

That effectively derails Eli's Valentine's plans.

Security shows up to escort Eli down to the locker room a few minutes later, and he sits in Alex's stall, absently playing with Hawk's ears—the left one will stay folded insideout, the right won't—while he waits.

The Hell Hounds lose in overtime even though, according to an irate Rushy, the goal shouldn't have counted due to goaltender interference.

Eli takes off Hawk's vest so she can be a consoling force, and Asher comes over while stripping out of his pads to ask Eli if he knows anything about peach glaze. It occurs to Eli, a little absently, that he's sitting in a locker room, alone, full of professional hockey players who know he's gay, and the most upsetting thing about the situation is the smell.

Regardless of social media and shitty people and refs who make bad calls—*We should replace all the refs with dogs,* Rushy says, smooshing the sides of Hawk's face. *You would have called goaltender interference, wouldn't you? Yes, you would*—regardless of everything else, the Hell

Hounds, Alex's team, their loyalty and defense, is something that shouldn't be overlooked.

Alex hobbles out of the trainers' room to several sympathetic noises as Jeff, fresh from the shower and toweling off his hair, sits down next to Eli.

"So," he says, "do you two have any big Valentine's Day plans?"

Eli throws a look at Alex, who's grimacing his way slowly over to them.

"Not anymore, I'm assuming."

"Yes, we do," Alex says.

"What?" Eli asks. "Watching Netflix and helping you ice your balls?"

"Romantic," Jeff says.

"Actually, we have real plans." Alex feigns affront. "I just had to change them a little."

"Care to share them?" Eli asks, dubious.

"I got you special permission for ice time from your doctor. Even though your eight weeks aren't up yet. And booked the rink from 9–10 tonight once free skate is over."

"*What?*"

"With stipulations. You have to wear a helmet and hold my hand."

"Really? The doctor necessitated handholding?"

"Well. The helmet was his primary stipulation; the handholding was more me, but he did say it was probably wise to have someone with you the whole time, at the very least close enough to catch you if you start to fall."

"Okay. But you can barely walk right now. If I fell, you'd just go down with me."

"Which is why I will be sitting on the bench with Hawk, and Matts will be the one accompanying you on the ice."

Matts?

"I'm not following."

"Well, he wanted to talk to you about something anyway, and he was just going to be all single and sad and alone tonight, so I figured—two birds, one stone."

"So Matts is going to hold my hand and skate with me tonight. On Valentine's Day."

"Matts is doing *what*?" Cookie asks.

"I'm doing what?" Matts says, coming out of the showers.

"Holding my hand during a romantic Valentine's skate tonight, apparently."

The locker room goes very suddenly quiet.

Matts looks like a deer in headlights. "Uh. That's not—I mean, yeah, I talked to Alex about—but I was thinking we could do more of, like, a ... prince arm thing?"

"A prince arm thing," Eli repeats. "What the hell is a prince arm thing?"

Matts bends one of his elbows at a ninety-degree angle, holding it out from his body, fist against his hip.

Wearing a towel and nothing else, he looks completely ridiculous.

"Ohhh," Asher says. "A prince arm thing." He hooks his hand through the bend of Matts's extended elbow, as dainty as a naked six-foot-four, corn-fed Tennessee boy can be. "Like this?"

"Right," Matts agrees, relieved. "Prince arm thing."

"How is this my life?" Eli asks no one in particular.

Eli has to help Alex get dressed that night, which is a fun change in the caretaking aspect of their relationship dynamic.

"Oh my god," Alex mutters. "I can zip up my pants myself; my hands work just fine."

"Let me love you," Eli retorts, and Alex rolls his eyes because that's his line.

"So is Matts really going to skate with me for an hour tonight? Is that really a thing that's happening?"

"Yup."

"You couldn't think of anyone uh ... better suited for the job?"

"He's one of the few single guys on the team, and he has a thing he needed to talk to you about anyway."

"A thing."

"A thing," Alex confirms. "Besides. He's been a lot better recently. You should hear some of the stuff he's been saying on the ice when guys on other teams talk shit about me."

Alex's expression dims for a minute, and Eli leans forward to kiss him.

"Okay. But he's not coming home with us afterward. I have a surprise for you too."

"Is this a sex surprise or a food surprise? Usually, I'd be happy with either one, but I'm pretty sure getting turned on would hurt right now."

"Food," Eli says, grinning.

They meet Matts at the igloo and put on their skates (and helmet, in Eli's case) in the practice locker room before walking down the hall to the public rink. The Zamboni is just finishing its final pass, and Alex waves to the driver.

"If you're curious," he murmurs to Eli, "bribing the Zamboni driver was what I spent my $200 on. Happy Valentine's Day."

"I knew you were going to combine the $150 with your monthly $50. That's cheating."

"No, it's not. It's only cheating if there's a rule saying I can't do it."

"I'm adding it to the whiteboard when we get home."

"I'm contesting it at our next relationship talk."

"I'll make a PowerPoint presentation defending my stance."

"You guys are weird," Matts says.

Once the ice is clear, Alex settles himself on a bench right next to the exit, where the Concerned Moms usually sit during free skate, and Eli leaves Hawk next to him.

Matts steps out onto the ice and then looks back at him, uncertain.

The PA system is still playing some godawful romantic song mix.

"So," Eli says sunnily, "this is really awkward."

Matts offers his bent elbow.

Prince arm thing.

"Right," Eli says.

He curls his hand around Matts's bicep and takes a step forward gingerly.

Matts almost immediately has to catch him.

Well, shit.

"Okay," Eli says, "this is fine. We expected this."

"We did?" Matts says, sounding a little panicked.

"Shut up."

Eli gets himself upright again, but apparently, all the improvement his walking balance has seen just ... isn't translating onto the ice.

"Here," Matts says, shifting so he's behind Eli. "What if we—"

He circles his hands around Eli's waist, propelling them forward a little, helping Eli find his center of gravity.

It's ... actually really effective.

Eli leans back into him a little, hesitant at first because—well. But Matts takes his weight, adjusts their course a little as they near the opposite end of the rink, and keeps going.

Alex might be glaring a little when they pass him on the way back.

After a few circuits, Eli straightens and lets Matts balance him with only his hands. And a few circuits after that, Matts starts to loosen his grip until he isn't touching Eli at all anymore, only hovering close behind him, hands a few inches from his sides.

"This is good," Matts says, "right? Like, this is really good?"

"Yeah," Eli says, "yeah, it is."

Fifteen minutes later, Matts moves to skate beside him, looking a little less overburdened with anxiety about Eli's ability to remain upright.

He offers his elbow again, but Eli waves him off.

"I think I'm good. And I'm not going to try to do anything more than this."

Matts nods, continuing to watch him with a slightly disconcerting level of focus, but doesn't argue.

"So," Eli says once they've made a few fluid circuits. "Alex said you wanted to talk to me about something?"

"Oh. Yeah. So, it's not a big deal. But do you remember Jesse from the Breaking the Ice event? The little kid who—"

"Wanted to figure skate? Prompted our dynamic duo moment? I remember."

"Well. I was kind of curious, afterward, if there was a program like the Little Hounds Scholarship fund. You know, that pays for poor kids' gear and waives their fees so they can play hockey? I was wondering if there was anything like that for figure skating here, and there wasn't."

"That sucks," Eli says because it feels as if Matts is waiting for a response.

"Right?" Matts agrees. "So I talked to Jessica about what it would take to try to start a program, and she set me up with some people to talk through specifics. Cost of ice time, gear, lessons, what the schedule would be depending on how many kids participated ... It's a lot more complicated than I thought it would be."

He licks his chapped lips, and Eli resists the urge to offer him the Burt's Bees in his pocket.

"The point," Matts says, "is that I'm going to start a program like that. Small at first, obviously. But maybe with some fundraisers and some sponsors, if I could get the word out, we could expand it within a few years—have different age groups sorted into different classes, pick up and drop off shuttles, stuff like that."

"That's really cool."

"It's not a big deal. It'll be good PR or whatever. But we're hoping the pilot program can start in the fall? It'll only be available to twelve students, grades 1–5, September to November, Tuesday and Thursday after school. But they'll get skates, a uniform, and any of the students can come in and skate for free during open-skating hours with a guest."

"That's amazing. Can Jesse come?"

"No. He lives too far away. But I already, uh, took care of that situation, so."

"What do you mean?"

Matts looks a little sheepish. "Oh. It's not a big deal. I had one of the PR minions put me in contact with his group home. I sorted it out with them, so he and his sister are both getting weekly lessons now. They sent me an email last week. Jesse won the "most improved" award at the end of the semester, and they moved him up to a more advanced class. Look."

Matts fishes his cell phone out of his back pocket and scrolls for a minute. He then shows Eli a picture of Jesse on the ice, knees together, skates snowplowed toe-to-toe, grinning with a missing tooth, and holding a slightly wrinkled paper certificate.

"That's great." Eli says, and maybe his voice cracks a little.

"Yeah. It's whatever. Not a big deal." Matts shoves his phone back in his pocket, a flush of color creeping up his neck.

"You realize you've said 'it's not a big deal' half a dozen times in the last two minutes," Eli points out.

"So?"

"So, there's this quote. I think from Shakespeare? About protesting too much—"

"Shut up. It's *not* a big deal. It's just a thing. It's whatever."

"Okay, fine. It's whatever." Eli makes sure the sarcasm in his voice is clear.

Matts rolls his eyes at him. "Anyway. I wanted to ask you. I don't know if you'd be interested—or if you can even do it with your class schedule or whatever, but—We think we're going to need two coaches. And obviously, you're the first person I thought of. We won't be able to pay you a whole lot, but it wouldn't be terrible either—"

Eli stops moving. "Are you serious?"

"Yes?" Matts circles around him, looking uncertain. "I think you'd be good at it. And it sounds like you'd enjoy doing it? And if things worked out and we could get more support for the program, maybe by the time you graduated, you could start teaching more than one class?"

"You're really serious."

"Yeah." Matts scratches the back of his still-pink neck. "We won't have an official job offer for you to come in and talk about and sign for another two or three months. I just wanted to ask you, um, informally, about it first, to make sure it'd be something you're into."

"You're asking me to teach kids how to skate. You're offering me *money* to teach kids how to skate. When I can currently barely skate on my own."

"Well, yeah," Matts says dismissively. "But the program wouldn't start until next season. You'll be better by then."

The confidence is heartening.

"Yes," Eli says. "Thank you. Yes. I'd love to be part of that."

"Cool."

"Uh, hey, Eli?" Alex calls from the bench.

They barely have a chance to glance over before Hawk barks, trying push past Alex to get to the ice.

"You've got to be kidding me," Eli mutters at the same moment that Matts says, "Oh shit."

And then Matts just—

Scoops Eli up.

Into his arms.

Into his actual, stupidly muscular arms, bridal-style, while skating hastily for the exit.

"What the fuck are you doing?" Eli asks.

"Doesn't that mean you're going to have a seizure?"

"Yeah, but not right this instant."

"Oh."

They get to the exit, where Alex is absolutely losing his shit, laughing so hard he's bent over on the bench, elbows braced on his knees, practically wheezing.

Hawk, whining, finds nothing about the situation amusing.

"Why are you laughing at me?" Matts demands.

"Okay, easy," Eli says. "I am super touched and all that, but could you maybe put me down?"

"Right. Sorry."

"Where do you think?" Eli asks Alex. "Locker room?"

"Probably best," he agrees, still grinning. "Matts, can you walk with him to our locker room? It's going to take me a minute."

"Yes," he says. "Yeah. Let's go."

"Deep breath," Eli says as they clip on their blade protectors. "This is really not a big scary thing. I'm fine."

"Sorry." Matts hovers anxiously at his elbow as they move into the hallway. "The only time I've ever seen someone have a seizure was at your competition. And that was—you know. A big fucking scary thing."

Eli goes ahead and wraps one hand around Matts's arm, just to be safe. Hawk keeps headbutting his knee which, combined with the skates, really isn't helping things. "That's fair. But that was also a worst-case scenario. Most of the time, I've got at least ten minutes after Hawk alerts to get somewhere safe and lie down. It's very chill."

"Seizures don't seem very chill," Matts says tightly.

Eli sits directly on the ground once they get to the locker room, just to be safe, and starts unlacing his skates. "Okay, can you hand me my backpack and then go wait outside?"

"Outside?" Matts repeats, handing over the bag. "No. What if something happens?"

"Hawk will take care of me. Go wait for Alex. He can talk you through things. Please."

Matts, thank god, obeys.

Eli manages to get his skates and helmet off, lays out his blanket, and is comfortably situated with a good portion of Hawk's body weight resting on him, when he gets an aura and closes his eyes.

Eight minutes later, Eli exits the locker room in a new pair of black leggings but, judging by Matts and Alex's grasp on fashion, neither of them will notice they're different black leggings than the ones he was wearing before.

"Hey," Alex says, clearly resisting the urge to physically check him over. "You good?"

"Yep. Head hurts a little. Can we go home?"

"Sure thing."

Matts walks with them to Alex's car, parked in one of the two north entrance handicapped spaces, Eli's placard hooked on the rearview mirror.

"Well," Matts says awkwardly, "later."

"Later," Alex agrees, opening the back door for Hawk. "Thanks for your help, man."

"No problem."

Matts starts to walk back toward the facility again—probably to head through the building to get to the players' lot—but Eli stops him.

"Hey, Matts?" he says.

"Yeah?"

"What you're doing—it's a big deal. And it's okay that it's a big deal. It's okay to care."

Matts swallows, looking somewhere in the vicinity of Eli's left shoulder.

"I'm serious," Eli says. "You're doing a really good thing. Don't pretend like it's not."

"Okay," Matts agrees, maybe just so Eli will let him leave.

"Okay," Eli says.

Matts books it inside, and Eli climbs into the passenger seat, groaning, half in exhaustion, half in ... complete bewilderment.

"Fuck me," he mutters.

"Um," Alex says, "I can try? But you probably shouldn't expect much."

"Oh my god, stop it," Eli says. "You know what I meant. Take us home."

"Okay." Alex reaches for his hand. "Home."

16

BY MARCH, IT'S CLEAR the Hell Hounds will be a serious contender in the playoffs. It's also clear they've reached a tipping point.

Overall, they're playing good, aggressive hockey. But as they creep closer and closer to April, on some days the "aggressive" is starting to outweigh the "good".

The late hits, the missed calls, the constant verbal abuse ...

Pretending they don't care and responding with sarcasm usually works, but they *do* care.

And Alex, at least, is so tired of pretending he doesn't.

The worst part is this might just be his life going forward. He might have to deal with this for the rest of his career.

It's exhausting.

And it's a good thing Eli has been progressing in leaps and bounds because Alex doesn't know what he would do if Eli still needed him the way Alex needs Eli.

Within a month, they've done a complete 180 in terms of who's taking care of who.

Before, in pre-Eli times, with the amount of stress Alex is under, Alex probably would have gotten off the plane from a roadie and headed straight to a bar. Now, he breaks speed limits to get to his condo and his couch, where Eli will have food and music and sweet commentary on the nuances of collegiate life. They've started taking baths together, too, and Alex discovers there is nothing quite as soothing as Eli slowly washing his hair, murmuring about how hard he's working and how proud Eli is of him.

Eli is the personification of a sigh of relief.

And the team is—the team is good too. Alex anticipates resentment, but instead, he gets anger. Not at him or Eli, but at the other teams. Other fans. Other organizations that send out pretty press releases but then say nothing about the hateful signs proudly displayed in their arenas.

"And captains *know*," Kuzy yells one night after a win that still left Alex with a bitter taste in his mouth. "Captains *know* players talk. Why they're not stop it? Tweet nice things—tape stick with rainbow for pride game—then pretend can't hear when fucking winger call Alex f-word. It's being *shitty* captain for not stop it. It's—" He devolves into Russian, and Oshie says, "Hypocritical is the word he's looking for, I think."

Kuzy just continues in Russian.

They get the gist of it anyway.

The following night, both Oshie and Kuzy end up in the box, red-faced and yelling incomprehensibly at a Russian player from the Islanders. A call-up who was not part of the group chat, Oshie later tells Alex, who has to be half carried off the ice, with a very clearly broken nose.

Neither of them will tell Coach or anyone else what the man said but, aside from that one instance, the Hell Hounds don't deal with any issues from other Russian players.

Asher and several of the younger players maintain this is due to Kuzy's mob connections.

There are a few good moments, though, like the Hell Hounds pride night.

It's against the Avs, one of the few teams that, blissfully, doesn't seem to have a single asshole player. Well. A couple of them are definitely assholes, but none of them are specifically *homophobic* assholes.

The stadium is sold out, and the game is preceded by a parade because it's Houston. So Eli invites the WAGs over to the apartment, and they bedazzle jean jackets with their player names and numbers in rainbow colors on the backs. They all sit together in the box and soon flood Instagram with selfies—most of them involving Hawk with her own bedazzled rainbow collar for the occasion. The internet loses its mind a bit.

Rushy covers his entire stick for warmups in rainbow tape and then signs it and auctions it off after the game with the proceeds going to You Can Play. Rads buys tickets for the Gay-Straight Alliance at Eli's university. Jeff and several other players donate to various LGBTQ+ charities. Alex, having already consulted with Eli during their March relationship meeting, and feeling very adult about it, offers to match any donations made over the following twenty-four hours to a GoFundMe campaign for a homeless LGBTQ+ youth shelter.

It's funded in half that time.

There's another good moment the following day, when a Deadspin reporter makes the unfortunate decision to ask Kuzy and Jeff if the team's environment has changed since Alex came out.

"Have you had to make any adjustments to having a gay captain?" the man asks.

"No," Jeff says evenly, making Jessica proud.

"Yes," Kuzy said seriously. "We make Alex wear blindfold in the shower so he's not see our dicks. Because no homo. Is rainbow blindfold though. Because Hell Hounds also pro-homo. You know?"

On Twitter later that day, *#prohomo* starts trending.

Jessica doesn't let Kuzy do media for a couple weeks.

Moments like that, though, the good moments, are getting more and more scarce. And Alex accidentally overhears Eli talking on the phone to Cody one day with a soft, terrible voice he's never heard Eli use before.

"I don't know," he says. "I wish there was a way for us to just ... take it back, which—No. I know. And I do. But Cody, you don't understand. I don't know how long he can do this without going crazy. This can't be the rest of his career. Or if it is, I've shortened his career by a decade. It's just not fair."

When Eli comes out of the guest bedroom, Alex is lying on the couch with his headphones on, listening to his pregame hype playlist, trying to act as if his world isn't very slowly falling apart.

The following week, after another win that feels like a loss, Rads won't let Alex change after practice. Kuzy and Asher stay in their gear too. Ten minutes later, after some Gatorade and a lot of deflection, they're pulling him back out onto the ice.

"I don't understand what's happening right now," Alex says.

"Well, kiddo," Rads says. "Tell me if I'm wrong, but it looked like you were about two seconds away from dropping your gloves out there last night. And in the interest of keeping your nose in the middle of your face, we thought we'd better teach you how to throw a punch."

Alex wants to protest, but he can't really argue that A. Yes, he nearly did try to fight someone last night, and B. No, he wouldn't have had the first clue as to how to go about the actual fighting.

He exhales. "That's probably a good idea," he allows.

The first week of April, Alex walks into Jessica's office and closes the door behind him.

"Alex," she says with raised eyebrows.

"I'm probably going to punch someone soon. I just thought I'd let you know."

She leans back in her chair. "Frankly, you've refrained from violence far longer than I anticipated. Do you have a clearer timeline for me, or—?"

Alex blinks at her. "You're not going to try to talk me out of it?"

"Not at all. This was, more or less, the plan, if you remember."

"I—what?"

"Alex," she says steadily. "Why do you think we've been micing you up every game since you came out? Micing up multiple other guys per game—generating hours of content we haven't been publishing on any of our social media sites. It's not because we enjoy hearing Rushy talk about sex toys—hilarious as that is. It's because those mics are picking up all the shit that's being said around you. At this point, we have an overwhelming amount of evidence that you're being mistreated, and most of the time, officials aren't calling the misconduct. I know the last three months have been terrible, but we have more than enough substantiation for an official complaint—even a lawsuit against the league if that's something you want to pursue. We just need an inciting event to deploy it."

"Oh," Alex says faintly.

"This was in the packet I sent to you back in January," she says, a little judgmentally. "You emailed me saying you approved. I take it you didn't actually read it?"

He'd skimmed it.

Mostly.

"Uh ... no."

She sighs, but it's her standard "I can't believe hockey players are paid so much money when they're this useless" sigh, not an actual annoyed sigh.

"We weren't just leaving you out to dry, Alex. We know this can't be the rest of your career. Or anyone else's. I've just been waiting for you to tell me when you've had enough."

"Oh."

"So," she says, tapping her tablet. "Do you have a particular game in mind, or—" And that's her calendar app.

"No. I don't want to *plan* a fight. I just know I won't be able to resist at some point soon."

"Ah. That's fine too. We have a press release ready, regardless."

"Right." He clears his throat. "So. Whenever it is, I should just make sure that my mic is working and I punch a guy who speaks clearly? Like. Really enunciates his slurs?"

"That would be preferable," she agrees solemnly.

"I can do that."

He gets home that afternoon feeling ... not relieved. But hopeful. Maybe. At least they have a plan. Things might get better soon. And then he won't have to spend so much of his time biting his tongue. But then again, part of that is his fault. He's been trying so hard to play good clean hockey and say the right things during media and avoid too much PDA with Eli where photographers might be present, and only make Jessica-approved Instagram posts, and ... Well, that's not what he wanted.

When he imagined the good parts of being out, he imagined being able to hold hands with Eli while walking Hawk, being able to tuck Eli under his arm and duck down to kiss him whenever he wanted; he imagined being casual with his affection. He's an effusive person.

Physically and verbally.

When he's in post-game interviews he wants to answer the "how are you planning to celebrate the win tonight" or "what are your plans for the upcoming break" questions honestly.

Well. Maybe not *too* honestly, but something other than the canned response that doesn't allow for references to his home life or who he shares it with. Pride night was a little taste of it, of being unashamedly gay, if that's a thing. And it made him realize what he didn't get to do otherwise. What he's missing.

He wants to post pictures on Instagram—not just the Jessica-approved ones of Alex and Eli sitting across the table from each other at dinner or Eli and Hawk wearing jerseys with Alex's name and number (adorable as that was). He wants to post the same sort of casually intimate photographs that Rads does with his wife or Rushy does with his girlfriend. Pictures of Eli at home, *their* home, sleep-rumpled and making pancakes in his boxers.

He wants to post disgusting romantic selfies.

Alex is Extra. He will fully admit that.

And right now, he feels like he's bursting with all the limitations that PR talked him through in hopes of mitigating any fallout from fans that were "uncomfortable" with the new developments in his personal life.

But it's *his* life.

And if fans are homophobic, they're going to be pissed off anyway. That's not Alex's problem.

He needs to stop acting like it is.

"Hey," he says to Eli that night as they're getting dressed. It's Asher's birthday, and the guys are all going out, families included, to a burger place.

"Hey," Eli agrees absently. He's in the closet, naked and considering his clothing options.

Alex pats Eli's butt because it's right there.

It's a very nice butt.

"Yes?" Eli prompts.

Right.

"Can I borrow a shirt?" Alex asks.

"Uh." Eli very obviously studies Alex's side of the closet—full of shirts—then his own side. "Anything of mine will be ridiculously small on you, but—Sure? Which one do you want to borrow?"

"The gayest one you own."

"Oh—kay."

He sorts through several hangers, considering, and Alex may or may not get a little distracted looking at his ass again.

"How about this one? Hey. Focus."

Alex focuses.

It's a plain white T-shirt. A little bigger than Eli's usual fare, with "I VIOLATE ARTICLE 27, SEC. 553-4 OF THE MARYLAND ANNOTATED CODE SAFELY, OFTEN, AND EXTREMELY WELL" in all caps on it.

Alex has never seen Eli wear it before.

"What's it mean?"

"Sections 553 and 554 of Article 27 of the Maryland Code prohibited sodomy, oral sex, and"—Eli makes quotes with his fingers—"any other unnatural or perverted sexual practice with any other person."

"That's fucked up," Alex says.

"Indeed."

"Not anymore, though, right?"

"No, not anymore."

Alex takes the hanger from Eli, rubbing the jersey-knit fabric between his thumb and forefinger.

"You're right; this is a very gay shirt."

"What you wanted?"

"It's perfect."

It's pretty small, clinging tightly to his chest and arms and just barely long enough to hit the top of his belt, but—It's definitely perfect.

He flexes in the mirror, grinning.

Eli gives Alex a retaliatory ass-slap, then fits himself to Alex's back, tucking his thumbs just under the hem of the shirt, and pressing his fingertips into the shower-heated skin over Alex's hip bones. He hooks his chin over Alex's shoulder. Leans his temple against Alex's jaw. "You know everyone will be taking pictures tonight."

"Yes," Alex agrees.

"I thought we were trying not to offend anyone's delicate sensibilities with our clothing and social media choices."

"We were. I just decided I'm done caring." Alex pauses, considering. "Unless you would rather—"

"No. No, if this is a 'fuck it' moment, you have my full support."

"This is definitely a 'fuck it' moment," Alex agrees.

"Oh, good," Eli says, kissing the hinge of Alex's jaw. "I love those. I will also need to reconsider my own clothes tonight, then."

Alex shifts to the side, pulling Eli to the front of the mirror, reversing their positions. "Wear the shoes," he suggests.

"To a burger place? No."

"Something sparkly?"

"It's 5:00 p.m."

"Leather?"

Eli sighs. "How about skinny jeans and something off-the-shoulder."

Alex considers this. "Which shoulder?"

"Either?" Eli laughs. "Do you have a preference?"

Alex lowers his mouth to the left side of his neck—the juncture between Eli's collarbone and shoulder. "This one," he says.

He sucks on the skin there, just a little, and then glances up, meeting Eli's eyes in the mirror, waiting for permission.

"Oh," Eli says faintly. "Yes. Yes, that one is good."

They're a little bit late for dinner.

The burger place is barely controlled madness. They didn't rent it out, but they did reserve a good portion of the booths, and nearly all the guys and their families or significant others are there.

It's not until they're mostly done eating that Asher asks, mouth still full, "Hey, Alex, what's your shirt mean?"

He lets Eli explain.

"Wait," Matts says, leaning over the back of the booth next to them. "Blowjobs used to be illegal in Maryland?"

"Blowjobs used to what?" Moose asks, popping over the back of the opposite booth.

Rads sighs, covering the ears of the toddler in his lap.

"Cunnilingus, too, depending on how a judge interpreted it," Jeff says.

Rads sighs louder.

"What's cunnilingus?" Cookie asks.

"Oh my god," Rushy says faintly.

All of the women stop eating.

"Okay," Jo says to Cookie. "That's horrifying. What state were you raised in? Because I need to write the representatives about their failed sexual education system."

"Here? Texas?" Cookie says.

"Who's surprised?"

"And, uh," Cookie puts down his drink, wilting a little under all the attention. "We didn't actually have sex ed in school? That I remember? It was just like—Don't do it. The end."

"Oh my god," Rushy repeats.

"Okay," Jo says. "Who has a mini whiteboard in their car?"

Several of the men at the table dutifully raise their hands.

"And markers?" Some of the hands go down.

"All right. Well, someone bring me a whiteboard and at least two different-colored markers, please. This booth is about to become the sex-ed booth."

"Have I mentioned I love you recently?" Jeff asks her.

"That's my cue to leave," Rads says, standing. He balances his daughter on one hip and picks up his drink with his free hand. "I'll send the other rookies over though. They could probably use a refresher."

"Good man," she says. "Hey, will someone go ask the milkshake maker guy for a banana? We'll give it back when we're done."

17

ALEX BRUISES EASILY.

He feels like that could probably be a metaphor for his life, or something, but it's also just true in the physical sense. Since he can remember, he's always carried the mistakes he's made on his skin: stubbed toes that turned purple, mottled knees from falling at the park, burst capillaries in his cheeks from forgetting his sunscreen. As he got older, the mistakes got bigger and so did the consequences: a twisted ankle that bloomed red and green over tight, swollen skin; fractured ribs that painted his whole back in a map of pain. He's used to seeing bruises as a bad thing. A reminder that he fucked up. Wasn't good enough. Needed to do better.

Be better.

So, the first time Eli leaves a hickey on his neck—probably an accident considering how careful he usually is about that kind of thing—it leaves Alex a little winded.

First, because it occurs to him he can let Eli do that now. The "fuck it" plan is in full swing, and he honestly couldn't care less if cameras catch him shirtless in the locker room with a clear indication of what he'd been up to with his boyfriend the night before.

But second ...

Alex likes leaving his marks on Eli. That's not new.

He's a possessive asshole, and he takes significant, maybe-more-than-is-healthy pleasure in seeing the places where his mouth has been on Eli's body. Places no one else's mouth will ever be.

But standing there in front of the mirror, toothbrush limp in his hand, noticing a bruise Eli has left on him ...

Well.

That's something else entirely.

He and James were always careful. No visible marks. No risk. Hardly any kissing, even.

But here he is, with his first ever hickey at nearly twenty years old, and it's—it's the first time he can remember that a bruise has meant something good. A reminder of something he's done well, done *right*. Not a mistake.

He pushes at it with one finger.

He wishes it was darker.

Eli stumbles into the bathroom, oblivious to Alex's existential hickey crisis, and squints his way over to Alex. He wraps his arms around his bare waist and presses a kiss to his shoulder blade. "Morning," he mutters.

Alex loves him so much. "Morning," he agrees.

Eli leans into him, harder, nose smushed into his neck, and meets Alex's eyes in the mirror. "Oh," he says, straightening. "I—" He brings one hand up and touches the bruise in question, washed out in the bright bathroom light, but still noticeable, still stark against Alex's pale skin.

Alex inhales sharply when Eli presses down.

"Sorry," Eli says. "I guess I got carried away. I didn't mean to."

"No," Alex says, maybe a little too loudly, a little too fast. "I—You can. Now."

"I can?"

"Mean to. If you want."

"Oh."

Eli presses a little harder. "Okay."

It's not even really a sex thing, Alex thinks, pulling Eli back into the bedroom with him.

Hell, even sex isn't just a sex thing. Sex with Eli is unlike any other intimate encounter he's had. Mostly, it's intimate in a way he can't even *equate* to something else.

They're both just—there. Which, obviously. But even their initial awkward fumbling was … more. Everything.

Whatever. Sex with Eli isn't just sex. It's being the closest he can possibly get to this person he loves so much and so desperately it scares him.

And having proof—right there on his skin—that Eli lets him get that close is—

Alex is a hockey player, not a poet.

He doesn't have words for this kind of thing.

But "love" seems really fucking trite for all the whatever that he feels. Or maybe other people shouldn't be allowed to use the word "love" because they can't possibly mean it the way he does.

"Alex," Eli says, and from his tone, it's probably not the first time he's said Alex's name. "Hey. I'm trying to kiss you; why are you frowning?"

"I love you."

"And that makes you angry?"

"No. I just … need a better word than 'love.' But there isn't one."

Eli folds his arms on top of Alex's chest and rests his head on them. "I'm not following."

"I more than love you."

He probably shouldn't sound so pissed off about it.

"Oh."

Eli sits up a little, elbow on Alex's sternum, chin cupped in his palm.

His hair is a riot of tangled curls and his eyes are kind of puffy and there are pillow creases on his cheek. He is quite possibly the most beautiful person Alex has ever seen.

"Well," Eli says. "I can't help you with terminology. But I more than love you too. If that helps."

It does.

Alex finally drops his gloves in the first period of their last regular season game.

He didn't plan it that way, though Jessica did call him with what amounted to a "hey, remember that fight you're supposed to have? Any idea when that's going to happen, and can it preferably be before playoffs?" inquiry the week before.

The thing is, once Alex knew putting up with shit on the ice had a purpose, he wanted to make sure the "inciting incident" was perfect. He wanted a sound bite that could encapsulate every bit of the rage he's been feeling for the past three months. A sound bite that could make people *understand*.

Jonathan Moyer gives Alex that sound bite.

He also gives Alex a black eye and a concussion.

Because Alex is a five-foot-ten-inch, 185-pound center, who's never dropped his gloves before in his life, and Moyer is a six-foot-three-inch, 225-pound enforcer, who literally gets paid to fight people.

Honestly, if Alex had been *thinking*, he wouldn't have chosen Moyer. Trying to fight an actual goon is stupidly dangerous for someone like Alex, and he wouldn't normally take a risk like that right before playoffs.

But the thing is, he's not thinking about uneven matchups or potential injury when he nearly breaks his hand on Moyer's face. He's not even thinking about the necessity of an inciting incident.

Mostly, he's thinking: *this man needs to die*.

They're playing the New Orleans Magic, one of their biggest rivals, and the first few face-offs are fine. The captain seems like a decent guy, from what Alex knows of him, and he doesn't hear anything particularly nasty from anyone on the ice for the first several minutes of play.

And then number 43, Moyer, presses Alex into the boards, battling over the puck, and spits out:

"Saw your boy toy in the box. Scraping the bottom of the barrel with that one, eh? You couldn't find some normal twink to suck your dick? Guess I'm not surprised the best you can do is a retarded nig—"

And suddenly Alex doesn't care about the puck anymore.

Alex doesn't even remember the first punch, afterward. He watches the film later and sees himself drop his gloves and his stick all in one go, use his right foot to hook Moyer's knee and take him down onto the ice.

All he remembers, though, is rage: straddling Moyer's chest and throwing furious, mostly ineffective punches, ignoring the two hits Moyer himself gets in—one that knocks off Alex's helmet, the second that blackens his eye—and the fact that his hand is screaming in pain.

He's not going to stop fucking hitting him until someone forces him to. And someone does within a few seconds, Alex's outrage is wild enough that it takes two refs to wrestle him off and haul him bodily away while he keeps on yelling—he doesn't even know what. Threats? Promises?

Except.

Moments after the ref has pulled Moyer to his feet, someone else tackles Moyer right back onto the ice, and it's—

It's not a Hell Hound.

It's one of the Magic players.

Number 32. Okezie.

His skin is several shades darker than Eli's, and he's nearly the same size as Moyer.

The refs are surprised enough that they don't actually stop it from happening at first. It's only the sudden shock of blood across the ice that gets them moving again, separating the two.

Moyer is screaming at Okezie. Okezie is screaming right back at him in French, looking like he's about ready to go after the ref holding onto him. Then the Magics' captain is there with a hand on Okezie's chest, shoving him, hands bunched in the neck of his jersey, talking low and in his face, and Alex is just—

Standing there.

Winded.

Dripping sweat and maybe a little blood.

Eventually, one of the refs remembers him and pushes him toward the tunnel, and he goes willingly.

He has a quickly swelling eye and ringing in his ears. His hand may very well be broken somewhere.

But he definitely has his sound bite.

The Hell Hounds win 4–2.

Alex listens to the game in the trainers' room with ice on his face, ice wrapped around his hand, and Hawk's head on his knee.

Eli paces through most of it with occasional interjections of "Did you have to pick the *biggest* man on the team? I mean honestly," while they do concussion protocol and manipulate his swollen fingers and make sure none of his teeth are loose.

They decide nothing is broken, but he does have a minor concussion, and he's maybe fucked up his middle extensor tendon, which means he'll miss, at the very least, the first game of the playoffs. Alex can't really bring himself to care at the moment though.

He stays with the trainers even after he's showered and the game is finished because he has a quickly building headache and a press conference to contend with. But the guys come back in quiet pairs to give him fist bumps and back slaps and then nearly all end up distracted by the fact that Hawk has her vest off and is available for petting.

When Coach comes back to say that Jessica is ready for them, he has a funny look on his face.

"What?" Alex asks.

"I'm not sure," he answers.

Alex doesn't understand until they get to the hall, where Jessica stands with multiple Magic players. There's Okezie, which isn't that surprising, maybe, but also the captain, Marlow; a second-line winger (number 23, Alex can't remember his name); the Magic's coach; and a tall, narrow man with a tablet and glasses and general air of resignation. Alex assumes the latter is the Magic's head of PR.

"Alex," Jessica says. "If you don't know them already, this is David Okezie, Aaron Marlow, Liam Martel, and Coach Jacob Thomson. They'll be joining our press conference."

"Oh—kay?" Alex says.

Because what the fuck.

"Thank you," Okezie says seriously, sticking out his hand. Alex reaches for it automatically because that's what you do when a massive defenseman—who just beat the shit out of his own teammate—offers you his hand.

They both realize at the same moment that Alex can't actually shake, though, seeing as his knuckles are still wrapped in an ice pack, and they grin, dropping their arms.

"I feel like I should probably be thanking *you*," Alex says. "I think you did more damage than I did."

"Yes," Okezie agrees solemnly, "I did."

Martel turns a laugh into a cough.

"I'd like to reiterate that I advise against this," Glasses-tablet-guy says.

The rest of the Magic players ignore him.

Clearly, he doesn't strike fear into the hearts of the team in the same way Jessica does the Hell Hounds. Alex would never dream of ignoring Jessica.

"They're ready when we are," Jessica says. "I want coaches on either end. Captains in the middle. Okezie, you'll sit between Martel and Marlow."

"What about us?" Rads says, drawing even with Alex. Kuzy appears a moment later, trying to get his still-wet hair to lay flat.

"Derek, I want you next to Alex. Dmitri, you'll be between Derek and Coach."

"You're letting Kuzy do media again?" Alex asks blankly.

"This is a Hell Hounds press conference," Jessica says. "There can't be more Magic players at the table than Hell Hounds. Besides. You need your A's with you."

She moves her attention to Kuzy: "Behave."

To Rads: "Keep them in line."

To Alex: "Turn your hat around the right way and try to keep your hand under the table. Here are your note cards. You're still speaking after Coach."

To all of them: "Are we ready?"

"No," the Magic's PR guy says.

Jessica leads them down the hall, heels clicking, and the coaches fall in line behind her, talking lowly to each other. The players from both teams glance at one another, cumulatively shrug, and follow.

"Elijah, right?" Okezie says, waiting until Alex and Eli have caught up to him and Martel.

"Eli," Eli says. "And your name is David?"

"Yes."

"We call him Davy," Martel says helpfully.

Okezie hip checks Martel, returning his attention to Eli. "Are you recovering well from your injury?"

Both Okezie and Martel have lilting French-Canadian accents that Eli clearly likes, judging by his delighted grin.

Alex is not jealous.

"I am, thanks," Eli says. "Skating again and everything."

"Oh, that's good," Okezie says. "It sucks you've had to deal with—" He gestures to encompass the hallway but clearly means more than their current surroundings. "—all of this, while trying to get healthy again too."

Eli tucks his hand into Alex's, lacing their fingers together. "It's worth it."

Okezie smiles, maybe a little wryly. "I'm glad to hear that."

"I've been watching your videos," Martel says to Eli. "Well. Honestly, I watch more of your friend Cody's videos."

"He has a strange obsession with southern American food," Okezie says.

"Excuse you. My *mother* has a strange obsession with American food; I am merely a devoted son."

"Oh, is she American?" Eli asks.

"Never even been. She's Chinese. And my father is Portuguese. And they named me Liam, of all things, so. And *he's* obsessed with German cars despite never visiting Germany."

"They don't need your whole life story," Okezie says gently. "I think you were going to tell them about the pie?"

"Right," Liam agrees. "So a few weeks ago, some of the guys got together, and we made the, uh, chocolate pecan pie Cody posted for your Independence Day? It was the best thing that has ever come out of Dumbo's oven."

"It was probably the *only* thing that's ever come out of Dumbo's oven," Okezie says.

Martel shrugs. "Also true."

"That's awesome," Eli says. "I'll tell Cody you liked it."

"He plays NCAA hockey, right? With James Petrov?"

Martel's face is perfectly innocent, but it feels like a loaded question.

Eli doesn't have a chance to answer, though, as they get to the conference room and Jessica opens the doors without giving them a chance to pause.

Eli lets go of Alex's hand, and Alex glances briefly at the others before remembering he's in full-on fuck-it mode and ducks to kiss him.

"Love you," he says, not even attempting to be quiet about it.

"More than love you," Eli answers.

"Time for gross later," Kuzy says and pulls Alex inside.

Jessica starts the conference by playing eight straight minutes of film on the projector: Five-, ten-, and fifteen-second cuts of audio from various Hell Hounds mics overlaying game footage. Late hits. Homophobic slurs. Refs ignoring slurs. Refs ignoring slashing. And hooking. And crosschecking. Threats. More slurs.

Seeing them, hearing them, laid end to end is infuriating in a way Alex hadn't expected. He realizes his hands are shaking as the last clip, the clip from the game that night—Jessica's inciting incident—plays over the speakers.

The audio is loud.

The room is uncomfortably silent afterward.

Alex notices that Martel's hands are curled into fists on top of the table.

Alex takes his note cards, two this time, out of his pocket and lays them flat on the table, trying to breathe evenly.

"Over the last thirteen weeks," Coach says, "my players, in particular Alex Price, have been the victims of harassment, injury, defamation, and ridicule. This abuse has been based primarily on Alex's sexual orientation but also, in some cases, as you just heard, on his boyfriend's race and disabilities. The league has neglected to address these issues up until this point."

He gestures to the now blank projector. "These were only highlights of the misconduct. We have over an hour of similar compiled instances, which we will make available to the public later tonight, as well as a list of names—players and referees who have perpetrated this misconduct. Up until this point, Alex has elected not to press charges against the league for willfully ignoring this abuse and failing to protect his health and safety. But should he decide to pursue legal action, the Hell Hounds will fully support him."

That causes the room to wake right up.

"I have faith," Alex says directly into the mike, loud enough that the reporters settle back down, "the league will take action now that the extent of the issue is beyond question. It's unacceptable that any player be targeted for their sexuality, race, or otherwise. I feel it's my responsibility to ensure that future players don't have to deal with similar treatment."

He looks up.

Tries to meet a few eyes, looks into a few cameras.

"This can't continue. The league can't purport itself to be inclusive, franchises can't hold pride nights and You Can Play campaigns, and then collectively ignore or oppose the same inclusivity they're preaching at fundraising events when a gay professional player steps on their ice or appears in their own locker room. It has to stop."

"I'm guilty of this," Marlow, the Magic's captain, says. "Most of the guys on the team were supportive of Alex when he came out. But there were a few who weren't. And I knew they would bring their mindsets onto the ice tonight.

"I'm a young captain. I've only had the C for a few months, and I didn't know how to handle it. So, I didn't. I didn't contribute to any of the shit that was said on the bus or in the locker room before the game today, but I didn't stop it either. I didn't want to rock the boat or seem weak or soft. That's not a good excuse, but I know it's one a lot of guys probably have right now. And I just want to say—we need to, even if it's uncomfortable or awkward. First, because it's the decent thing to do, but second, because it's likely there's a player on your own team who's affected by it." He swallows. "And if we as captains and team leaders are afraid to do that—maybe we don't deserve the letters on our jerseys."

"And coaching staff is responsible for picking up the slack if their team leaders aren't handling things," the Magic's coach says. "I knew I had a few guys with views I didn't agree with, using language I didn't agree with. I even pulled them aside and spoke to them, but I didn't make it clear that prejudice and bigotry would not be tolerated on my team. If I had, tonight would not have happened. I take responsibility for that, and I promise you it won't happen again."

A couple reporters start to yell questions, and he raises his voice. "Speaking specifically about the incident tonight, and Jonathan Moyer—"

The room goes quiet again.

"This is not the first disciplinary issue we've had with Moyer. The New Orleans Magic have elected to place Moyer on waivers. I've got no idea what the league's punishment will be for his actions tonight, but I hope it similarly sets a precedent."

Martel and Okezie turn to look at each other—surprised, maybe? Alex sees Okezie kick his toe against Martel's heel under the table. The press conference version of a fist bump.

"Okay," Jessica says. "Questions?"

There are a lot of questions.

Most of them are for Alex: Why did he wait this long to say anything? Was he intending to sue the league? Was he intentionally building a case to sue the league? Were the Hell Hounds compiling evidence at his behest? Is he injured? Will he be able to play in the first round?

Mostly, his answer is the same: He just wants to play hockey.

He waited because he wanted to focus on hockey. He thought things would get better on their own, but they didn't. He's not currently planning to sue the league, but he's waiting to see how the league responds. He just wants to play hockey, and right now, he can't play to the best of his ability unless something changes. He wasn't building a case. He did not ask the Hell Hounds to compile evidence; he was too busy trying to play his best hockey. He has a concussion that will mean he's out for the first game or two of the playoffs. He hopes he's back on the ice soon. He just wants to play hockey.

Rads and Kuzy take a couple questions to give him a break. Rads takes ones about the Hell Hounds unity: they all completely support Alex; they don't blame him for the shit they've been dealing with; they hope the league institutes necessary changes.

Kuzy takes one about the fight itself, a softball noting that Alex has never dropped his gloves before, "I teach Alex to punch. Maybe shouldn't say because his aim not so good. Makes me look bad. But we don't need for practice if the league do the right thing." His easy smile fades a little. "But I have warning for other teams if the league do the wrong thing. Anybody say bad things about Eli, *my* aim very good." Jessica clears her throat, and Kuzy grins sunnily again. "But I'm sure league do the right thing. Make best decision." Okezie gets several questions about locker room behavior, anger management, which is frankly laughable all things considered, and whether or not physical violence on game ice was the "appropriate forum" for addressing intrateam disagreements.

Okezie takes a deep breath.

"I'm the child of immigrants. I'm proud of that. Growing up in Montreal, diversity was a good thing. I was embraced by the hockey community at a young age, and my teammates were like family. But other teams—even as a kid, other teams never let me forget that I am Black.

"That's followed me to the NHL, to some degree. It's an easy chirp. An easy dig. Guys know it will piss me off. Usually, my own locker room is safe, but for some reason, people think it's okay to say things to opponents about race that they would never say to teammates' faces. Even when it amounts to the same thing. While he was in the locker room, Moyer hadn't ever said anything like what he said tonight on the ice. If he had, I would have punched him then."

Several reporters try to jump on the "unnecessary violence" aspect of that answer, while others yell out questions about why Moyer is being put on waivers if this is the "first time" he's said something like this.

"Oh, he's said plenty," Okezie retorts. "Vaguely racist stuff. The kind of thing you can't call out without making yourself a bigger target. The homophobia was less vague. The ableism even worse. I sat there and gritted my teeth through a year and a half of it—the last two months being the worst. I'm not a proponent of violence in most situations, but I'm also not sorry I hit him. I'll take whatever punishment the organization and the league believe I deserve, but I'm not sorry. I'd do it again. The Magic can trade me. I don't care."

Glasses-tablet-guy pinches the bridge of his nose, looking heavenward.

Apparently, Okezie is having his own little fuck-it moment.

"We won't be trading him anytime soon," the Magic's coach notes dryly. "And he won't receive any punishment inhouse. Had I addressed the problem sooner, it wouldn't have come to this."

"Liam! Mr. Martel!" a man in the front row calls. Alex recognizes him. He's the *Washington Post* reporter who usually manages to come across as not completely incompetent.

Martel leans forward, expectant.

"You've been very quiet up until this point," *Washington Post* guy says. "Is there a reason you've joined your teammates and coach at the table? Is there anything you'd like to say?"

"Oh, me?" Martel throws his thumb, cavalier, toward Okezie. "I'm just here as moral support for my boyfriend."

18

FOR THE FIRST TIME in maybe ever, ESPN has more hockey-related coverage than any other sport for a solid forty-eight hours.

It starts with the press conference.

The press conference where the Magic's top-performing defenseman and one of their rising-star rookies casually inform the world they've been in a relationship for *four years*.

Since they played together in Rimouski for the Océanic.

"Not that we were ever really on the ice together during games then," Martel says. "I was sixteen, third line, and still figuring out what hand-eye coordination was. He was eighteen, star of the show, and headed for the draft. I had no game to speak of, on or off the ice, but I won him over eventually."

"They had us rooming together," Okezie says. "It was probably Stockholm syndrome."

"That doesn't explain the three years we were long-distance," Martel tells Okezie, "but nice try." Martel turns to address the cameras. "He loves me."

Okezie rolls his eyes.

Alex feels like he's stepped into an alternate dimension.

The reporters take a moment to shift gears, and then the questions start again full-force. For the first time in three months, Alex, despite sitting at the center of the table, feels completely invisible.

It's nice.

Alex buys Okezie and Martel's drinks that night, along with a good portion of the Magic and Hell Hound players who go out with them.

He's feeling particularly benevolent.

The Magic have an early curfew because they're leaving at the crack of dawn. But Alex, Okezie, and Martel have forty-five minutes after the press conference to find a club, have a beer, yell in one another's faces about how much they love their boyfriends, and then yell about how cool it is that they can be in public yelling about how much they love their boyfriends. They pose for selfies with a couple dozen people, Martel loses his shirt, they drink some multicolored shots, and then Okezie and Martel promise to keep in touch as Marlow drags them out the door with the rest of the Magic to meet their Ubers.

Alex goes home to Eli—who declined the invitation to get drinks in favor of prefinals studying and avoiding potential flashing lights.

But when Alex gets home, Eli isn't doing schoolwork. He's sitting on the bed with both animals and a tub of icecream, TV on. He's watching the press conference which has apparently gone viral.

But things escalate, minutes later, with the Instagram post.

It's from Martel's account—a picture of Okezie carrying him piggyback down the hallway of what looks like a hotel. Martel—still shirtless from the club—has got his face tucked into Okezie's neck, laughing. There's no caption, just a hashtag: *#prohomo.*

Okezie posts his own photo a few minutes later with their positions reversed, Martel making an exaggerated pained face, pretending to stagger under Okezie's weight. It has the same hashtag: *#prohomo.*

And then things get downright unreal.

Fifteen minutes later, Rushy makes his own Instagram post. He's wearing a tank top that says "Let me be perfectly queer," while toasting the camera with a beer. It has two hashtags:

#bisexual and *#prohomo.*

Ten minutes after that, a retired player, Brian Andrews (two Stanley cups and one Conn Smythe, fifteen years in the league), posts a picture on Twitter of two clearly male hands with interlaced fingers.

Both are wearing matching wedding rings.

#prohomo.

Ten minutes after that, one of the Rangers' veterans, Max Clarke—probably going to retire this year but still killing it in PPG—posts a selfie on Twitter of himself sitting up in bed, arm slung with casual familiarity around another man's shoulders. They're both wearing old T-shirts and glasses, and the top of a large dog's head and shoulders is visible, laid out across their laps.

#prohomo.

And then there are NCAA players:

One who's leaning over the boards, goalie helmet tipped up, to accept a kiss from a man in pedestrian clothes.

Two who are out cold, wearing their team colors, spooning in a single dorm room bed that looks like it's struggling to accommodate their combined weight.

#prohomo.

And then there are the juniors:

A gangly kid posts a video of himself doing sit-ups, getting a kiss for every rep he completes from an equally gangly guy holding his feet.

One posts a picture of himself with his arm around empty air, followed by *The Fairly OddParents* trophy meme, which has been adjusted to say "This is where I'd put my boyfriend ... IF I HAD ONE."

#prohomo.

And then there's another NHL player: a Falconer.

And then a Wilkes-Barre player.

A Chicago Wolf.

A Penguin.

A Marlie.

#prohomo.

Eli and Alex sit on the bed in quiet, baffled amazement, with the TV on and their laptops open.

By sunrise, eight additional NHL players (five retired, three active), seven AHL players, six ECHL players, twelve NCAA players, and eleven juniors have all come out.

#prohomo.

And that's just the men.

There are women, too, though there were already several out female players—NCAA, NWHL, and Olympic players and—

Alex is glad they have the day off because he's not sure he'd be able to function properly on the combined lack of sleep and euphoria.

Eli screams when Alex is in the shower.

"Fuck," Alex yells. "What?" And then, maybe the better question: "Who?!"

He turns off the shower, grabs a towel, and waddles, dripping, back into the bedroom. "Who is it?"

Eli turns his laptop so Alex can see and—

It's James's Instagram.

James's Instagram which, until this point, has been entirely empty since Cody convinced him to make it three months before. There's a picture, now though.

The picture is of James's bed. And the bare, sunlight-striped back of a man—a man who is decidedly not James—sleeping in it.

There's no caption. Just a hashtag:

#prohomo.

"Holy shit," Alex says.

"Cody *Edward* Griggs," Eli yells.

Cody, still shirtless, still in James's bed, answers Eli's FaceTime call with a grin so wide it makes Alex's face hurt by proxy.

"Hey," Cody says, all shy and demure.

"Hey? *Hey*?!! I cannot *believe* you didn't tell me," Eli says. "I called you, like, the minute Alex kissed me. Okay, not the minute. But you knew before anyone else! I am—not hurt; honestly, I'm so happy for you, but once I'm done congratulating you, we are going to have *words*."

Alex, sitting awkwardly next to Eli, leans in so Cody can see him.

"Hi," he says. "Congratulations. We're really happy for you guys."

"Well, thank you, Alex," Cody says. "And I didn't ... *not* tell you—it only just happened."

"What do you mean?" Eli asks.

"Well. We were watching the game last night. And then the press conference after. And then Twitter and Instagram—and James and I—"

Cody's face goes pink. "We. Uh. Talked. About things. And then, when we woke up this morning, he said he wanted to come out. And asked if I wanted to be part of it. And I said yes. I haven't even—" His smiles dims by several degrees. "I haven't had a chance to call Mama yet."

"That is the shortest possible version of a very long story I need to hear in full," Eli says.

There's a noise on Cody's side of the conversation—a door opening and closing—and Cody glances away from his phone, smile jumping right back up to full wattage.

"Hey," James says, somewhere off-camera. "Someone put vodka in the coffeemaker again, so that's not going to happen. But I brought you some orange juice and one of those protein bars. Do you want to go out for coffee or—oh. Hi."

And there's a mostly naked James Petrov, kneeling on the bed with his arms full of breakfast items, looking charmingly bemused.

"He—llo," Eli says slyly as James settles next to Cody.

"Hi, James," Alex says.

"Hi, Eli. Hi, Alex."

It should probably be awkward, all things considered, but it doesn't feel that way.

"So," Eli says, "Cody was just telling me about how you two both put out on the first date."

James chokes while trying to take a sip of orange juice.

"Technically, there wasn't even a date," Cody says.

"You slut," Eli says cheerfully.

"I *am*, aren't I?" Cody agrees, delighted.

James mutters something in Russian that sounds like disagreement.

"But only for you," Cody assures him.

"Does that really even count as being slutty, then?" Alex asks.

Eli elbows him. "Okay. Alex, James, can you two give Cody and me a couple minutes, or can we decide a time later today where you two can be somewhere else? We need to talk about our boyfriends."

"Oh," Cody says. "We're not—um."

"We're not?" James asks.

"Oh my god," Alex mutters.

"You sure as hell *better* be," Eli says.

"I'd, uh, like to be?" James says.

"Oh," Cody says. "Really?" He glances between James and his phone screen. "Eli, I'm going to need to call you back."

"Yes," Eli agrees. "You do."

The call abruptly disconnects.

"Jesus," Eli says, closing his laptop. "Were we ever that useless?"

"I fake-dated you for three months, and said I loved you in my head before I ever pined my way into kissing you in a fit of rage. I think we were worse."

Eli considers this for a minute. "Yeah, okay. That's fair. On the plus side, that means they'll probably be just fine, then. Look how great we turned out."

Alex tackles him.

Gently.

Things get better.

The NHL, likely under an enormous amount of pressure, releases a statement later that morning. It says there will be an internal investigation into the misconduct that had occurred, and the league will remain in close contact with individual management teams as the situation develops. In addition, they will require all refs to undergo "intensive" diversity training before the playoffs begin, and they will be imposing a "zero tolerance policy" going forward that will dictate anything from steep fines to multi-game suspensions for homophobic or racist infractions.

This is followed by similar statements from various franchises about their "renewed" efforts for curbing prejudicial behavior and their dedication to ensuring that "hockey is for everyone." Only a few claim responsibility for not doing something sooner despite knowing intolerance was taking place, but ...

It's something.

In the following week, sports news programs and magazines and blogs don't seem to know how to handle the situation. Most of them put out hasty stories that closely mimic the information in all of their competitors' stories, rehashing how many players have come out, often lingering on Martel and Okezie and speculating about the potential effects intrateam relationships might have on cohesion and performance. The articles range from unbiased and contemplative, to cautiously supportive, to heralding the end of "real" hockey (and "real men") as the world knows them.

The day of the Hell Hounds' first playoff game, Brian Andrews invites Alex to a group chat. Alex figures out pretty quickly that the occupants of the chat are the newly out NHL, AHL, and ECHL players.

The veterans and retirees have taken up paternal roles, checking in and making sure everyone's teams are treating them all right, fielding questions, giving warnings, recommending agents, and occasionally bemoaning the youth.

It's everything Alex needed at eighteen, newly drafted and resigned to a career of loneliness.

He refuses to get emotional about it.

Eli gets an extension on one of his final papers from an understanding history professor, so he can attend the game that night. The professor is, conveniently, a Hell Hounds fan and, coincidentally, now also has a ticket to the first game in their playoff run.

That would probably be frowned upon by collegiate administration if they knew, but Alex isn't going to tell anyone.

So, his boyfriend is in the stands, wearing Alex's jersey and screaming his head off when the Hell Hounds win that night.

It's not an easy first period; the Kings are hardly an easy team, but the Hell Hounds take the lead in the second and sustain it through the third.

Most importantly, through all the standard chirping and swearing—heightened a bit as it is, hey, playoffs—there isn't, or at least Alex doesn't hear, a single homophobic comment. Not even hissed to him, out of ref earshot in between plays. Or mouthed from the bench. Or said through smiling teeth in the handshake line.

It's not so much a relief as it is a catharsis.

Media afterward is more or less as hellish as usual, but then he goes out with the guys for a celebratory drink and, even better, goes home to Eli afterward.

Eli, who is on the couch, compellingly rumpled, still wearing Alex's jersey but wrapped in the extra soft blanket from the bedroom, squinting angrily at his laptop.

Alex is pretty sure Eli is going to need reading glasses soon, if he doesn't already, and he frankly can't wait.

Alex is 100 percent certain Eli in glasses will be adorable. "Hey," he says, leaning over the back of the couch to kiss Eli's temple.

"Hey," Eli agrees, twisting a little to grin up at him. "1–0 feeling pretty good?"

"It is. How's it feel to be dating a winner?"

"Pretty good. It'd feel better to date a Stanley Cup champion, I think."

"Don't jinx it." Alex moves into the kitchen, pours a glass of Gatorade over ice and then more or less collapses next to Eli. "Do you need both your hands?" he mumbles, somewhere in the vicinity of Eli's thigh.

"I could spare one."

Alex chooses to ignore that he's being laughed at and says stoically, "I'd appreciate that."

Eli's fingers make a first, slow pass down Alex's scalp, and he closes his eyes, sighing.

"Have I mentioned I love you?" Alex murmurs.

"Once or twice," Eli says.

19

THEY WIN THE FIRST round against the Kings in five games.

Coach gives them the weekend off to recover from game five; they narrowly won in overtime, leaving Alex so wired he couldn't sleep.

So, after staring at the ceiling for a few hours and then staring at Eli's sleeping face for a couple more hours, he goes to the rink.

Because he's Alexander Fucking Price, and he just led the Hell Hounds to a first-round win in the Stanley Cup finals, and no one is going to tell him he can't.

He means to just skate.

It's 6:00 a.m., and the place doesn't open until 8:00, and he means to just do some gentle laps and clear his head for an hour. He'll give a substantial tip to the rink admin who let him in and sneak back home for breakfast with Eli.

Except once he starts skating, his breath is harsh in the silence and his heartbeat is loud in his ears and it's bright and cold and echoing, and he starts to think about all the little things he'd done wrong in the last game. The little things that could have turned into big things. He thinks about all the ways he nearly let his team down. And he knows he's not perfect, and that anyone striving for perfection will inevitably be disappointed. He knows, objectively, he's playing some of the best hockey of his life. And he knows—he *knows*—that punishing his body for being human will only hurt him more in the future, and that his therapist would likely scold him if she knew he was letting these thoughts percolate and fill his chest until he can hardly breathe.

But his therapist isn't here.

And a pile of pucks is.

He starts with inside edge circles, the scrape of fresh ice loud and familiar and a comfort to his oversensitive senses. And then he scatters a bucket of pucks, picks four that are more or less in a square and does outside edge work, figure eights, until his thighs are burning and he can't tell if his breathlessness is from anxiety or exertion.

He nudges the pucks into a different formation to do more inside edge work, dropping for a one-hand touch to the ice with each turn, then switching back to outside, then doing inside one more time because the first just wasn't good enough. The next round he does edge transitions with knee touches, repeating the same mantra he's been repeating since he was twelve years old and his coach made him drill so much he dreamed it at night:

Head up, Price, chest up, left foot turn, right knee down, back up, right foot turn, chest up, left knee down, don't rely on the stick for balance, chest up, left foot turn, right knee down, chest up, chest up, chest up.

He makes a noise—unintentional and strangled and feral in a way that should probably frighten him. It echoes back to him, and he snowplows to a stop, letting the aggressive rasp of his breathing overshadow whatever that just was.

He's fine.

He just.

Needs to work harder.

You did not come this far to only come this far, he thinks. Another mantra. Another thought his therapist would probably want to unpack.

He's fine.

He starts again: outside punch and tight turns, double punch and tight turns, back to inside edge work.

His legs are burning; his lungs feel hot despite the chill; he's sweating; his fingers are nearly frozen—but the tightness in his chest is earned now.

He scatters more pucks.

He'll just do a little stick handling, and then he'll leave.

He's fine.

Alex is not fine.

Eli knows Alex is not fine. He has quite of bit of experience with being not fine and Alex—

Alex is not fine.

His sleeping schedule is getting more and more fucked, and he's losing weight, and the circles under his eyes are growing, and he's chewing absently on his cuticles in way Eli recognizes from his own time spent deep under the blanket of anxiety.

Except Eli doesn't know how to tell him, in a gentle, non-confrontational way: *Hey, maybe you should be talking to your therapist more about coping mechanisms or something because you're kind of falling apart.*

So, he puts it off. Playoffs won't last forever.

The morning after game five of the first round, Eli wakes up alone at 7:00 a.m. Alex's gym bag and keys are gone.

He narrows his eyes at the empty spot on the key hook by the door and then goes back into the bedroom to pull up Alex's location on his phone.

He is completely unsurprised to find Alex's icon, foreboding despite the bright glow of the screen, at the Hell Hounds practice facility.

Eli makes a cup of coffee.

He'll deal with this after some caffeine.

And a dog walk.

And maybe a quick batch of muffins.

Except after caffeine and a dog walk and a quick batch of muffins, Alex still isn't home. Eli is now pursing his lips at the calendar where the next relationship-meeting heart indicator isn't for another two weeks. He snags the marker from on top of the refrigerator, uncaps it with his teeth, and draws a big heart on the current day.

"Great," he tells Hawk. "Now I have to figure out how to stage an intervention before he gets home."

She has no advice to give.

He cleans the already pretty clean apartment because that is something he knows how to do. Then, when the Windex fumes haven't given him any clarity, he calls Jeff.

"Why," Jeff answers blurrily.

"Sorry. I know it's early," Eli says. "But I need help staging an intervention for Alex."

"I hate you," Jeff sighs.

"I know. He's at the igloo, and he has been there for at least two hours. I woke up alone."

"Ah, fuck," Jeff says. "I've been worried about him. I caught him in the weight room in LA last week after that loss. Looked like he was trying to kill himself on the treadmill."

"Fantastic."

"You want me to come over?"

"I don't know. Maybe I'll try this morning, and you can invite us over to your place this afternoon so we can double down if needed?"

"And if not, you can just come over for dinner minus the intervention," Jo says.

"Oh, yeah," Jeff says, "you're on speaker."

"Got that."

Eli groans, drapes himself over the freshly cleaned island still smelling of lavender, and knocks his forehead against the granite a few times. Gently, all things considered.

"Yeah, that sounds good." He swipes over to check Alex's location and is relieved to see he's left the practice facility. "Hey, Alex is on his way back, I'll text you later."

"Ok. Hey, Eli?"

"Hm?"

"You're doing good, kid. This—Alex during playoffs—is a lot, and you're handling it really well even if it doesn't feel like it. He's so much healthier now than he was this time last year."

Eli hopes Jeff is exaggerating but is afraid he isn't. "Ok, thanks, bye."

He slides his phone back and forth between his hands a few times and then stands decisively. "All right," he says, pointing first at Bells on top of the refrigerator and then at Hawk. "Team meeting in the living room. We have ten minutes to come up with a plan."

The plan mostly consists of Eli shoving a muffin into Alex's hands and then shoving Alex onto the couch and then crossing his arms and staring at him until Alex wilts.

It's weirdly effective.

"Is this an intervention?" Alex says, picking at the muffin.

His jaw is so sharp, Eli is tempted to go get a second muffin.

"It would be, only I don't know how to—" Eli gestures helplessly for a moment. "Intervene. Eat that."

Alex dutifully takes a bite, makes a little noise of pleasure, and takes another one.

"Have you been skating?" Eli asks.

"Yeah."

"In a healthy, productive way?"

Alex chews for what feels like a needlessly long time. "No," he admits.

"Do you ... want to talk about it?" Eli asks hopefully.

"Also no."

Damn. Worth a try.

"Okay, well. I'm calling an emergency relationship meeting about it, so you're gonna have to. Or, I guess if you want to call Anika and talk to her, that works too." He points to the calendar. "I made it official and everything, so."

Alex takes another pointed bite of his muffin, and Eli resists the impulse to roll his eyes. He anticipated this.

He fishes the bottle of lube out of his pocket and tosses it into Alex's lap. "Also, if you're good, it can be a sex thing."

Alex stops chewing.

He considers.

He starts chewing again, swallows, and then says, "So you're bribing me to talk about my feelings with sexual favors?"

"Whatever works."

Alex sighs. "What if I promise to make an appointment with Anika?"

"What if you make the appointment right now?"

Eli swipes Alex's phone from the couch cushion next to him and proffers it, with ceremony, on his open palms.

Alex sighs again, louder, but texts Anika, asking to meet with her at the soonest next availability. He turns the screen to show Eli once he's done.

"Very good, thank you." Eli sits, shoulder leaned into the back of the couch so he can face Alex. He tucks his feet under Alex's thigh. "I'd still really appreciate it if you'd tell me what's going on in your head, and if there's something I can do to help though."

Alex finishes the muffin before speaking because, of course, he does. "It's just—the usual gifted child syndrome stuff."

"Gifted child syndrome stuff," Eli repeats.

"You know. The whole—" He gestures wordlessly for a minute and then starts over. "So, Anika says most people skew one of two ways as kids. They're either encouraged to do things themselves, or they have things done for them. The kids who are encouraged to be independent will try things and fail and grow, or they're given too much freedom and end up feeling lost or abandoned. The kids who have things done for them are typically not as good at taking risks or dealing with the consequences of their actions once they're adults. But they do feel more comfortable asking for help and are more likely to feel a sense of safety or confidence in a lack of judgment from their family."

"Okay," Eli says.

Alex looks down at his hands. "Sometimes, there's a third kind of kid, though, who's marked as gifted early on. In sports or school or whatever. And *that* kid is encouraged to do things themself. Except when they fail, which is normal, their failures are criticized, and the kid is told they should have been successful. When the kid points out that others are failing, too, they're told those people aren't ... their peers, I guess. Because the kid had already illustrated with previous successes that they should be held to a higher standard. Now, they're competing with their own perception of self as described to them by an authority figure. And then they internalize that they must have become lazy or aren't working hard enough, or maybe they've somehow lost the thing that made them special to begin with."

Eli exhales at nearly the same time Alex does.

"Shit, ok. Definitely following," Eli says. "So every time you succeed at something, you feel good because success is supposed to feel good. But you also feel like you're digging your own grave as, inevitably, that success will be used against you at some point in the future."

"Yeah," Alex agrees. "And as an adult, your self-worth is all tied up in your accomplishments. So even when you're successful, you don't feel as if you're good enough. The minute you've achieved something, the achievement gets added to the list of things that make any failures even more noteworthy. And when you *do* fail at something, it feels like the end of the world. Since you're certain you should have, and could have, succeeded, even if you don't know how."

"And you don't want to ask for help," Eli says. "Because it feels like admitting to failure. You don't like relying on other people, in general—it feels like 'cheating'."

"So," Alex says, quiet and breathless and honest, "you're really only confident when you're doing something you're exceptionally good at. But even then, you live in constant fear of somehow losing your ability. Not necessarily because you love the thing, but because you've separated the very concept of joy from an activity and attached it instead to your ... perceived success at the activity."

Eli does understand. He so, so understands.

"What can I do? Tell you you're doing a good job? Not just with hockey but other things too? Point out the ... little victories or whatever?"

Alex grimaces, then makes a contemplative face. "Actually, that might help. Stupid as it is."

"It's not stupid if it helps. And I know it helps for me, so you'd better not call it stupid, or I'll be insulted."

Alex smiles, genuine and soft and vulnerable. "I don't deserve you."

"Ah," Eli says, climbing into Alex's lap. He links his hands behind Alex's neck. "You do. Because you're so good. And you try so hard. You haven't left your clothes on the floor in weeks. And you rinse the sink out every night instead of letting nasty crusty bits of food hang around until the cleaning service comes next. And you remember all my favorite foods for the grocery list without asking, and dote on Hawk and Bells, and you've been so damn attentive to me and any possible way you could help with my recovery."

"Maybe too attentive," Alex mutters.

"Maybe too attentive," Eli allows, "but it's because you care."

"I do."

"And you do such a good job caring. *Such* a good job taking care of me and the girls. You're a good partner and a good pet parent and a good friend. And you're also a damn good captain and hockey player, and I'd be happy to call up the boys who can speak on that with authority if you need me to."

Alex's ears have flushed pink by the time Eli is done with his little rant, and Eli is delighted to see it. He ducks to kiss one such ear, just because.

"Not necessary," Alex says.

His phone buzzes with a response from Anika asking if he wants to talk in two hours.

He dutifully answers *yes please* and tips the screen to show Eli.

Eli kisses his mouth this time. "Thank you."

Alex slips one hand up the back of Eli's shirt and pulls their bodies flush, breathing into his neck. "Thank you," he says, maybe a little cracked, maybe a little more honest than he meant to. Eli just squeezes him back and pets the back of his head until Alex's grip loosens.

"Hey, Eli," Alex says, tone conspiratorial. "Have you showered yet?"

"Mmm? No. Not yet."

"I need to take a shower."

"You definitely do."

"Okay, asshole. I'm just saying. I made an appointment with Anika. And I talked about my feelings. And we both need to take a shower."

Ah. Eli understands, now.

"All of these things are true, yes," he agrees, wide-eyed and feigning confusion.

Alex shoves Eli, laughing, off his lap so he can find the lube and then throw it, gently, at Eli's face. "Are you coming or not?"

"Not right now, but I assume I will be shortly," Eli answers beatifically. "Also, we're not having shower sex during playoffs when my balance is still shit."

"How about shower foreplay, followed by very safe doctor-and-NHL-sanctioned bed sex?"

"Done," Eli says, seriously extending one hand to shake. Alex takes his proffered hand and drags him to the bathroom, and Eli thinks maybe he's pretty good at interventions after all.

20

THEY WIN ROUND TWO against the Sharks in four games.

It's a brutal series, even if it's short. Nearly the entirety of the first and second lines are playing with injuries—Jeff's ankle, Kuzy's knee, Alex's shoulder, Matt's wrist—the list goes on. But none of them are bad enough to bench them, and even while the trainers despair, they don't prohibit them from playing as long as they feel up to it.

Shockingly, they all feel up to it.

Alex still can't sleep the night after game four, but he doesn't get up at 5:00 the next morning to go to the rink. He's trying to make healthier choices or whatever. Also, Eli is sleeping on him.

It's nice; Eli, so still and heavy and warm, bathed in watery morning light and completely unaware that Alex is staring at him like a creeper.

But how can Alex not stare at his perfect curls and the scar that cups his ear and the lovely slope of his nose; the way his cheek is pressed to Alex's sternum, his upper lip pushed up a little to expose one white canine. His bottom lip is wet.

The moving, living, protective thing inside Alex's chest likes that, for whatever reason. He doesn't want to suppress it; why should he?

One of Eli's hands rests, fingers curled, just above Alex's belly button. Alex tucks his own hand around it.

He focuses on the soft web between Eli's thumb and forefinger: a small, manageable part of him.

Alex drags his own thumb along the skin there: reverent, maybe.

He thinks about how, a year ago, he was so desperately unhappy.

And now—

Alex can't remember ever being so content. Or so scared.

Eli makes a little noise, fingers curling around Alex's, and Alex has to close his eyes for a moment.

To breathe.

Was it possible to miss a person before you lost them? To want them back before they were gone? Alex knows that part of every adventure is the end, except he doesn't want this one to end. He wants Eli in his bed and in his clothes for—forever, maybe. And that's terrifying. He's pretty sure Eli feels the same way. And he's pretty sure Eli would never intentionally walk away from him. But Eli also has a traumatic brain injury and a seizure disorder. Alex knows—he's seen all too closely how tenuous Eli's existence is.

God, how do people in love ever stop worrying? People are fragile. Two hundred and six bones. Skeletons held together by sinew and skin. And perfectly healthy people die every day. Accidentally. In car crashes and muggings and freak accidents. And now, some days, all Alex can think about is the statistical probability of Eli and his horrible human body being caught up in the mess of chance. Half of him wants to lock Eli up where there can be no accidents, no danger; when he is hurt, Alex is hurt. He knows it's stupid, but if Eli were to die today, he thinks he would die tomorrow. Because Eli is ... Eli. Because there is only *one* of him.

He's never loved someone like this before. The thought of losing him is—Alex can't even think about it without his lungs seizing up. No one has ever had this power over him before, and it's likely no one else ever will.

He presses a kiss to Eli's knuckles, to the protruding bone of his wrist, to the scar bisecting the second tendon on the back of his hand.

Eli inhales sharply and pulls away, turns over, and Alex drags a hand slowly up the landscape of Eli's back, taking in the everything of him: the dip of his spine, the terraces of his ribs, the wings of his shoulder blades, the goosebumps that trail in Alex's fingertips' wake.

He is objectively beautiful, but it's been a long time since Alex could be objective about Eli.

Alex presses his mouth to Eli's temple, not really a kiss, just breathing in the clean smell of his hair; the new rosewater toner he's started using in the evenings; the subtle bite of mint from his toothpaste, nearly gone after a night of sleep.

He presses his lips with more intention to Eli's cheek, the hinge of his jaw, the soft pocket of skin just below his ear.

And then Eli is rolling to hook one elbow around Alex's neck and shove their mouths inelegantly together. Alex kisses him back, hard and rough and controlled in a way that doesn't feel very controlled at all. Like maybe Alex is losing his mind a little. He remembers, suddenly, a line he read in a book somewhere: *Love is the fire of life; it either consumes or purifies.*

Eli kisses him again, just as desperate as Alex feels, and Alex—

Alex is consumed.

"So that was a relatively dramatic way to wake up," Eli murmurs over breakfast, nudging his elbow into Alex's side. "Not that I'm complaining or anything. You okay?"

"Not really," Alex admits.

"Is it hockey? Or feelings?" Eli rubs the heel of his hand into one eye, considering. "Feelings about hockey?"

"Feelings about you."

Eli goes still.

He resumes rubbing his eye after a beat, then props his elbow on the counter, resting his chin in his hand. "Well. I'd be worried, but the incredibly hot sex just now was a pretty thorough demonstration of your, uh ... continued interest in me. Unless it was some sort of really fucked-up goodbye."

"What? No. I'm not—It's the concept of having to *say* goodbye to you that's causing the problem."

Eli blinks. "Are you thinking I'm going to lose my mind and leave you, or are you planning my funeral already?"

"Little bit of column A, little bit of column B. Maybe mostly column B."

"Woof," Eli says. "Okay."

"Sorry," Alex adds, and Eli knows it's because he feels like he should.

"No, it's fine. I know I'm not exactly the picture of a healthy life partner. But technically, of the two of us, I think I should be the most worried. I'm a college student and soon to be children's figure skating coach. You let people slam you into walls for a living."

"I think you'll find I don't *let* them slam me into walls. I spend a good portion of my energy trying to avoid that."

"Huh," Eli says, "I stand corrected; you try, and fail, to keep people from slamming you into walls for a living. Clearly my occupation is the one most fraught with peril."

"I hate you," Alex mutters.

"No, you don't."

"No, I don't."

They eat in companionable silence for several minutes until Eli puts down his fork.

"Do you wish—would you change it? If you could? Change me, I mean. My injuries. My seizure disorder. All of it."

Alex looks stymied. "Would *you*?"

"I asked you first."

"But my answer depends on yours. I mean, I want you healthy. I want you not in pain. If I somehow was given the ability to make all the shit you deal with go away, I—obviously, I'd want to. But only if *you* wanted me to. It's your body."

"Jeff would approve of that answer. Hashtag consent."

Alex snorts into his coffee.

Eli clarifies, "I guess what I really mean is, do you wish you could be with someone you didn't have to constantly worry about? Is being with me just super draining for you and your anxiety?"

There's not anything he can do about it. And he's way too selfish to end things, even if Alex is dealing with a shit ton of worry on his behalf. But it'd be nice to know. Even if the answer sucks.

"If you're asking if I resent you or something—no. And I'd probably worry more than a normal amount about you getting hurt or sick, even if you didn't have a TBI. But if getting a healthy boyfriend meant getting a different boyfriend, absolutely not. You're it for me." Alex gestures to him with his fork. "Regardless of whatever physical state you're in. Sickness and health and all that."

"Sickness and health is for marriage," Eli points out, forcing himself to be so, so casual as he says the word.

Alex stills, cuts his eyes over to meet Eli's, and then immediately looks away again. "Yeah."

"Alex."

"Yeah?"

"Do you want me to pretend you didn't say that?"

Alex slumps, burying his face in his folded arms on the counter. "I mean, I feel like it should be pretty obvious at this point that I want to marry you."

And maybe that's true, but Eli still feels winded. "Really?" he says, just to make sure.

"I—" Alex looks up, as if he can't help but respond to the surprise in Eli's tone. "Yes. Obviously, yes. I've already started looking at rings. Except I think you're just going to have to pick it yourself and then look surprised because I know you have opinions and I have terrible style sense. And also, you'll probably kill me if I spend more than a couple thousand dollars."

Eli processes this.

"Are you ok?" Alex asks. "Do you—" His voice goes suddenly uncertain. "—not want to marry me?"

Eli would throw himself at Alex if not for the fact that Alex is already a walking bruise. So instead, he calmly stands, brackets Alex's worried face with both hands, and says, "I want to marry you *so bad*."

"Oh," Alex says. "Good. Cool."

"Are you done with your breakfast?" Eli asks.

Alex tries to look at his plate without displacing Eli's hands. "Not really, why?"

"I need to lie on top of you for a few minutes and have feelings. Can we come back to breakfast later?"

"Absolutely. Can we do the lying thing naked?"

"We literally just had sex."

"And?" Alex says.

That's a valid point.

Alex helpfully pulls Eli's shirt over his head as they walk to the bedroom. "Just to confirm," Alex says as Eli is finding the exact place he wants to tuck his face in Alex's neck, "for 100 percent certainty. You *do* want to marry me."

"Yes. But you are also correct that I have opinions, and if you spend more than a couple hundred dollars on a ring for me, we will have words."

"A couple *hundred*? That's less than your skates."

"My skates are beautiful and useful and not something I could potentially lose when I'm washing the dishes."

"We have a dishwasher."

"That is not the point, and you *know* it."

"Two thousand cap," Alex says staunchly.

"This isn't a debate."

"Of course, it is."

Eli sighs. Of course, it is. "One thousand cap."

"One and a half, and I won't get you any other gifts for ... three months after the proposal."

"One thousand, and I don't complain when you buy us business class seats when we fly for the first year of our marriage."

Alex considers. "Make it two years, and we have a deal."

"One thousand cap, two years, and if there are diamonds and shit, we only get ethically sourced ones. And we're getting you a ring, too, for the engagement."

"Deal," Alex agrees.

Eli props himself up on Alex's chest long enough to shake his hand. "Pleasure doing business with you."

Alex shifts his hips. "It could be ... *more* pleasurable."

Eli groans into Alex's neck. "Regrettably," he says to no one in particular, "this is who I've chosen to love."

"On *purpose.* You've chosen to love me *on purpose.*"

"I have," Eli agrees, not laughing anymore. "Kinda hard not to though."

How could people know Alex and have the absolute gall to *not* love him? Eli thinks briefly of the news articles and the Reddit threads and the talking heads, and wonders, not for the first time, how so many people can look at Alex without bothering to *see* him.

Alex makes a considering noise. "I wouldn't, you know?" he says after a minute of silence.

"Wouldn't what?" Eli murmurs; he could easily fall back asleep.

"I wouldn't change anything about you."

Eli opens his eyes. "Nothing?"

"Maybe your elbows."

"My elbows?"

"Mm," Alex confirms. "Make 'em less pointy."

Except even that's a lie, Eli knows. More than once, Alex has pressed gentle little kisses he probably wouldn't want to acknowledge to the tips of his pointy elbows.

"You love my pointy elbows," Eli says with conviction.

"I do," Alex admits morosely. "In fact, I love ... " He shifts his hips again. " ... all the pointy things about you."

"Oh my god, Alex. Why are you like this?"

"The combination of you naked and the promise of orgasms is really good at distracting me from my crushing anxiety."

"Oh, well, if the sex is for your mental health ... "

"The sex is absolutely for my mental health," Alex confirms.

"Guess we'd better get right on that, then."

"I'd like to get right on your—"

"*Alex*."

"Kiss me?" he asks innocently.

Eli does.

21

THEY WIN ROUND THREE against the Jets in six games.

And hoisting the conference cup on opponent ice doesn't make the victory any less sweet. The Hell Hounds are going to the Stanley Cup final.

For the first time in franchise history.

Alex manages to make it back home from the airport, to his own apartment, to his own bathroom before having one of the worst panic attacks of his life.

Eli is gone when Alex finally stumbles inside, shedding his coat and bags on the way to the medicine cabinet.

A Xanax takes the edge off. But then he feels awful and lost and like he *should* be struggling to breathe but can't, which is nearly as bad as not being able to breathe in the first place. And then, since his brain can't focus on the static of panic, it focuses on all of the mistakes he's made in the last series—the kind of mistakes that could cost them the championship if repeated.

So instead of struggling to breathe on the bathroom floor, he's suddenly crying on the bathroom floor.

For no particular reason that he can determine.

He also can't seem to stop.

Fantastic, he thinks absently, pressing his eye sockets into his knees. *I've finally lost it*.

Bells comes to sit with him, which is nice, but what he needs—

Well. He needs to call Anika. He should call Anika.

But what he *wants*—

He checks his phone.

Eli's last final exam was an hour earlier. He should be finished by now. But then he had a meeting with his advisor to talk about his schedule next semester.

Can you come home? Alex texts him.

And then:

Now.

And then:

Please.

Less than two minutes later, Eli calls him.

"Hey," Alex says, and it's rough and a little desperate, something he would be embarrassed about if he wasn't so—whatever he is right now.

"Hey," Eli says. "What's wrong? Are you okay?"

"No. I had a panic attack. Took a Xanax. Now I'm just—" He breathes, and it doesn't rattle in his chest, but it doesn't feel right either. "I don't know. Something is wrong."

"Okay. Okay, I'm walking out to the parking lot right now. Are you at home?"

"Yeah."

"Where are you at home?"

"Bathroom. Bells is with me."

He doesn't know why he adds the last part. It seems important.

"Okay, that's good. We'll be there in fifteen minutes. Can you do something for me?"

Anything.

"Yeah."

"Call Anika. Tell her what's going on and see if she has any advice. If she doesn't answer, call me right back, though, okay? And I'll keep you company while I ride home."

"Okay."

"I love you," Eli says. "I'll see you in just a few minutes. We'll figure this out."

"Love you," Alex agrees.

He hangs up and calls Anika.

It's good the Hell Hounds have a week off while they wait for their final opponent to be determined.

For five days, Alex wakes up in his own bed to Eli's soft hands, soft voice, soft mouth.

"How's your brain today?" Eli asks every morning, and Alex answers "Better," and it's the truth.

He eats. He sleeps. He does light workouts and attends practice and talks to Anika almost daily.

Eli starts a six-week online summer-school course to make up for the one class he dropped during the semester. He hates it, and he's vocal about it.

"Trouble in paradise?" Jeff asks one day, sitting at the kitchen island and eating guacamole in a way that means the counter will be covered in chip debris later.

Eli sits on one side of Jeff, decidedly ignoring Alex, who's on his other side.

"Alex is being homophobic," Eli mutters.

"Oh?" Jeff says.

"I won't kiss him until he's done with this paper," Alex explains.

"Ah," Jeff says. "You should call HR, Eli. The NHL is very serious about homophobia now; I'm not sure if you've heard."

"Shut up," Alex says, and then, to Eli, "I'm just trying to provide incentive. It's for your own good. Don't sulk."

"I'm not sulking," Eli says sulkily.

Later, when Alex is lying on the couch, not napping, but not really awake either, Eli drops down onto the cushion beside his head, jostling him.

"Hey, Alex. I want to try something."

"If it's a sex thing, can it wait until after playoffs?" Alex says, not opening his eyes.

"If it's a sex thing, can it wait until I'M NOT HERE?" Jeff yells from the kitchen.

They ignore him.

"What?" Alex asks, squinting up at Eli.

"Encouragement kisses. That's incentive too."

"Oh my god," he says, closing his eyes again. "Just go finish the stupid paper."

"I've got eight out of ten pages. I think that deserves a reward. Something to bolster me through the last two."

"You're ridiculous."

"And you're lucky I want to kiss you at all considering the way your face looks right now."

"He has a point," Jeff says.

He does.

Alex can't grow a playoff beard to save his life. All he has right now is horrible itchy blond stubble that gets wispy around his chin and jaw and the corners of his mouth, and it's a miracle Eli will even look at him right now much less want to get anywhere near him.

Alex sits up, considering his boyfriend. His beautiful boyfriend, who does not have terrible facial hair but does need to finish his paper. "Are you trying to take advantage of me because I'm exhausted and ugly and my defenses are down?"

"Yes," Eli says.

"Okay," Alex agrees magnanimously. "Come take advantage of me, then."

Eli grins, climbing into his lap.

"All right, well, goodbye," Jeff says.

When the Caps win their conference and the final series schedule is announced, Alex asks Eli if they can have a midmonth relationship meeting.

"I need you there," Alex says, picking at the jagged edge of one of his fingernails. "At all of the games. Home and away. And maybe that isn't healthy and maybe it isn't actually true that I need you there, but my brain is saying I do, and it's the Stanley Cup finals, so."

"Okay," Eli agrees.

"Okay?"

Maybe Eli doesn't understand.

"And you have to let me pay for it," Alex clarifies. "Flights and hotels and food and everything."

"Okay," Eli repeats.

"I don't understand. I thought this would be an argument. I made notecards."

"Well, you can read them to me if you want. But Alex. This isn't a vacation or a pair of shoes. It's the Stanley Cup finals. It's—you. Your health. If you say you need me there, I'm there."

Alex should probably start looking for rings.

It's been six months. Eight, if you count their original not-dates.

That's enough time, right?

They had a conversation about getting engaged at the end of April. Well. Sort of. The conversation mostly consisted of Alex saying, "You're it for me, and I'd like to marry you at some point, cool?" and Eli saying, "Cool." And then they'd moved on to arguing about whether or not Eli would let Alex pay for a two-week trip to the Dominican Republic over the summer.

"But think how happy it would make Abuela!" he'd argued. "I need sun and beaches and no stress as part of my recovery, and if you don't come with me, I'll be stressed the whole time. Also, if you don't come with me, I'll spend two weeks with Aba, and I'll have her tell me every embarrassing story from your childhood. Do you think she has pictures?"

Eli eventually agreed that Alex could pay for their trip provided that they, A. stayed in Abuela's guest room, not at some horrible resort, B. Alex didn't buy him any gifts until their departure date.

He agreed.

They shook on it.

And since then, Alex has been so preoccupied with hockey and planning their vacation that he hasn't done much thinking about the marriage situation. He starts covert internet research the weekend before the first final game, primarily while using the bathroom.

Eli casually inquires about Alex's bowel health.

"You know, you could just say you're planning something secret, and I'd leave you alone in the bedroom or the living room or something," he says. "At this rate, you're going to get a permanent toilet seat indent on your butt, and I'll be very sad. I like your butt the way it is."

Apparently, Alex is not very covert after all.

Apparently, his boyfriend is also the worst.

Alex decides to set aside his research until the summer anyway.

He needs to focus on hockey now.

The Hell Hounds win the first game of the series at home against the Caps.

They lose the second.

Lose the third in DC.

Lose the fourth.

Win the fifth.

Win the sixth.

The final goes to seven games because, of course, it does.

At least that means they're on home ice.

It's not really a consolation.

The night before game seven, Alex is in the bathtub, soaking aching muscles in Epsom salts, when Eli gets home from the library.

"Hey," he says, kneeling beside the tub, rolling up the sleeves of his shirt. "How's it going?"

"Everything hurts. And I'm afraid I won't be able to sleep tonight.

But I *have* to sleep tonight to play well tomorrow, and I *have* to play well tomorrow, but if I *can't sleep—*"

"I know," Eli says lowly. "Shhh. It's okay." He somehow manages to shush Alex without sounding condescending.

Alex isn't sure how he feels about that.

Eli kisses the corner of Alex's mouth, then wets a washcloth to rub along the line of his collarbone.

Alex closes his eyes again.

"Do you want me to wash your hair?" Eli asks a few minutes later because he's the best and Alex can never hope to deserve him.

"Yes, please."

"Okay. Do you want me to make pancakes and omelets again tomorrow?" Eli murmurs, fingers working against Alex's scalp in a vanilla-scented lather.

"Yeah," Alex says. "With—"

"Blueberries," Eli agrees. "And I picked up more spinach for the omelets on the way home too."

They've been eating the same thing for breakfast for the last several days. It's what Alex had to eat the morning before game one, and then again before game five, and then game six. And now it's part of his routine.

"My superstitious weirdo," Eli says affectionately, tugging at the shell of one of his ears. "You're lucky I love you."

"So lucky," Alex agrees. "But I'm not that superstitious. There are a lot of guys who are worse than me."

Eli snorts, scratching at the nape of Alex's neck in a way that makes him feel wobbly and limp. "Don't think I haven't noticed you've been wearing the same pair of underwear every day since game three of the second round."

Alex was, actually, hoping Eli hadn't noticed that. "I've been washing them," he says defensively.

"Thank god for small mercies. Did you know you've become a meme?" Eli asks conversationally, tipping Alex's head back to rinse the suds out of his hair.

"A meme?"

"Mmm. That screencap I posted on Instagram of you sitting in the sin bin looking all grumpy from the last game. Someone paired it up with a picture of Bells sitting in a box from your Instagram, and now everyone is making 'if I fits, I sits' jokes."

That actually sounds pretty great. "Can you show me?"

"Mm-hmm. Got it pulled up on my laptop. It's waiting on the bed."

"Is that where we're going next?" Alex says hopefully, trying not to groan out loud as Eli starts to work conditioner into his hair.

"Yessir, I'm going to rub you down with your fancy version of VapoRub because it seems that's a service I provide now, and then tuck you in and make sure you get to sleep."

Alex pouts. "You know, I've read," Alex says, "from very official scientific sources, that orgasms make people sleepy."

"Alexander," Eli says sternly. "I am not going to encourage you risking a sex injury the night before game seven in the Stanley Cup final."

"We could be really careful."

Eli rolls his eyes. "Tilt your head back," he says, turning on the water to rinse Alex's hair again.

"Is that a yes?"

"It's a maybe."

That means it's a yes.

Alex grins and ends up choking on a mouthful of water.

Alex honestly doesn't remember much of the final game.

He remembers taping his stick. Retaping his stick. Taping it a third time because it has to be perfect.

He remembers sweating in the Hell Hounds' mirrored tunnel, the itch of anxiety at the back of his throat and clenched around his stomach, waiting for the announcer to shout, loud and at last over the PA system, *And now, your captain: Alexander Priiiiiiiiice.*

And then his skates hit the ice and things go a little blurry.

He remembers chewing on the front of his jersey during the anthem.

He remembers assisting Kuzy on a goal in the first.

He remembers fury when the Caps turn right back around and score less than a minute later.

He remembers taking a hard check in the second.

Screaming Rushy's name over a fantastic block in the third.

Getting slashed.

Two broken fingers.

Getting treated on the bench and shoving them back in his glove.

Scoring on a breakaway even though his hand feels cumbersome with pain.

He's not on the ice when the clock runs out.

He's just finished a shift, and he's leaned onto his elbows over the boards, breathing hard, shaking sweat out of his eyes, watching the puck, which is uncomfortably close to their net. The Caps are on the power play, and the Caps only need one goal to tie, to go into overtime. Alex doesn't know if he'll survive that if it happens; he's so damn tired, and his hand hurts and his head hurts and—

Please, he thinks.

Please.

Please.

Please.

The horn sounds and for a moment, he closes his eyes—relief rather than ecstasy—until he remembers:

He did it.

They did.

They're Stanley Cup champions.

Holy shit.

He doesn't remember most of what comes next, either, but he

does remember holding the cup. He remembers kissing the cup—cold against his chapped mouth.

He remembers passing the cup to Rads, who's probably skating on a broken ankle.

Who isn't coming back next year.

Who's definitely crying when he lifts the cup out of Alex's hands and pushes it straight up into the air, yelling.

The cup is both heavier and lighter than Alex expected.

There are a lot of pictures and hugging and the tacky residue of spilled champagne everywhere and Eli throwing himself into Alex's arms.

It's probably good he doesn't have a ring yet. If he did, he'd be on one knee right now, and even if Eli didn't kill him for proposing in front of approximately a billion cameras after less than a year of knowing each other, Eli's mother definitely would.

He manages to make it to the locker room, to say a sound bite for some reporters, and strip mostly out of his gear before the adrenaline wears off enough that he realizes he's breathing harder than he should be, and his hands are shaking.

He looks around and can't find Eli.

Hawk is there, a few feet away, and Jeff is telling Cookie that *no* he cannot give the dog beer, *what the hell is wrong with you?* which would be funny if Alex wasn't—whatever he is right now.

He doesn't even know.

He has so many emotions that he can't even—

He is a *hemorrhage*.

Leaking feelings everywhere with absolutely no idea how to contain them or even if he should and—

Oh.

There he is.

Alex's mind quiets down a little when he sees Eli talking to Jessica just outside the open door of the locker room.

Alex pushes his way through the guys, grabs Eli's wrist, and pulls him farther down the hallway.

Past camera crews and security and a concerned-looking Jeff with his arm around Jo.

Alex doesn't know where he's going but—

Yes.

Perfect.

"Oh my god," Eli says as the door closes behind them, "are we in an actual utility closet? I thought that only happened in movies. What are we doing? Are we going to make out? I really don't think the guys will care if we do that in front of them at this point. They're already three beers deep, and your gay ass just won them the Stanley Cup, you know?"

"Hey," Jeff says outside, knocking on the door. "I thought your whole thing was about being out of the closet?"

"Shut up, Coops," Alex yells back, and his voice might actually crack.

"Oh," Eli says, serious all of the sudden. "Hey, what's going on?"

And Alex just ... wraps himself around Eli.

Tucks his face into his neck.

And maybe sobs a little.

"Okay," Eli says. "Okay. This is good too. Hey. Whatever you need. I'm so proud of you, you know? I'm so proud of you and you worked so hard and I love you so much. More than love you. So much more than love you. Oh shit. Okay. Well, I'm crying too, now. Thanks for that."

They cling to each other for a few minutes until Alex's breathing has evened out.

The hallway slowly gets louder, and then Matts opens the door to peek inside. "You guys," he yells to the assembled group outside, "they're not even fucking. They're just crying all over each other."

"Fuck you," Alex says, smearing his sweaty, tear-streaked face against Eli's. "We just won the Stanley Cup. I'm allowed to have feelings about it."

"That is fair," Moose says seriously, leaning against the wall outside the closet, wearing his compression shorts and only one sock.

Moose is definitely already drunk.

Rookies.

"You want to have feelings in the locker room with everyone else, Captain?" Rads asks. He's got a crutch under one arm and a massive grin on his face.

"Yeah," Alex says. "Yeah, all right. Where's the cup? I need to drink some fucking champagne out of it with my boyfriend."

That gets a cheer.

Alex wakes up the following day just after 11:00 a.m., his phone buzzing in his hand. It's a text from Kuzy: *Everyone is hangover*.

He blinks at his phone in agreement.

He's in his own bed, which is good.

Eli is asleep on one side of him.

Also good.

The cup is tucked under the covers on the other.

So good.

Bells is half inside the bowl of the cup, and Hawk is sprawled across their feet, cutting off Alex's circulation.

He grins at the ceiling for a solid minute before getting up, slowly, to use the bathroom. He takes some heavy-duty painkillers because his hangover is eclipsed by the throbbing of his broken fingers, drinks an entire Gatorade that drunk-him was kind enough to leave on the nightstand, and takes a shower. By the time he's brushing his teeth, damp and feeling a little more human, the ache in both his head and his hand have subsided enough for the euphoria to take back over.

When he returns to the bed, he has to climb over the cup to get to Eli, to press fresh minty kisses all over his scrunched-up grumpy face.

"What?" Eli mutters. He has a magnificent case of bedhead. There might be confetti in his curls.

In a few minutes, they'll need to get up. Make sure everyone is still alive and figure out when the parade is and hash out the schedule for the whole post-final media circus. He's already thinking he wants to take the cup to Pride and invite all the other out players from the group chat—he'll need to call Jessica and maybe You Can Play? And he should also probably—

But not yet.

All of that can wait.

The shades are blocking the morning sun, and the duvet is crinkly around them.

Eli is warm and soft and beautiful, and he smells like peppermint schnapps for some unholy reason, and Alex loves him so, so much.

For now, at least for the next few minutes, it's just them.

And *just them* is his favorite thing.

"What?" Eli repeats, a little bemused now.

Probably because Alex is staring at him like a dope. "Nothing. Just." Alex kisses him one more time.

"Hi." Eli blinks up at him. Smiles a little. Kisses him back.

"Hi," he agrees.

Epilogue

ONE YEAR LATER

Alex isn't exactly surprised when he gets a call from Coach three days before the draft and Coach asks, with studied calm, "What are your thoughts on Patrick Roman?"

Patrick Roman. A polarizing six-foot-three, 200-pound eighteen-year-old center from one of the top hockey boarding schools in the US. He was all but nonexistent until nine months before. It was as if he suddenly appeared from the ether his senior year, breaking records and dazzling scouts with absolutely no paper trail of his career up until that point. Alex knows that makes some teams nervous. But Alex has also watched Roman's tape online, and it's hard to argue with talent, regardless of where it came from. If Patrick Roman isn't a prodigy, he's sure as hell something like it.

Patrick Roman is also bisexual and, according to social media, currently dating a man.

Which, yeah. That might make some teams nervous too.

Over the last year, the NHL has gotten better. Ish. But they've yet to have an out queer player drafted. Roman would be the first.

Alex takes a breath.

"He's a solid center," Alex says. "Fast, despite his size. Like, shockingly fast actually. Great chemistry with his wingers. Doesn't try to be a glory hound. Seems like an all-around team player."

Alex tries to remember some of the scouting reports he's read. "Sounds like he might have a temper, but I wouldn't blame him.

And that's something we can work on. And we need another center. Obviously. From what I've seen, we probably wouldn't even need to send him down for a year. He looks ready for the show."

"So you'd draft him?" Coach asks. "Over, say, Dupont? Or Federov? Baker?"

"Dupont is a serious contender for sure. But, yeah. If I had my choice, I'd take Roman."

"Even with the increased scrutiny his presence might bring the team?"

Alex resists the urge to laugh. "Coach, nothing anyone might say will be new. Or worse than anything I've heard before. I can't speak for the team. But I'm not worried about that."

"Noted."

"You think we have a chance of getting him?"

"I think he scares most teams, so they'll pass in the first round. I think he scares our GM, too, if we're being honest. No promises. We'll see."

"Right. Of course."

"If we do get him, though," Coach says, "I want you on the phone with him day one. I want him staying with you during training camp. You're senior enough to start babysitting the new ones at this point. And who better to start with?"

"Sure. I mean, I'd have to check with Eli but—"

"Eli would love having a kid stay with you," Coach says.

Which is absolutely true. Though a muscle-bound eighteen-year-old who dwarfs them both isn't exactly the kind of kid Eli would really like. But they're working on that.

"Just be ready to make that first call on Thursday," Coach says.

"Yessir," Alex answers.

Three days later, Alex watches from his couch as Patrick Roman pulls a Hell Hounds jersey over his shaved head on the draft stage and shakes hands with the GM. His face and arms are so densely freckled that he looks darkly tanned, even in the harsh white lights. His jaw is a set line. His eyes are dark and serious. He doesn't smile the entire time he's on the television screen.

"Whoo boy," Jeff says from where he's sprawled on the rug. "Let it begin."

Half the team is at Alex and Eli's place, taking turns eating and lounging and making commentary on all the kids being drafted, remembering their own draft days.

"They're already calling us the Gay Team," Rushy says, tossing his phone onto the couch before following it. "I mean, like, lots of people."

"It isn't exactly surprising," Jeff says, "but it is disappointing. It's not like they didn't have time to plan for this potential eventuality. That's the best they could come up with? Gay Team?"

"Gay emphasis-on-A-team," Matts says, dipping a carrot in so much ranch it negates the healthy concept of a carrot. "Actually. That could be good. *The Gay Team*, but with the A capitalized. We could make shirts. I bet they'd make a killing if we posted some pics of us wearing them on IG. Someone text Jessica."

"Mm," Eli agrees, half sprawled over Alex's lap. "We could even bedazzle the shirts. Just to drive the point home."

"Subtlety, thy name is Eli," Jeff says.

"It really isn't," Alex murmurs.

"You love my lack of subtlety," Eli informs him confidently.

"I do," Alex agrees, kissing him because he can.

"What's bezazzle?" Kuzy asks.

"Bedazzle," Asher corrects. "It's like when you put rhinestones, those little sparkly things, all over everything. Oh, like that horrible pair of jeans you have. With the pockets? Like that."

"Ah," Kuzy says approvingly. "Yes, we could bezazzle shirts."

"Bedazzle," Asher corrects again.

"Bezazzle," Kuzy agrees, this time definitely on purpose.

Alex's phone rings, and they all go quiet because they know what that means.

"Hey, Coach," he says.

"Alex, you ready to make that phone call?"

He is.

They talk for a few more minutes, and then Alex meets Eli's eyes and nods toward the bedroom. One, because he hates doing stuff like this alone, and two, because he wants the kid to be able to talk to both the people he'll potentially be living with.

They settle on the bed together, Hawk at their feet and Bells perched on the headboard, grumbling her disdain about so many uninvited people in her house. Alex dials the number Coach has just texted him.

He links his fingers with Eli's and rubs his thumb against the base of his engagement ring.

"Hello?" The voice that answers is deep and steady and doesn't seem nearly as anxious as Alex felt when he had a similar conversation three years ago.

"Hi, this is Alexander Price? The, uh, captain of the Hell Hounds."

"I—yeah," Roman says. "I know. Hi."

Right. Alex hasn't gotten any better at this. "I just wanted to tell you congrats and welcome. We think you're going to be a real asset to the team."

"Thanks. I'm excited to join you. I ... appreciate that you were willing to take a risk on me."

Now Alex can hear the nerves. It's subtle, but the word "risk" cracked in a way Alex recognizes. "Yeah, of course. Hey, so, full disclosure, you're on speakerphone. My fiancé Eli is here too."

"Hola," Eli says. "Nice to meet you, Patrick."

Roman huffs what might be a laugh. "Full disclosure. You're also on speakerphone. And my boyfriend is also here."

"Well, hola to your boyfriend as well, then," Eli corrects.

"Hola," a new voice says. "Damien Bordeaux. Encantado de conocerte."

"Ayy," Eli says. "¿Hablas español?"

"Here we go," Roman mutters. "Yeah. He speaks Mandarin and French too."

"Oh, I like him," Eli says, sotto voce. "Can we keep them both?"

"Um," Roman says. "We're kind of a package deal, so."

"Nice," Eli says approvingly. "Well, just so you know, we've been instructed by Coach to let you stay with us during training camp. Maybe y'all want your own space though? There are a couple units available in our building. That might be a nice compromise."

"I don't—" Roman says, sounding a little winded. "That's—uh."

"Very kind of you to offer," Damien cuts in smoothly. When he's not speaking Spanish, he has an accent that sounds as if France and England had a deep-timbred baby. "We'll need to discuss it, but we appreciate the kindness. And living close would likely be convenient. Can you send us the information about your building?"

"Sure thing," Eli says. "I can email you the details in a minute."

"Maybe we should just let Eli and Damien talk," Alex says to Roman. "Seems like they're better at it."

They all laugh, and Alex sags a little against Eli's side. He's already looking forward to meeting them in person. He's imagining shared dinners with another couple like them, and it feels like something tightly spooled in his chest starts to loosen.

"How are you doing?" Alex asks. "Overwhelmed?"

"Yeah," Roman admits.

"We're hiding," Damien says. "There are a lot of photographers waiting, so we're ... hiding for a while."

"I'm taking important calls privately," Roman says mulishly.

"Of course you are, darling."

"So we should drag out this important call with your future captain as long as possible then?" Eli asks. "Well, if there's one thing I'm good at, it's talking."

"True," Alex whispers.

Eli elbows him in the ribs. "Hey, before we start hashing out hockey things, how did you two meet?"

"I suppose we're high school sweethearts," Damien says. "Well. 'Sweethearts' probably isn't the right word. We were more like high school adversaries at the start."

"Oh god," Eli says. "Is this an enemies-to-friends-to-lovers situation?"

"The definition of the trope," Damien agrees.

"Well, now you *have* to tell us the story," Alex says. "Sorry. I don't make the rules."

"I do," Eli agrees. "And yes, you have to tell us. But only if you're comfortable."

"I'd love to," Damien says.

"You would," Roman mutters. "*You're* not the one who was a massive asshole for the first three months."

"Mmm." Eli grins at Alex. "When you're done, I'll tell you about what a massive asshole Alex was the first day we met, if that makes you feel better."

"Or not," Alex mutters.

"Sounds great," Roman says.

"Well," Damien begins. "It started the first day of term ... "

Alex squeezes Eli's hand, presses a kiss to his curls, and settles in to listen.

Acknowledgements

I DEDICATED LRPD TO fic writers. I'm going to acknowledge the same folks here for the latter half of Alex and Eli's story.

Fic was the first place I ever found stories about LGBTQ+ characters that had happy endings (often written by real-life queer adults!), and for a confused queer middle-schooler absolutely drowning in spiritual guilt, this discovery may very well have changed my life.

So I'd like to acknowledge all the Livejournal and Fanfiction.net and Dreamwidth writers who introduced me to the wonder of writing, the GeoCities and print zine folks that came before them, and the Tumblr and AO3 creators now. I wish I could thank every commenter on every fic I've written and every friend I've made through fandom, but that would take too long. So instead, I'll list a few that have been particularly encouraging in my writing journey: labelleizzy, plagues-and-pansies, the-lincyclopedia, vibraphone1o1, beaniebaneenie, parrishsrubberplant, emmalovesdilemas, cesperanza, david_of_oz, emmagrant01, venomwrites, protectorowl, shutupsavannah, nearlydeparted, aulophobia, maybeitstimetoearnmybluebead, a-isoiso, actual-corgi, draskireis, ursamajorstudio, littlewhitedragonlet, aussietwat, onetwistedmiracle, echrai, sleepanon, pcr-and-glamour, pianosinthewild, glutenwitch, sexydexynurse, springbok7, gnomer-denois, ohdarlingwatson, zzledri, oatdog, sparrow-ink, sadkazzoosolo, lambbabies, beyondmrsbossladymom, balaenopteraricei, and everyone I've forgotten to add or who has changed their username. Also shout out the the various OMGCP Discord servers I've been part of over the years, primarily the Parse Posse and Haus servers.

I like your shoelaces.